06a

5.00

THE MAN WHO WANTED SEVEN WIVES

Being the Account of a Famous Murder Mystery of 1897
Supposedly Solved by the Testimony of a Ghost,
 Together with an Explanation of Same

by KATIE LETCHER LYLE

Algonquin Books of Chapel Hill
1986

Algonquin Books of Chapel Hill
Post Office Box 2225
Chapel Hill, North Carolina 27515–2225

LIBRARY OF CONGRESS CATALOGING-IN-PUBLICATION DATA

Lyle, Katie Letcher, 1938–
The man who wanted seven wives.
Bibliography: p.
1. Shue, Erasmus Stribbling, 1861 or 2–1900.
2. Crime and criminals—West Virginia—Greenbrier
County—Biography.   3. Shue, Zona Heaster, d. 1897.
4. Murder—West Virginia—Greenbrier County—Case
studies.   I. Title.
HV6248.S56184L95   1986   813'.54   85-28597
ISBN 0-912697-35-0

Once more, for Louis Rubin,
with love and gratitude

Contents

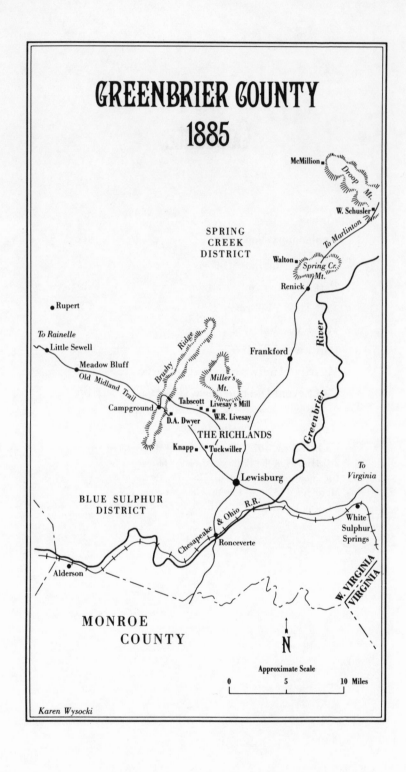

GREENBRIER COUNTY
1885

McMillion

Droop Mt.

W. Schusler

To Marlinton

SPRING
CREEK
DISTRICT

Walton

Spring Cr.
Mt.

Renick

Rupert

To Rainelle

Little Sewell

Brushy Ridge

Frankford

Meadow Bluff

Old Midland Trail

Miller's
Mt.

Tabscott

Livesay's Mill

Campground

D.A. Dwyer

W.R. Livesay

Greenbrier River

THE RICHLANDS

Knapp

Tuckwiller

Lewisburg

To
Virginia

BLUE SULPHUR
DISTRICT

Chesapeake & Ohio R.R.

White
Sulphur
Springs

Ronceverte

Alderson

W. VIRGINIA

VIRGINIA

MONROE
COUNTY

N

Approximate Scale

0   5   10 Miles

Karen Wysocki

Preface

Early in the year 1897 in Greenbrier County in West Virginia, a bride of three months was found dead by a neighbor child. Within a month her ghost appeared on four successive nights and described in great detail the fact that her husband had killed her and just exactly how. On her mother's insistence, the young wife's body was exhumed, the cause of her death confirmed, and her husband brought to trial, convicted of murder, and sentenced to life in the penitentiary.

Convicted in a court of law, because of evidence furnished by a ghost?

That is what the natives of Greenbrier will tell you.

Who was she, the girl who was killed? Who was her husband? Why did people believe her mother's story? What really happened?

When I first heard of Zona Shue's death from my friend Paul Shue, a distant relative of the convicted murderer, I wanted to investigate and write about this locally famous story. So, on a summer day in 1982, while in West Virginia on other business, I stopped to read the road marker. Near where the uncompleted Interstate 64 ends in the rolling hills of Greenbrier County, and traffic is returned to old Route 60, there is a state historical marker that would stop even the most driven traveler. There today's motorist must begin the slow trek of ninety twisting miles to get from just about anywhere in Virginia to Charleston, or anywhere west of it in the continental United States. Unless he should happen to glance to his left, back up Route 60, the modern driver is likely to miss this marker altogether. There it is, just visible, three or four hundred yards away, by the side of the old Midland Trail. It reads:

Greenbrier Ghost

Interred in nearby cemetery is Zona Heaster Shue. Her death in 1897 was presumed natural until her spirit appeared to her mother to describe how she was killed by her husband Edward. Autopsy on the exhumed body verified the apparition's account. Edward, found guilty of murder, was sentenced to the state prison. Only known case in which testimony from ghost helped convict a murderer.

Standing there in the hot sun, I knew at once that I wanted to know more about this, and I figured, as I have done before, that the best way to learn about something is to write about it.

I don't believe in ghosts, yet of course they appear in stories told by men through the ages. So do a lot of other things that I believe do not exist.

In January 1897, the world was turning faster than anyone could dream of towards the twentieth century. You could have seen the gaslights of Broadway if you'd taken the train to New York. It left Ronceverte, five miles away, in the morning, and with some changes, you'd have been in the big city before midnight. London already had a subway system. Steam locomotives could run at speeds of 100 miles an hour, and more. Thomas Edison had discovered a practical way to light rooms, buildings, even whole cities. Sigmund Freud had already begun publishing his shocking theories, and Darwin's revolutionary views of mankind's origins had been around for nearly four decades. Yet, in mountainous West Virginia in 1897, education was limited; people relied on country school teachers and preachers for knowledge; and superstition stalked the land. The power of the printed word then as now was strong, and specters of all sorts appeared in stories printed every week in newspapers in West Virginia during the last decade of the nineteenth century. Furthermore, Scripture was accepted literally, and those who were students of the Bible could show you where there are spirits in that book. All in all, it must have come naturally to Greenbrier folks a century ago to believe in ghosts.

But very shortly, I was struck with the irony of such a thought. We today are probably no farther from witchcraft than they were just before the turn of the twentieth century. Irrationality holds the world in thrall even now, on the brink of space exploration, in the midst of burgeoning scientific and medical advances, and it is this irrationality that poses, to my mind, a threat to civilization greater than communism or nuclear war. A strong personal reason for wanting to write this book was to see if I could, by investigating this ghost story, shed some light of reason on a story generally accepted even today as supernatural, and thereby perhaps to cause others to view such claims with a salting of skepticism. If reason was then, as it still is, in shorter supply than mindless gullibility, why should that come as a surprise? Greenbrier County, West Virginia, in 1897, was, in worldly terms, a tiny place indeed. But it was a place and a time big enough for one's heart to get lost in.

All my life I've heard, or read, ghost stories—with no way to check them for truth. A name in a book or a newspaper article is impractical and usually impossible to follow up. Or it becomes a case of an earnest friend's word against one's own—and who is willing to call a friend a liar?

Here was a ghost story I could check on. If there was a trial, records were kept. The events happened within two hours' driving time of my home, making an on-the-spot investigation possible. Surely there must be relatives still alive of both the woman who died and the man convicted of murdering her, and there must be folk-memories of the event still extant. For it is a story not easily forgotten, with all the elements a writer could wish for: love, death, passion, betrayal, murder, the supernatural.

Superstition is tenacious. Even when confronted with facts, people often wanted to reject them, to refuse to even consider the truth. For example, one man in Greenbrier County, when shown newspaper clippings confirming facts that disagreed with his version of the events, flatly declared that the newspapers were lying.

Another told me, "They say wolves howled when Zona was killed."

"Oh," I replied, "were there wolves in this part of the country then?"

And his reply was, "I don't think so. But that's what they say."

"Do you believe in the ghost?" I asked, many times.

"Well, I don't, but there's no other explanation there could be," would be the reply. Or, "No, of course not, but how else could she have known?"

A Pocahontas woman advised me, "Let the dead rest. Don't be mixing around with the dead. That's just trouble."

And someone else said, by way of proving the ghost was real, "Y'know, the sheets turned to blood when Trout went to wash them." (Trout was the husband, Edward, who was first called Erastus and also went by the name Erasmus.)

My research has revealed a world in some ways like our own, yet in other ways quite different. I have sometimes felt as if I have been trying to peer backwards down a telescope at figures so tiny or so dim I can hardly see them, or trying to listen desperately through space and time in the hope of hearing just a few remarks, a few words, from those days. The diction, words, thoughts, and day-by-day activities of the inhabitants of this book are all almost entirely lost to us. We are spoiled today, with our cameras and tape recorders and home movies and photostatic copying machines. Movies exist of Teddy Roosevelt and Adolf Hitler; today we can actually see the dead alive; if civilization survives, it will presumably be possible in five thousand years to see accurately five thousand years into the past. Yet only a brief century ago my characters had few ways to record themselves, left precious few written words, hardly any photographic likenesses that we can be certain of, and only one strange drawing. The transcript of the murder trial mysteriously disappeared from the Greenbrier County Courthouse about half a century ago. I have found no one who could describe Zona or Trout in any but the most general terms: "He was tall, big, powerful, handsome." "She was pretty, with long black hair." I have not one word that Zona ever spoke.

Yet the characters in this book were ordinary people, and people whose society and probably whose genes I share. They lived only seventy miles west of where I do, were of the same northern European extraction, of Scots-Irish-German lineage. They were probably originally from Virginia, and their speech patterns must have been similar to those of my grandparents. I trust that their emotional reactions were of the sort that I understand. They were rural folk, like my people. They were ordinary people who were, of course, like all of us, not ordinary at all.

It is February 13, 1983. Surprisingly, the tombstone is new, sharp-edged, shiny: "In memory of Zona Heaster Shue, 'Greenbrier Ghost' 1876–1897." The congregation of the nearby church put it up in 1979, raising the money themselves, perhaps believing still in the ghost, or believing at least that the cemetery's most celebrated occupant ought to be acknowledged in some permanent way. Apparently no grave marker ever existed for her until then. The West Virginia Highway Commission erected the nearby roadside marker as a concomitant of their efforts.

Some plastic daisies have been stuck in the ground in front of the gravestone. The grass is brown, with islands of snow. Yucca plants spike out of the ground, ever green. Yews and boxwoods grow here and there among the unkempt gravestones, and many of the markers are leaning or toppled over. I have followed the deserted winding road up Little Sewell Mountain to Soule Methodist Church, which is very small. I wonder idly if the names derive from the same root: Soule and Sewell sound exactly alike on the tongues of the folk hereabouts. (They do not: Soule was a nineteenth-century circuit-rider, and Sewell a railroad magnate who would also give his name to a boom town, now a ghost town, on the C & O main line.) I have come in winter to see the little cemetery more or less as it was when the hapless woman died nearly a century ago. Moss grows on what must be the north sides of the trees, and the ground is spongy in the early thaw.

The modern stone, carved with flowers, stands out in sharp contrast to the time-softened ones nearby. There seems to be no schoolhouse, or any other sort of house, near enough to have been Nickell schoolhouse, where I have heard the autopsy was performed, and no indications of any building foundations. There is only a farmhouse nearly out of sight down the road, from which unseen dogs send their frantic, accusative warnings in my direction. Go, go, go-go. Stay away. Stay away!

I have never particularly cared for historical novels, simply because it bothers me a great deal not to know what is fact and what is fiction. Even the names of such works are odious to me: "docudrama" is the new one, but "faction" (factual fiction) and non-fiction novels (a patent contradiction in terms) have been around awhile. All allow for dangerous half-truths that muddy real historical issues, and all allow writers to attach real names to our fantasies, which end up becoming realities in readers' minds. I am very much aware that I now have in my mind clear pictures of the characters I have been working on, which may not be accurate.

As a researcher, I have for more than two years been committed to discovering and telling the truth of this story. Yet as a writer, I had finally to admit that defensible facts alone did not always tell the story to my satisfaction. A factual historical account did not enable me to evoke the feeling of the times, or to portray the minds of people or the details of their daily lives. These facts taken by themselves left all my characters as two-dimensioal as cardboard figures, primitives in some quaint regional puppet show.

To tell the story of Zona Heaster Shue, her mother Mary Jane Robinson Heaster, her husband Trout Shue, and the "ghost" who supposedly solved a murder case in the state of West Virginia in 1897, I saw that it would be necessary for me to get myself inside the imaginations of these people, as a novelist must do, and to try to understand what they were feeling, thinking, imagining. I would have to attempt, out of my knowledge and experience of the region that I have spent my life in, from which all my people sprang, a mere sixty or seventy miles to the east of Greenbrier County, to reconstruct the characters with something of the complexity that I know they possessed as human beings.

Let me say here that I have invented no facts or motives that would in any way distort or change the historical record. I have filled in, but not altered. My solution to the problem of fictionalizing history, imperfect though it may be, has been to provide copious notes at the end of each chapter, by which I have tried to be scrupulous in distinguishing for the readers facts from factually based fiction. The truth is, there is a great deal about this story that can no longer be known, such as how Trout Shue and Zona Heaster actually met, and so I have invented a plausible meeting for them. If I have occasionally, or often, told more than the reader wanted to know, I apologize. The account that follows, though some details of it cannot be proven, is, I believe, as honest an account as anyone could possibly write. I have been as objective as I could, and as fair as I could, and I have no bones to pick. I merely find the story interesting, and wanted to ferret out what really happened.

I believe I have done that. I believe that I have solved the mystery of the "Greenbrier ghost." For in the course of my investigation, and with the help of a friend, I turned up a piece of evidence—circumstantial to be sure, but to my mind quite conclusive—that will indicate what really must have taken place.

I am not the first to observe that fiction is, or can be, more real than truth. Thus I feel that the purposes of history, in this instance at least, are better served by a carefully documented account interspersed with invented scenes based on the best information I could find, than by an account so dry no one would have wanted to read it. Where I have been given the freedom to do so, I have credited people who gave me information. In some cases, people have asked that I not print their names.

When I make a dress, I take pains to hide the seams, to make the outside of the garment appear all new and smooth, as if it was done by magic. Yet in writing history, I think that the story will be more interesting if I let the seams show, allowing the reader to see the process, as well as the result, of several years of work and pleasure.

I am indebted to the many people who helped me with this book. My first thanks go to Paul Shue, whose grandfather and Trout Shue's father were brothers. His unflagging companionship, objectivity, and help I depended on from the start. He is retired from a career that included both the postal service and radio. It was he who first told me this story, and then found relatives who helped enormously. Through him I got in touch with Wenona Shue McNeal, whose explanations of various events in Trout Shue's life and career have proven extremely interesting.

Charles Robert Adams, Jr., whose great-grandfather was Johnston Heaster, brother to Zona's father Jacob Hedges Heaster, is the self-appointed genealogist of the Heasters. A retired lawyer who was an insurance investigator during his career, Bob knows his way around courthouses, and spent days going through court records for me and with me. Without Bob Adams and Paul Shue I simply couldn't have written any more than what's been written scores of times. Yet although they guided me to valuable information, the conclusions in this book are my own, and neither of them is responsible for anything written herein.

I owe special thanks to Mrs. Daisy K. Hume, who when I met her told me that she was ninety-nine and a half. She lived at the time of the incidents I describe, and has helped me with a thousand details of daily life that have enriched my narrative. To my regret, though she was twelve at the time of Zona Shue's death and lived only three miles from Livesay's Mill, she never knew or saw either Trout or Zona. But she knew, or knew about, nearly all of the other characters in this story, and her descriptions and observations have been invaluable. She knows where the road ran, where the store was, what kind of house Anderson Jones lived in (he was the boy who found the dead woman). At least as important, she knows how people lived at the time, their customs, their habits, their daily activities, how everyone dried corn and fruit spread out on sheets on the tin roofs, for example, and a million other details I could neither write down fast enough nor make use of. Those years, nearly a century ago, are clearer to her than the present.

Trout Shue's next brother, John Patrick Bruffey Shue, and his wife Josie had a son, Emery, who with his wife Pearl had eight daughters and a son. The seventh daughter, Wenona Shue McNeal ("Nonie"), has always passionately believed in her "Uncle Trout's" innocence because of the stories passed on by relatives whose first duty, she is sure, was to tell the truth. Nonie is the Shue family's main spokeswoman in this book.

Linda Susan Hyatt suggested to me the direct narrative technique; I am in her debt.

To Fred Long of the *Hinton News-Leader* I am indebted for a small but crucial piece of information that he kindly shared with me.

Many other people either allowed me to interview them, or answered my letters to area newspapers, or agreed to talk with me on the telephone, or in other ways opened doors for me. Some assisted me by reading and commenting on the manuscript at various stages. I am extremely grateful to them all. They include Frederick H. Armstrong; William M. Baker; Dr. Charles Ballou; Lola Hill Beam; Susan J. Beates; Brack V. Campbell; Newton Campbell; Dr. Joseph Carter; Charlotte Cavender; Greetha Morten Childress; Mrs. Floyd Clark; Edwin C. Coffman, Sr.; Jim Comstock; Leslie Conradi; Nina Shue Cutlip; Barbara Dailey; Liz Darhansoff; Dr. Joyce Outten Davis; Lillian Davis; George W. Deitz; J. Dennis Deitz; Violet Rapp Deitz; Tom Dixon of the C&O Historical Society; Mrs. Shirley Donnelly; Alice Donovan; Jeanne Tracy Eichelburger; Harry Fields; Harold M. Forbes; Dr. Dean Foster; Thomas Garlow; Dr. J. Michael Gilmore; Gladys Goodwin; Dr. Jim Gray; Mrs. S. C. Griffith; Dr. Roger Groot; Col. Oscar Gupton; Mary Frances Hanger; Tod Hanger; Shelby D. Hanna; Alma E. Harless; Mrs. E. R. Hawkins; Sheldon "Don" Haynes; H. G. "Bill" Heaster; Brenda Heaster; Rosalie Hicks; Bob Holliday; G. Harwood "Woody" Huffcutt; Blanche Humphreys; Dr. Julie A. Jennings; Dr. Jules Karpas, M.D.; Frieda M. Hendrick King; Dr. Janet H. Lee, M.D.; Mrs. Barclay Leef; Julia A. Legg; Betsy Letcher LeGassick; Shelby Lewis; Judge Charles M. Lobban; William D. Lomax; Joy Radford Loudermilk; Mrs. Elmer Loudermilk; Harry D. Lynch; John F. Massie; Joe McCoy; F. Witcher McCullough; Glenn McKeever; Ivan McKeever; Mr. and Mrs. J. C. McKinney; Virginia W. McLaughlin; Wenona Shue McNeal; William McNeel; Lonnie S. Miles; Dr. William W. Old III, M.D.; Zona Carr Osborne; Edwin Ott; Ann Parker; Mrs. Millard Parker; Gertrude Patterson; Carolyn Phipps; Mary Odell Phipps; Lou Robinson; Dr. Louis D. Rubin; Lee Smith; Bobby L. Shafer; Pauline Sheppard; Darleigh D. Shue; Louise Simms; Edgar Smith; Thomas C. Spencer; Frank L. Spicer; Jesse Stanley;

Margaret Stanley; Laura M. Stearns; Frances Alderson Swope; Nancy C. Thomas; Lisa Sweeney Treat; Grace K. Tuckwiller; Gray Tuckwiller; William D. Tuckwiller; Mrs. and Mrs. Fred Viers; Nelle Watts; Bonnie Wells; Lacey F. Wells; Brenda West; Elizabeth B. Wiseman; Dr. James Worth; and Dr. Maureen Rousset Worth.

I wish also to thank my colleagues at Southern Seminary who so patiently taught me word-processing, and helped me out of endless "glitches": Paul Wilson, Nick Mathis, and Lowell Cooper. I am in the debt of a remarkable little magazine that ought to be required reading for everyone, *The Skeptical Inquirer*. Since its inception a decade ago it has helped me keep my balance against irrationality. And last but not least, I want to thank my dear husband Royster Lyle for all his help, encouragement, and truly amazing patience.

Explanatory Note

In the pages that follow, certain devices of typography and ornamentation have been used to indicate to the reader the nature of the information being given.

Material that is factual, documentary material, quotations from printed sources, and statements made to me by living persons have been printed in standard typography, with even margins left and right.

Imagined scenes and sequences voiced directly by myself as storyteller are preceded and concluded by distinctive ornamentation, thus:

and are set with "ragged" right margins, as is also true for the imagined speech or thought of characters, whose names are identified in ornamental period type, thus:

 Maud Dawkins:

Each part of this seven-part narrative is followed by a set of endnotes that describe the source and nature of the material.

K. L. L.

Part One
JANUARY 1897

I would ask of you, my darlin', a question soft and low,
It gives me many heartaches, as the moments come and go;
I know your love is truthful, but the truest love grows cold,
And it's this that I would ask you: will you love me when
   I'm old?

        "Will You Love Me When I'm Old?" Anonymous, c. 1850

Saturday, January 23

Andy Jones looks at the sky. Though no sun shines through a cloudcover the dull color of old tin, the look of the air tells him it is after noon—that and the gnawing in his belly. He looks over at the other hill, a quarter of a mile away, just a few minutes' walk. Mr. Shue was very insistent this morning that he go at once to Mrs. Shue, as she was ill. But Mammy was insistent, too. She told the man that Andy was promised out today to Dr. Knapp. Across the way, in the Shue house, the boy can see no activity, no lights, nothing moving. Now finally he is done with cleaning out all of Dr. Knapp's fireplaces, with scrubbing to whiteness all of the linen from the physician's office. For a moment more he stands with his back to the doctor's house, looking across the valley at the Shue house. He calculates the distance to his own little house at the top of the hill, just about midway between the two. Dinner will be waiting, hogmeat and corn pone and coffee boiling hot to thaw him out. He spreads his lips and blows into his cupped hands. It will take only thirty minutes more to go now, instead of after dinner, to see about Mrs. Shue. He heard Mr. Shue tell Mammy that he was not going home for dinner today. Funny about white folks, Mrs. Shue always drooping around, sick-like, but not with any sickness he knew of. And Mr. Shue staying away at dinnertime.

Wearily he trots up the path leading around the side of the hill. Mammy needs the money he makes doing chores, especially now with baby Reuben in the family. And Mr. Shue had insisted. Twice during the morning Andy had seen him running up the hill to the shack they lived in, him and his mama and Reuben, as he had been at work at Dr. Knapp's chores, carrying out cinders, hanging out the cold wet linens. Didn't see how a man could get much smithing done always running around like that. And what was wrong with the man that he couldn't go home and check on his wife himself?

The chicken coop is no warmer, but at least it is protected from the wind inside. Andy feels under each setting hen, but there are no eggs today. Two other scraggly hens peck around stupidly in the barren dirt outside the coop.

Of late Andy has been taking Mrs. Shue's extra eggs to the store for her. He is very hungry now. He will go in and tell her that there are none today, and that he will come back after dinner and do whatever else she needs. If he runs, he won't be so cold.

First he knocks on the kitchen door, lightly, as the contact causes his knuckles to ache. After a moment the wind seems almost unbearable, and he knocks again, this time with his open palm, which makes a louder noise. And a third time, he bangs on the door and calls.

There is nothing but silence from inside the house. Cautiously he tries the door. It is not locked. She is ill, her husband said. Maybe she really does need help.

The kitchen is dark, and cold. There has been no recent food preparation here. The next room is the dining room, from which the stairs lead up to the second floor. He has never been upstairs. Should he go? He pushes open the door to the dining room.

The child is unprepared for the sight before his eyes. There, lying on her back, her head slightly to one side, her brown eyes staring blankly, her mouth wide open, is Mrs. Shue, right on the floor at the bottom of the stairs. She is stretched out perfectly straight, her feet together. One hand is lying by her side and the other lies across her belly. Her clothes are all neat. He does not understand. What is she doing here?

He reaches down to help her up, but withdraws from the icy cold of the hand he has just grasped. This is wrong! For just a second, the expression on her face makes him think she is laughing at him. Did she fall down the steps? But no, she is too straight. A person who falls is not straight.

She is dead. Shocked and uncertain what to do, he backs away, out of the room, turning his back on the horror only when he is outside the door, stumbling backwards over the door sill in his haste to get out. Before he is off the porch, his mouth is open and a voice is coming up from way down deep in his frozen lungs, where he is trying to call, over and over, "Mammy! Mammy!"

The Richlands section of Greenbrier County where the Shues lived is cattle country: lovely rolling hills, limestone outcroppings, contented slow-moving cows grazing the slopes, meandering creeks, springs bubbling up from underground, limestone caves, neatly tended farms. The small cluster of buildings—mill, store, smithy, and a handful of dwellings, where Trout Shue took his bride to live and where the blacksmith shop in which he worked stood—was called Livesay's Mill.

Shue had come to Greenbrier only a few short months before, in the autumn of 1896, to ply his trade of blacksmithing in the shop of James Crookshanks, located just off the old Midland Trail, now U.S. Route 60, seven miles or so west of Lewisburg. All the public roads in those days were still unpaved and had gates across them to keep cattle from roaming from farm to farm. Miss Gray Tuckwiller of Fairlea, born soon after the events of this story, reports that the new blacksmith took care of shoeing the horses on her father's farm. She believes that it was her father, Charlie Tuckwiller, who owned the land on which Crookshank's blacksmith shop stood. The old Tuckwiller house still stands, a local landmark.

Hard by the smithy stood Livesay's Mill, which gave the area its name. There, corn and wheat were milled for the farmers of the area for roughly three miles around, or as the old-timers like to say, "from the foot of Miller's Mountain to Brushy Ridge." Across Milligan Creek, on which the mill stood with its big water wheel, was the small general store, which stocked groceries and dry goods, among them cotton, calico, and "outing" or flannel, hooks and eyes and needles and thread. Hats sold for about a dollar apiece. A good stout rope was eight cents, and a broom seventeen. There was nothing in cans at that time, but at the store one could buy coffee (Arbuckle's cost sixteen cents a pound) and tea, hard cheddar-type cheese manufactured locally (as opposed to cottage cheese, or soft cheese, which was made at home), rice, candles, oatmeal, soap, and dried fruit and vegetables—apples, peas, beans, corn, cherries, raisins, peaches, and pears—as well as candy out of jars: coconut candy, chocolate candy, barbershop pole stick candy, and vanilla stick candy a child could insert into a whole lemon and suck the sweet-sour juice through. Local eggs, like Mrs. Shue's extras, were usually available at five cents a dozen. Sometimes there were peanuts for sale, as well as staples like sugar, baking powder, soda, and salt. Some spices, exotic and highly prized, were to be had from time to time. A few patent medicines were available, and certain chemicals, such as copperas, used to make fertilizer and ink and to purify water. Probably arsenic and strychnine compounds were available, as they were useful for controlling pests.

At the top of the hill to the south about 300 yards distant from the store stood the white frame house where the local physician, Dr. George W. Knapp, lived and had his office. He is an important figure in this story. He always sat in the "Amen corner" of church on Sundays, and was very well thought of. To the northeast of the mill and blacksmith shop on another hill about a quarter mile away was the house Shue rented from the estate of Mr. Will Livesay, who had recently died. It was a two-story log house, "hewed up to the square." Roughly in between these two dwellings was the schoolhouse where young Charlie Tabscott taught the area's white children, all eight grades in the same room, for the princely salary of forty dollars a month, eight dollars of which went to pay for room and board with the family of one or more of his pupils, who attended school five days a week from nine to four. One of his future colleagues would be Mrs. Hume, then Miss Daisy Kincaid, age twelve.

Near the schoolhouse was a tiny dwelling, hardly more than a shack, that was home for a black woman whom the Civil War had freed from her owner, Col. Samuel McClung. The woman was "Aunt" Martha Jones, and she had two children, both boys. Anderson, or Andy, was about eleven at the time of these events, and Reuben was just a baby. In the neighborhood, too, were prosperous farms and elegant houses, like the home of the Tuckwillers who owned the blacksmith shop where Shue worked and the land on which it stood. The prosecuting attorney of Greenbrier County, John Alfred Preston, who was to play an important part in the events to come, lived in a large house with white columns on a big farm down the road from Livesay's Mill, about a mile back towards Lewisburg. He is remembered as an elegant, fine-looking man, bald and spiffy, who rode a snappy black horse around Greenbrier County.

Col. Sam McClung's handsome farm was nearby. He had a stillhouse and made whiskey, and some of his sons grew up to be topers, running themselves into debt. A story goes that one time one of the McClung boys had Dr. Knapp to the house about a sore throat, and when he said, peering down his throat, "I can't see a thing," Mr. McClung's wife retorted drily, "Well, look again. There ought to be two or three good farms down there."

Andy cannot run any faster. His mammy hears him coming, panting and trying to holler her name. When he looks up from running, out of breath, she is already outside, standing in the dirt yard, and she places a finger on her mouth to shush him so that he will not wake the baby. Then she is holding him by the shoulders, her large hands firm, commanding him to slow down and explain. And it's like a nightmare; the words won't come out right. Finally she understands, and she has him by the hand, dragging him across the frozen ground, down the hill, into the hollow, his side with a stitch fit to kill and her apron flapping in his face.

Inside the blacksmith shop it's warm, heavenly warm. There are mountains of scrap metal for a boy's pleasure, and Andy usually loves coming here. The smith is wearing only his sheepskin vest above the waist, the woolly side against his skin, and the muscles in his arm bulge with every motion. It makes Andy shiver to look at those bare arms. Andy has never been so cold in his life, and his entire body is trembling violently. Mr. Shue won't pay attention, has his back to them, with a determined, set stance as if he never even heard them when they burst in the door. From this angle Andy can see nothing of the blacksmith's face except that lick of falling hair in front of his forehead. But Andy sees the look on Charlie Tabscott's face as he holds his old mare while Shue peels her toenail away in a big curl. All the while Mammy tries to explain, spreading her hands out as if to soothe away the information she has to convey.

Eventually Aunt Martha makes Shue understand what she is trying to tell him, and he leaps up, flinging the hoof parer with a great clang, and shouts so loud it echoes in the shop. The horse shies, its eyes rolling. The blacksmith flings off his sheepskin vest, grabs his shirt and greatcoat, and begins to run while he is still half-out of his coat. Behind him, Charlie Tabscott watches them go, his mouth open, fallen into a perfect O. Then he grabs his coat and follows.

At the house, the kitchen door still stands open, and Shue turns on them angrily. "Boy, why did you leave the door—?"

But Aunt Martha steps close and pushes Andy behind her skirts. "The child was frightened to death!"

With no comment, Shue goes on in at a run, directly through the kitchen and into the dining room. They hesitate for a moment, for who knows what to do when there is a death? Andy is reluctant to go back in. But Aunt Martha near yanks his arm off, and when they get there the powerful smith is kneeling on the floor with his wife's lifeless form in his arms, keening loudly. There are tears on his cheeks, and a wild look in his eyes. "Why didn't you get Dr. Knapp?" he shouts.

Andy backs off, rebuffed by the anger. "I-I—" But Shue doesn't wait. "Now!" he yells. "Go get him!"

*

Dr. George W. Knapp could barely make out what the two of them, mother and boy, were saying. Then, "Oh, my God, no!" He had been eating his dinner in his shirtsleeves, and had to leap up, leaving unfinished the beefsteak and corn pudding, bank the fire and dress for outdoors, still picking bits of cornsilk out of his teeth, calling to the Negro girl in the kitchen that he would be back as soon as he could, as he struggled into his overcoat, helped by Aunt Martha. Hastily he rummaged through his bag looking for his stethoscope, and finding it missing, had to go scrabbling for it amidst the clutter of bottles and pillboxes and papers on his desk before he could go. He grabbed some ammonia in a vial with the notion of trying to revive her. Finally he snapped closed the brass lock. Then, the black leather bag swinging, long coat flapping in the fierce wind, he hurried down the hill and across the valley, followed closely by Aunt Martha and Anderson.

By the time Dr. Knapp arrived "a short while later," by most accounts near an hour, Trout had carried Zona's body upstairs and dressed it up in Sunday best. Shue had, contrary to local custom, laid the body out upon their bed instead of waiting for "the women" whose task it usually was to wash and dress a corpse in preparation for burial. All versions of the story mention a large scarf or a big bow tied over a high-necked, stiff-collared dress, and a veil added on top of all that. Mr. Shue had seated himself by his dead wife's head, cradling her head and upper body in his arms, apparently stricken with desolation. Everyone's heart went out to this poor, distracted man. His show of distress, then and later, impressed everyone who observed it.

Dr. Knapp's job as coroner was to determine the cause of death. But Trout Shue held his wife's head in his arms and sobbed, appearing so distraught with grief that Dr. Knapp, moved by intimidation or delicacy, made short shrift of his examination of the dead woman. Judge J. M. McWhorter, the judge who would preside at the trial the following July, said in a letter to the editor of the *McDowell Recorder* in 1903 that Knapp had been treating Mrs. Shue for two weeks, for some unknown sort of "trouble." The newspaper later reported that Dr. Knapp said that she had "died of an everlasting faint." An account in the *Pocahontas Times* at the time of the trial, the following July, reports, "There were slight discolorations on the right side of the neck and right cheek. The Doctor unfastened the collar and examined the front of the neck and right cheek and was about to examine the back of the neck when [Shue] protested so vigorously that he desisted from further examination and left the house." Judge McWhorter wrote simply that Knapp "made a cursory examination."

Dr. Knapp had to send someone out to tell Zona's parents. Word of the young woman's death spread like brushfire throughout the area, and by late afternoon, two young fellows who had known Zona and her family stepped forward to be the ones to ride out and tell the Heasters. Dick Watts had been a friend of Zona's, and Lewis Stuart agreed to keep him company on the long bitter ride. Bundled up to the eyes, to prevent windburn and frostbite, the two men mounted their horses.

About fifteen miles to the west of the Richlands, where Livesay's Mill was, are two fair-sized mountains called Little Sewell and Big Sewell, with the town of Rainelle in between them. On the east slope of Little Sewell is the area called Meadow Bluff, or the Meadowlands. That is where Zona grew up, where Watts and Stuart had to go. Even today the farms are small here, with flattened brown grass in winter, scattered cedar and scrub-pines the green-blue-gray of cold seas, small orchards of arthritic apple trees, their ugly gnarls exposed on the wintry hillsides, and the hillsides themselves seemingly scraped down to the bone in places. In the low areas between the hills the water table is in some places actually above ground, creating marshy areas that ooze up from underground and sometimes freeze, treacherous bogs of slime concealed under tufts and tumuli of stiff weeds. No real town has ever grown up here, though there are enough scattered cabins, farms, and small houses in the area so that nowadays there is a post office. It is a tiny building at a crossroads, probably no more than ten feet square, with a sign over the door:

just the name, "U.S. Post Office, Meadow Bluff, WV," and the zipcode, 24967. Homes are scattered up and down along mostly unpaved and winding roads. The dwellings stand separate from their neighbors in the aloof way often found in mountain country.

In one of these isolated homes in 1897 lived the Heasters. Jacob Hedges Heaster and his wife Mary Jane Robinson Heaster, both in their forties, were Baptists. Heaster was either a farmer or a laborer, appearing with different occupations on different censuses. The Heasters, like most of their neighbors, were poor but respectable. Out of eight children, only one, their second, was a girl. Lively and popular, she was called Zona. She had been married in October, just three months before, and gone to live on the other side of the county with her bridegroom. The Heasters had not seen their daughter since her wedding to Erasmus Stribbling Trout Shue.

When they arrived at the small house where the Heasters lived on the side of Little Sewell, Watts and Stuart were windburned and half-frozen. They surprised the woman; that was clear. Her eyes grew large at once, and she looked startled and pleased. Then her eyes narrowed as she realized this was no social visit, and she stood in the door forgetting to invite them in out of the cold. Dick gestured that they would like to come in, and she stepped aside. Inside the house, she at once said the name: "Zonie . . ."

Dick nodded. "Someone had to come. Better it was me. Is your husband home?"

She shook her head. "No one but me. What happened? Is she sick? What—? Where—?"

Both men shook their heads, and haltingly, reluctantly, brought themselves to tell her. "Don't nobody seem to know. Dr. Knapp was treating her—a nigger boy found her—it was about noon. Knapp said she died of an everlasting faint. I don't reckon that means he knows what it is. She was at the bottom of the stairs . . ."

And Mary Jane Robinson Heaster's face grew dark as the

news sank in. She swallowed, then spit out the words, "The devil has killed her!"

All day the skies had been heavy and threatening, with a damp cold that penetrated all the way down into her bones. Now, in addition, behind the two men standing in her doorway, the world was turning into night, and outside it was beginning to sleet.

She would keep the men over, cold as it was, but there was not even elbow room in the little house, with the boys growing so fast. The two smallest had moved over into Zonie's old room when she left. Automatically, shocked beyond feeling, Mrs. Heaster offered Dick and Lewis what hospitality she could. She gave them whiskey and made them coffee, though they protested that they needed nothing. She brought them to the kitchen fire. As she sat, too shocked to think, their conversation halted, took up for a moment, died, took up again, halted. What she later recalled them talking about: how woods burn, a good subject and safe, as they stared into the fire.

"You have maples . . ." Lewis began.

"Yes . . ."

"Real nice trees."

They all nodded.

Watts spoke. "We have maples too, but they ain't good for climbing. You need oaks to climb. Or elms."

"But it burns nice. Maple. Nice and steady."

"And real hot."

"I like how that sap boils up with a nice friendly sound."

"Not like pine."

"No. Pine, it burns fast. You think it's finished, and then it flares up again, later, and you know it wasn't dead, just resting."

"Well, oak burns good. Real slow and hot. Not like pine."

"No, not like pine . . ."

She broke in. "Can't I go back with you now? I need to go to her—"

And gently, they dissuaded her; Zona's body would be brought home in the morning; it was bitter out there; she would need to conserve her strength; besides, her family would need her now. She gave in, nodding.

She thought later that she'd held up real well as long as there was someone else there, someone to talk to. But they had to get home before the night got too dark, and as soon as they left, she sank to a chair, her knees like jelly, nausea rising into her throat. She tried to pray, to try to stop the trembling of her body. Her own first blurted-out reaction still shocked her. She hadn't known she could have said it until the words were out, clear on the winter air, staying to echo even after the smoke of her breath was gone. The boys had shuffled their feet and looked down, embarrassed. Yet it must be true. That blacksmith was as false as Indian summer. She had gone to the wedding, just three months ago. Even then, Mary Jane Heaster had been full of a mother's uncertainty. But Zona, eyes sparkling with defiance, had marched proudly by her to go stand at the side of the new blacksmith who had been causing a commotion ever since the day he first showed up. Then, her daugher's color had been high, and her face full of hope, and if she hadn't been happy— and who could say?—at least she'd been a perfectly healthy young woman.

How, how was it possible that now, so soon, precious Zonie lay lifeless in that stranger's house?

He killed her. She knew it deep down, as deep down as she knew that flowers bloom after rain. In the fireplace in front of her the pine log suddenly ignited, as if rising from the dead.

Sunday, January 24

On Sunday, January 24, Zona Heaster Shue's body was taken by carriage to her parents' home, fourteen miles away from Livesay's, on Little Sewell, in an unfinished coffin provided by the Handley Undertaking Establishment in Lewisburg. (Their newspaper ads offered plain coffins for five dollars.) Mrs. Shue's grieving husband and "some neighbors" attended the move. Shue showed extraordinary devotion, keeping a vigil at the head of the open coffin the entire time that Zona "lay a corpse" in her mother's house, which must have been from Sunday morning when the body was moved there from their home at Livesay's Mill through Sunday night and into Monday until time for the burial. Such "wakes," as they were called, were common at the time. Neighbors came to pay their last respects to the dead and give solace to the bereaved, brought food to the family, and visited with one another.

The recollections handed down from that day are many. Every time anyone came near, Shue would say, "Isn't she pretty?" He told everyone he had dressed her himself, and appeared nervous about people coming too close. He was agitated and distracted, wavering between debilitating grief and moments of intense, manic energy, in which he talked energetically with the visitors. He didn't want anyone else near her, they said, and he lovingly placed a pillow at one side of her head, and some "wrapped sheet or garment" at the other, saying that she would "be able to rest easier." He told someone that the dressing at her neck was her favorite scarf and that she had "wanted to be buried in it."

Despite Shue's ministrations and watchfulness, many people noticed an odd looseness of the head on the neck at the time that the corpse was moved. The peculiar wadded supports in the coffin at the sides of the head probably also indicated to observers that the head must have been unstable. Yet all accounts contend that those who saw him after Zona's death were deeply touched at the bereaved smith's attentions.

Leaving the house, back in their own homes, or meeting along the winding country roads, neighbors exchanged remarks as neighbors will:

"I have seen a lot of corpses in my time, but what were those bundles by her head?"

"Someone said he was married before. I heard Mary Jane thinks he killed her. You have to wonder what happened to his other wife."

"He never left her once the whole time she was in her mother's house. Like he didn't trust anyone. Heard he never even went to the outhouse."

Monday, January 25

Mary Jane Robinson Heaster, forty-eight, had gone nearly all day without speaking to anyone. She was numb. First the shock of hearing, like that, of her only daughter's death, then the pain of seeing Zona lying there looking just as she had in life. There had never been a day so miserable, as if all the heavens were weeping freezing rain for her Zonie, her wild high-spirited girl. Zonie, who had always held her own with all the boys in the family, the fat little girl with black curling hair who would have defied God if He'd crossed her. The sunny child who laughed her way into everybody's heart. Mary Jane's hands had never got warm all day until she went to bed and clasped them between the flesh of her upper legs, curled into herself for warmth. Finally, comforted by her own doughy smell, she had fallen into a fitful sleep. In the night, a dream had found Zonie next to her bed. She had cried out to her, "Zonie, Zonie, I've lost something!" And Zonie had only said, "For everything you lose, you'll find something." That was what *she* had always told Zona, when she'd lost her china doll, when she'd broken her Fast Flyer, when her pony had died.

Now she trudged heavily with Hedges and the boys, silent, up the path towards the chapel, her heavy woolen cloak eventually weighing down her shoulders with rain. Behind her trooped grimly what neighbors would come out in all this; for two days now they had stopped by to take her hand or call her by name, and she had perhaps responded, but if she had, it was without knowing a thing she said. She recalled the men who dug the grave saying it was a good thing that the ground was still not frozen.

A good thing? It seemed to her that there was no good thing left any longer in God's world.

She had, before it was time to close the coffin, removed that sheet that her son-in-law had stuffed in at the side of Zonie's head. She had tried to give it back to him, as it was from his house, but saw how in his pride he would not take a thing from her, not even his own sheet. "Mother, you keep it," he had said loudly, smiling a wan, sad smile where others could see and hear.

Mother? She was not his mother, had never been, never would be. He only said it for appearance, to be heard by the others.

She had asked him to give her back one thing only, Zonie's little gold ring that had come from her mother, and which she had passed on to her only daughter, who would now never have a daughter of her own. And Shue had taken off his little finger some ring she had never seen, that didn't even look to be real gold. "Oh, I meant to. Yes, she said when she was sick that she wanted you to have this," he said.

But she had stared at the ring. "That isn't Zonie's. I never saw it before." As she looked at his face, she saw him hesitate, look frightened, then recover. "Oh, yes, I forgot. Of course. Her death has undone me." And he took back the ring, and put it back on his little finger. And had said nothing more about Zonie's gold ring.

She looked up, and saw to her surprise that already they were at the cemetery, the winter ground spongy underfoot. Just looking at that gaping hole made her weep anew. Soule Methodist Chapel had been her haven since she was a child, and now to be burying her only daughter here! Why, oh, why, couldn't Zonie ever have listened? Mary Jane Robinson Heaster stared up at the oaks and poplars at the edge of the cemetery, at the scrubby bushes nearer where the ground had been cleared for burying. Headstrong. Why couldn't she have married George Woldridge and raised that baby of theirs like she was supposed to? Why at least couldn't she have then married Al Carr? He was a nice boy, and somebody they knew. Ah, but it was too late now.

It had all been wrong, all wrong. She realized how very little she had known now that it was over, yet how it had nattered at her all along. It had happened too fast, the meeting, the courtship, the marriage, all in less than three weeks! She had begged Zonie not to. He was too biggity, cutting up so that everyone had a story about him. Some of them not too good, either. And all that talk! Someone had even said that he was a horse thief!

The preacher spoke words of comfort, of a Heavenly Home where they would all be together again, where already Zonie was joyful in the presence of the Lord. The words only made her angry. How could he know? They had all drunk from wells they did not dig, he intoned, and warmed themselves at fires they never built. It had nothing to do with Zonie. Nothing! That smith had robbed her of her daughter! Brother Sills spoke of Zonie still being among them. But it was a lie. There was nothing but the here, the now, and the absence. Zonie was gone.

She watched Shue hammering down the nails on Zonie's coffin himself, weeping loudly. He had pushed back the others who tried to help, insisted on doing it alone. She was never going to see Zona again. That thought occurred for the first time. Never. Never. The word had no meaning. She wanted to cry to him to stop, to hurl herself upon the coffin, to lay her own feverish cheek on the cool wood, to go down herself into the sweet oblivion of death. But of course she did nothing of the sort. She looked around, desperately hoping for some help from somewhere. This was all wrong; the world itself was askew. Beside her, Hedges's head was bowed, the children stood patient and quiet, some of them sniffling, two of the older boys near to cry-ing, holding the littlest ones by the shoulders. It's all wrong! she wanted to tell them. If she screamed loud enough, maybe it would wake Zona up. How could she be dead? There was something wrong!

Her neighbors stood by patiently, huddled miserably in their coats, some with oiled cloths over their shoulders, and she herself felt helpless, watching the freezing raindrops spot the unfinished coffin, staining and finally soaking it before they could throw down enough clods to cover it up, so she thought, forever. She felt a terrible fire inside her; and looking at the wailing blacksmith, she knew that the only way she would ever be free of it was to do to him what he had done to Zona.

Mary Heaster sat rigid and cold staring at the candlelight long after the others were abed. She had never known such rage, and did not know what to do with it. At the cemetery it had risen like seawater into her throat, pushing out sadness. She could not even pray. If he had not killed Zonie outright, then he had somehow made her so sick that she died. Mary Jane Heaster had not liked him from the beginning, even before Zona had admitted that he'd been married before. And what had happened to his wife? She'd died. Well, and fair enough, she had thought at the time: she knew it happened. Some women weren't made for bearing children. It couldn't be helped. Zonie was all right in that regard, certainly. Outside, she could hear, if she attended, the soft shirr of snow falling. She could see the snow gathering in a graceful curve at the bottom of each window pane.

Died. All right. But not twice. It had taken Ira Pritt from up Spring Creek to tell her, just a few weeks back, about the other time, the other marriage. Two marriages—and what had he told them about that? Exactly nothing, that's what. And Zonie had never answered the letter Mary Jane had gotten one of the boys to write for her about it. That blacksmith was a stranger, a thieving, murdering stranger. Just sashayed smack-dab into the country on the first crisp autumn day, so cocky and smart-aleck, not a stick to his name, two wives dead and gone. Others had told her how he bragged.

Mary Jane remembered well the day Zonie had first set eyes
on him. They had needed to have the axe repaired, of a Saturday. They had gone to the shop at Livesay's, really only because
it was on the way to Lewisburg. Charles Tabscott and Maud and
Vic Dawkins had been there too. You met everyone at smiths'
shops, as everyone had some kind of business there. Mary Jane
loved the pleasant clutter of wheel and tong and blade, of pot
and hinge and nail. At a smithy there was warmth from the forge
in winter, and in summer relief from the sun's glare. And they
had, of course, all heard there was a new blacksmith, and they
were curious.

A simple errand. Mary Jane had seen Zonie stand aside while
they waited, admiring the shine on the powerful muscles in
Shue's back and shoulders as he hammered the glowing yellow
iron on the anvil into a horseshoe or stove-lid lifter—she could
no longer remember what he was working on, that day while
they waited. Zonie wasn't blind. When they left, he'd told them
to come back sometime. And that was the first night she'd come
home late . . .

From the beginning, he had twisted Zona around his finger,
like he had some charm or magic. It was those muscles, that
brag, the wicked stories he told, that slow grin of his, the way
the dark hair fell down in a lick onto his forehead. He was good-
looking, all right, with those blue eyes. He told Zonie he had a
child, but that her mother had abandoned them. She bet he was
older than he'd said. He couldn't have done all those things he'd
said he'd done—plus Lord knows what things he wasn't saying—and still be only twenty-nine, but that was what he'd put
down on the marriage certificate. The child, he claimed, lived
with her grandparents, because a father couldn't properly care
for a little girl all by his lonesome. But there was no talk of the
child coming to be with him and Zona.

A man twice married—no, she corrected herself, three times
married—whose wives had somehow got discarded in the years,
who had a child he didn't take care of? He was as foreign as the
man in the moon!

Yet how could he have killed her? There didn't seem to be a

mark on her, only maybe that reddish place on her cheek, the kind of bruise anyone might get from a fall. Zonie did not look pale or thin, despite Dr. Knapp's admission that he had been treating her for almost a month. It was just plain unnatural, Shue dressing Zonie himself. But people were falling all over him, saying to each other how grieved he was. It was so very confusing—the boy said she was at the bottom of the stairs. Had she perhaps fallen?

Mary Jane tried to turn to Christian thoughts. She found the Twenty-third Psalm and read it slowly to herself, even though the words blurred more with every passing year, and every passing month, it seemed like she had to hold the Bible farther out beyond her lap . . . Yea, though I walk through the valley of the shadow of death . . .

Somehow, some way, she would find the answer. She was sure Zona had not died naturally. A perfectly healthy girl didn't just keel over after three months of marriage. For hadn't she been with her when a year before, Zonie had sailed through a pregnancy, giving birth almost before Dr. Rupert got there, and got up to her chores the next day, as if nothing out of the way had happened to her? Mary Jane still thought it was awful how Zonie let them just come and take the child. But Zonie didn't want him, said she was too young. Said she didn't want to marry the Woldridge fellow, either.

She reckoned that Zonie couldn't have kept the boy baby and gone on like she did, dancing and going to parties and all. But Zonie was not a girl to be sickly, never had been; in fact she had always scorned friends who took to their beds at the slightest twinge.

Somehow, she had to find out. Every time she tried to pray to God, she found a picture of Zona before her mind's eye. She found herself praying not to God, but to Zona, to come back and tell on him. Because only Zona knew what had really happened, what went wrong, and how it was that the west wind changed into a killing north wind.

Maud Dawkins:

"I am with Mary Jane. I will never believe that Zonie went naturally. After she met Shue, poor Albert Carr didn't stand a snowflake's chance in Hell. First off, he was good-looking in the way of an older man, and Al he still had his freckles and that skinny chicken look. I do not hold with gossip, but I said to my husband, I says, 'Mr. Dawkins, I don't see what harm could come from seeing what I can find out. Do you.'

"So I asked around, that is what I did. Turns out he lied. Told them twenty-nine on the marriage license, but sure enough he turns out to be thirty-five. That's according to that other marriage, the one to the Tritt girl? They got it right there in the courthouse. Anyone can look. I don't think you can change a born liar any more than you can make a rattlesnake act nice.

"And I heard too that she—that's Mary Jane—tried to wash that sheet or whatever it was he put in the coffin with her to keep her head straight, because it smelled funny. And it turned pink.

"But you couldn't of kept Zonie away from that man any more than you can keep hogmeat from coming back on you. Chicken is more tolerable, it don't come back on you like pig.

"It was the same way with the Woldridge fellow. We all knew, but didn't nobody talk that much about it. Not out in the open.

"Found out the other wives' names too. Like I said, Isaac Tritt's girl, Lucy, was one. She died—mysteriously. I'm working on that. They lived up on Droop then. The one before that was called Estie—one of them Cutlips from up Spring Creek way. Somebody said she died too. Looks like he had his way with the ladies. For all I know there might of been half a dozen others."

 Another neighbor:

"You know, she tried to wash the sheet that was in the coffin, and it turned blood-red. She washed it again, and boiled it, and even hung it out and froze it, but it wouldn't come white again."

Maud Dawkins:

"Wasn't the blacksmith supposed to be corresponding with another woman while he was still married to Zonie? Do you know, he bought a pair of shoes at Leef's for three dollars the day he and Zonie got married, and he never paid for them!"

 A Livesay's Mill neighbor:

"They were such good neighbors! I just don't believe he killed her."

On October 15, 1896, there had been announced in the *Greenbrier Independent* a "Grand Barbecue" to be held in the "grove near Big Clear Creek" on Saturday, October 24. There would be Republican and Democrat speakers, and food enough for 5,000 people. The *Independent*, on that same day, admonished young ladies to "hurry up and find husbands, as it is now leap year, which will not come again for another eight [*sic*] years."

Whether Zona proposed marriage or Trout did, the October 22, 1896, edition of the *Independent* announced that "Mr. E. S. Shue and Miss E. Z. Heaster, of the Meadow Bluff district, were married by the Rev. T. W. Brown at the Lewisburg Station Parsonage Tuesday afternoon." The date would have been October 20. Zona's mother, Mary Jane Robinson Heaster, probably attended, though local residents tell that Zona's father was ill at the time. Very probably no one of the groom's family came, as a fifty-mile trip would have been no afternoon's jaunt but a major journey, farther than most people in those days ever went in their whole lives. No mention is made in the paper of a reception or celebration, though these were commonly reported in detail at the time. The marriage records of Greenbrier show E. S. Shue as twenty-nine, and E. Z. Heaster as twenty-two. Actually he was about thirty-five, and she was probably twenty-three.

It is tempting to suggest that since social events and entertainment were rare at the time, the newlyweds, along with most of the other residents in the vicinity, probably attended the big barbecue on Saturday, perhaps strolling hand in hand through the milling crowds, listening to the political rhetoric of the day. There would be a presidential election in less than a month. Grover Cleveland was the incumbent, a Democrat; the candidates to be voted on in only a few weeks were William Jennings Bryan, Democrat, and William McKinley, Republican. Mrs. Alex McVeigh Miller, a local writer then living in Alderson, wrote, ". . . Greenbrier County, near the Virginia line, was a little bit of the old south [sic] and considered that it was not altogether respectable to be a Republican." It was an age of golden rhetoric. "Burn down your cities and leave your farms, and your cities will spring up again as if by magic," Bryan had said in his famous "Cross of Gold" speech during the presidential campaign, "but destroy your farms and the grass will grow in the streets of every city in the country!" This message would of course have appealed to the farmers in eastern West Virginia.

We can imagine the young couple waving or calling to friends and neighbors, feasting on the barbecued beef, roast corn, bread, butter, fruit preserves from the summer just past, squash pies, apple cider, perhaps even some homemade whiskey. Perhaps they would have joined a crowd listening to a fellow in a long-tailed suit speechifying loudly and passionately about how the Republicans were sacrificing their farms and businesses to the great god gold!

Trout and Zonie would have enjoyed the autumn scenery, and been admired and envied by other young people of the area. According to older residents, he was seen as a great "catch." And she was to become remembered as "the wild rose of Greenbrier." Perhaps they thanked a cousin for the new umbrella Zonie was holding above them to keep the sun off, or "mirated" to a neighbor on the set of flowered plates she had given them to set up housekeeping, or expressed their gratitude for the fat pig nearly ready to be butchered for winter. A close relative, perhaps an older brother and his family, might have given the couple a spice-box, a treasured gift with which to begin housekeeping: of tin, painted or punched, they contained little jars of cinnamon, cloves, mace, pepper, nutmegs, and such, which were hard to obtain at the time, and dear even when available. Zona would have blushed at the well-wishers, while Trout winked and grinned at his male friends, hinting at the dark mysteries of marriage and probably strutting a bit. We have heard that he was something of a braggart. Other likely gifts would have been a broom, a few yards of sheeting, a cord of wood for the coming winter. As it was not customary to write thank-you notes to nearby neighbors, possibly this was an opportunity for the young couple to mention their appreciation to friends.

Wenona Shue McNeal:

"Around Christmas, my grandfather—that was Trout's brother John Patrick Bruffey Shue—and his wife Josie, and their sons Oliver and Emery, visited Trout and Zonie. Emery was my father. I still recall him telling me what 'Aunt Zonie' gave him for Christmas. Having been born in 1894, Emery was about two and a half in December of 1896, and Aunt Zonie gave him one of those little flat round box puzzles with beebees in it. He always said Zona was pretty, with long black hair."

 ## Mary Jane Heaster:

"I knew he was trouble the first time I saw him, that first day yonder in the blacksmith shop. It had to be early in October. I remember how the leaves were beginning to turn orange and red, and the special feel of the mellow sun that day, and later just the hint of frost to the air. There's always one day every year like that. I saw him glance at her, then just as quick as he turned away, he looked back again. And I saw Zonie, suddenly aware of herself standing among all the men, in a man's place, and feeling awkward. And when he finished shaping the axe edge, and moved his foot off the treadle, the grindstone slowed and stopped, and he said, 'It'll have to do. Still a little uneven. Last person to work on this thing come near to ruining it. All crooked along the side.'

"'Hard to get decent work done around these parts anymore,' Hedges said. 'Come all the way over here from Meadow Bluff. Heard you was good.'

"'Well,' the blacksmith says, slow and deep-voiced, 'you got to treat things real gentle.' His voice was as golden as the day. He was looking down at the axe blade, but he was talking to Zonie. Children always think old people can't remember, or never knew, about things like that.

"So when she came waltzing home that night, and I said, 'Where have you been' and she said, 'Nowhere,' and I said, 'Nowhere! You come riding in here an hour after supper is over looking like you have been through Hell and High Water, and I say, Where have you been, and you say, Nowhere?'

"And then she said, 'Well, I guess it did get kind of late. A bunch of us was talking to the new blacksmith over at Livesay's.'

"'A bunch,' I said. 'And who, may I ask, was in that bunch?'

"And she can't recall but only one name: Albert. But it just so happens I seen Albert go by two hours ago with his father. So I know she has been up to something. And my heart got tight then, and I remembered how it had been with that George Woldridge fellow."

Trout Shue:

"She comes in talking to Al Carr, that skinny little no-account, to see when her folks will be ready to go. I heard. Al wants to take her to some play at Meadow Ground Saturday night; they are going to play 'Sister Feeby,' and 'David and Goliath.' She wasn't much interested, it looked like. There was just something about her, a sashay to her I liked. But then she left and I didn't think one thing or the other.

"But it was really something. The way she came back to the shop late that afternoon, just stood in the doorway until I felt her there and turned around and saw it was her. How in less than no time, no talking at all, we were in the back of the shop, the door bolted from inside, on the old horse-blanket, and her out of her dress and petticoat and tugging me down on the blanket.

Amazed—that was how it made me feel. She told me she knew where the sinkhole pine lilies grow. She made them sound like the rarest, prettiest things in the whole world. And she promised to take me to see them in the spring. I reckon I made more love to her before dark than I'd ever made to anyone else in a month, and then, quick as she'd come she was up and leaning over, her breasts swaying, to pick up her petticoat and saying, not one bit embarrassed, but bold as brass, 'You wanted me to come back, didn't you.' Never even looked at me for an answer. And as I lay there on one elbow in the dimness feeling dumb and helpless for the first time, and wondering how she was going to get home, and not wanting to ask, she turned to me and said, 'Is Trout your real name?' Then, because she might never come back, I leaned up and reached for her, nodding, but she only said, 'Button me up the back. I have to get home before it's too dark.'

"'How?' I asked, wanting her to stay.

"'I have a horse,' she said, and smiled and went out quick, only the smell of her left on my hands to say it was no dream. Heard her leave as I pulled my trousers on. And outside, the stars just coming out, a streak of orange deep down the sky, and the first crispness that said autumn was here. And as I started up the hill to that old empty house, a sadness that maybe nothing like that would ever happen to me again. But it did."

 ## Mary Jane Heaster:

"Slowly I slid up from sleep, grasping for information. The rooster that had awakened me crowed again. I am alone, is the thought I had. I could see blue night bleaching to day, hear Hedges snore on, as oblivious as if he was the one dead. I had a dream of a baby lying naked on a red sheet, and I was young. But then I come to know: I am old, and my Zonie is dead. Her head was so floppy. Even now it makes me weak to think of it.

"You start with a baby, and you never once think about how it will turn out. So soft and helpless, and all turned to you for every need, every idea. Hugging you, loving you, hanging on every word. And when did it start to go wrong? In the paper, just those few words, that's all that's left.

"Her life is nothing anymore, just a few lines in the middle of page three of the *Independent*. I already know it by heart. 'Mrs. E. Z. Shue, wife of E. S. Shue, died at her home in the Richlands of this county on Sunday last—' They even got the day wrong—'the twenty-fourth, age twenty-two years. Mrs. Shue was the daughter of Mr. Hedges Heaster of Meadow Bluff District. Mr. Shue formerly lived in Pocahontas County.' By heart. That's how I know it.

"That's all that's left. Reading is not easy when you have only gone to school for three years, when a Bible is the only book you ever owned except for the first reading book. But sometimes I try to read the paper. Sometimes there is a name I recognize. The advertisements are in bigger writing than the columns, like the one for those Candy Cathartic Cascarets. Sometimes I even read a story, if I can find an hour to sit. I reckon that I have read every word of that one by now.

"How can Zonie's entire life be reduced to a few words in the newspaper? Is this God's will? Zonie!"

John Alfred Preston:

"As County Prosecutor, I suppose it is inevitable that sooner or later I will hear everything. Gossip. Rumor. Out at Livesay's, they say, some poor woman died a week or so ago. A bride. A girl, apparently married only a few weeks. For several days now I have been hearing of suspicions that some foul play was involved. It is very likely just the excitement caused by a sudden death in a small area, nothing more than winter boredom. Of course they are ignorant folk, uneducated—the husband, as I understand, a blacksmith come to the area only recently, reportedly a big man, tall and powerful, and something of a rogue. The mother of the girl now believes she has seen her daughter's ghost, because some sheets turned bloody after the girl was buried, though any logical connection between the two occurrences escapes me. She has told all her neighbors that the wraith of her daughter told her that the blacksmith, the husband, killed her. And now I have a message saying that she is coming to tell it to me.

"I have said it before and I will say it again: they ought not to publish those frivolous works of fiction in our newspapers that serve only to confound and confuse already weak minds!"

Trout Shue:

"When I come here, it was to begin a new life, and all of this would never have happened if I'd just gone farther. A good smith can find his way anywhere, and it's always been the thing I did best, and I was always the best blacksmith wherever I was. And the best in a lot of other things, too. The smithing part is easy here, for there have been no smiths since Jacob Boone died in the spring. That's what I wanted: work, and fire, and sweat. I and the crack of dawn are good friends, always have been. Things just never seem to work out. Erastus, father named me first: after some Swiss. But then my mother saw that picture in *Harper's Weekly* of Erasmus, while I was still a babe. He was Dutch, a preacher, a scholar, a traveler. She told me about him every living day of my life. But I didn't turn out to suit her . . .

"Maybe it was too easy. Maybe if I'd just come quietly into some place that already had a smith or two, it would have been better. But I cut a wide swath, and that was how it was. I always have. If there was some girl had a mind to go off the bridge, I'd go along with her. All of them, bringing pies, inviting me to eat with them, all those girls walking real slow past the shop . . .

"There's always folks against the best, jealous and mean, always looking, hoping to see you fall. The higher you are, you more have got to watch, and they always want to put the worst face on everything."

Maud Dawkins:

"Well. It says in the deathbook she died of childbirth. I looked, yesterday, when we was in town. Course I didn't tell my old man. I don't tell him everything I do. But that blacksmith was a nervous wreck while Zonie lay a corpse. I said it to Mr. Dawkins at the time. I said: 'Mr. Dawkins, did you notice how skittish he was when we went around?' I do not believe in gossip, as I said, but the sheets turned bloody when she went to wash them. Course, everyone knows the way to bleach white woolens is you hang them out and freeze them, but I don't know if it works on sheets.

"And I'd still like to know: did he ever pay for them shoes?"

The newsboy, out early to catch everyone, watches with interest as the three alight in the empty street. Country folks, from the looks of them. In an hour the town will be alive, the men all greeting each other in front of the feed store and buying his papers, the women looking for dry goods and chatting while the children cling to their mothers' skirts whining for candy. Usually he is the only one abroad this early to see the winter sun rise red as blood to tint the frozen puddles on Court Street.

The lady rights her hat with one hand, a straw hat smack-dab in the middle of winter! She steps firmly down from the wagon seat onto the mounting board and then to the ground. Her face is gray and drawn, and her cloak is a man's, all the way to the ground. Neither the boy nor the man helps her. She shakes her head sharply as he catches her eye, indicating they will not buy a paper, and lifts her cloak like a queen to clear the ground. Her hands are gloveless and workworn, square nails blue with cold, yet she is pretty, with fading hair a mixture of gold and silver. Meanwhile the thin child in a coat way too big for him is busy unwrapping a long gray woolen scarf from about his neck. The man pays no heed to either of them, instead busies himself with tying the horse, a chestnut mare in her fuzzy winter coat, to the hitching post. The man's coat is black and shiny with wear.

Country folks. The newsboy has never seen them. Breath-clouds before their faces, they do not speak—not to each other, not to him. He blows on his hands, trying to catch the man's eye to sell him a paper, but instead, they all troop past him across the street and into the courthouse.

 Mary Jane Heaster:

"The night was as black as a January night could be. You could hear the wind whining like a dog outside trying to get in. Every now and again a blast of wind shook the walls, like some beast out of the night was trying to get at us. I could feel it along my back as it came in at the cracks. I pulled the quilt up around my neck. I was praying, like I do every night until sleep overtakes me. I was of course thinking of Zonie, my murdered girl. During sleep I have had some strange dreams since her death. Hedges was snoring beside me, like he always does unless I nudge him and make him turn over.

"I guess I had been praying near an hour, looking into the blackness of the room and wondering if the grave was as black to my Zonie, when I heard a noise. Whenever I been in that room lately, I get a strange cold feeling. But this sounded like a sigh, maybe, or a movement like maybe a cat would make on a midnight prowl. But we don't have a cat. I strained my ears, but couldn't hear no more and I decided it was my imagination.

"Suddenly, the sound came again, like a hollow rustly noise maybe like a person would make trying to come through a narrow place. 'Til then, I had not been afraid, but then my heart began to pound fast, and I cut my eyes in that direction, but all I could see was only blackness. I would've cried out, but I was too scared. Yet I—I don't know how to say it—felt that something—someone—was there. A breath in the darkness—or—a beast, maybe—I don't know what I thought. I was like a blind person, you know how they question the darkness with their hands—only I did it with my blind eyes—I wanted to pull the covers over my head, or wake up Hedges, but I didn't dare to move. I recall about that time an owl hooting out acrost the dark, and I lay still for a long time, terrified, I didn't know why.

"It must have grown lighter, or the moon rose, 'cause after a while I could make out something. I could begin to see that it was a form, and that it was coming slowly towards me, just creeping acrost the floor towards that bed. I was froze to the marrow of my bones. As the shape approached, I elbowed Hedges sharply to wake him up, but he only groaned and turned over away from me, still asleep. Then, in a flash I knew it was Zonie, and I seen she was dressed in that blue homespun dress we made for her a year to two by. But Zonie was dead! I reckon until that moment, I never knew what shivering was. I was trembling so bad I couldn't hardly stand it.

"But then, finally, I just had to put my hand out to touch her. When I pulled it out from under the covers, it felt like putting it in ice water. I wanted to see if such people came in coffins, but there wasn't nothing there but her, her hand as cold as clay, colder than a living hand could be. The light, whatever it was, stayed in the room for as long as she was there.

"When I knew it was Zonie, I said, or thought, Is it you? And she only stared at me, looking sad. But I got my courage back. Come, I told her, and get in bed with me, honey. As a child she was used to coming into my room when a nightmare waked her up.

"But she still stood there and stared at me like she was in a trance, like she wanted to speak. Then she left, and it was the strangest thing, but I'll swear to it on a stack of Bibles a mile high: she turned to go, but then turned her head all the way back around to stare at me. Not just over her shoulder, but all the way around. I was horrified, and after she left, I did what I'd wanted to do earlier: pulled the covers over my head, and backed up to Hedges just to have something to touch, to try to feel warm again. It wasn't 'til the second night she finally started talking.

"She came the same way four nights in all. And every time when she left to go back she turned her head all the way around to look at me, and her head was just as loose as it had been in the coffin! And every night I learned more. The blacksmith had been cruel to her, and thrown her clothes out into the cold, and came at her in a fury and broke her neck. That's how she died. Wasn't no natural death, the way he said. He killed her, that devil! Zonie was murdered. My daughter is murdered!"

NOTES

p. 3: Information about the day of Zona Heaster Shue's death and the several days to follow comes from the *Greenbrier Independent*, January 28, 1897, February 25, 1897, and July 8, 1897; and from the *Pocahontas Times*, March 12, 1897, and July 9, 1897. Also, late in 1903, Joseph A. Swope, then editor of the *McDowell Recorder* in Welch, West Virginia, wrote to the presiding judge, J. M. McWhorter, seeking "an account for my readers of the trial of E. S. Shue in June of 1897 for the murder of his wife." McWhorter obliged him with a letter, dated December 1, 1903, which Mr. Swope published soon thereafter in his paper. I have drawn heavily from it, since of all sources, this one seems among the likeliest to be objective. It is printed in Appendix V.

The July 9, 1897, *Pocahontas Times* description of the child finding the body is more detailed than most; clearly they had a reporter at the trial.

Shue . . . went to the house of a negro woman and asked the son of this woman to go to his house and hunt the eggs and then go to Mrs. Shue and see if she wanted to send to the store for anything. This negro boy went to the house of Shue, and after looking for eggs and finding none, he went to the house, knocked and received no response, opened the door and went in. He found the dead body of Mrs. Shue lying upon the floor. The body was lying stretched out perfectly straight with feet together, one hand by the side and the other lying across the body, the head was slightly inclined to one side. The negro boy ran and told his mother that Mrs. Shue was dead. . . .

p. 5: Information about the area around Livesay's Mill is from Daisy Kincaid Hume, in interviews on June 16, 1983, October 22, 1983, March 23, 1984, and July 1, 1984, in Ronceverte, West Virginia. On October 22, 1983, Mr. William Tuckwiller took Miss Daisy and me on a drive through the Richlands, and Miss Daisy pointed out and described to me the area and landmarks, most of which are gone now. Knapp was her doctor when she was a child. She knew the McClung boys well. I also consulted newspapers and magazines of the time, especially the *Greenbrier Independent* and the *Pocahontas Times*.

p. 9: On the day of the murder, it took Knapp around an hour to arrive at the Shue house.

p. 9: To this day, it is not known what Knapp had been treating Zona for in the weeks prior to her death. As "childbirth" is the stated cause of death, it seems likely he was treating her for some malady connected with a pregnancy. To the general public he stated "she died of an everlasting faint," which tells us exactly nothing. Judge McWhorter, writing six years later of the trial, makes it clear that the trial brought out no reason for his treating her.

p. 9: Elva Zona Heaster was born probably in 1873, though her tombstone says 1876. In the June 1880 Greenbrier census she is listed as Elva Z., age seven, a schoolgirl, adding at least three more years to her life. The birth records of Greenbrier County indicate that she was twenty-two on November 29, 1895, when she bore an illegitimate child, whose supposed father was a worker named George Woldridge (Book 1, p. 230, line 310). It appears that people guessed at ages, rather than keeping accurate account. From the dates on Zona's tombstone, 1876–1897, it appears that she was twenty-one at the time of her death, not twenty-two, as her death certificate reads. Actually, she was probably twenty-four.

Records on the Heaster family are extremely confusing. The June 1880 census lists the children of Hedges and Mary Jane Heaster as Alfred, eight; Elva Z., seven; John M., six; and Lennie, three months old. The 1890 census has been destroyed. Other documents indicate several other boys born later, and one girl, Lanie, born July 10, 1888, or boy, Lennie, also listed as having been born on the same date, who seems not to have survived as she or he is not mentioned in the father's will in 1916. They may have been twins, but it seems more likely to have been one child, with one clerk making an error in reporting the child's sex. Lanie and Lennie are so close together in sound that reason dictates it was the same baby. Jacob Hedges Heaster's will mentions AN, LE, HC, JE, JL, JM, and JA, all sons. The last, James Arnett, adopted, was actually his grandson, the illegitimate son of James L., if the marriage book is accurate. James Arnett was born in 1906. The first Lennie, from the 1880 census, must have died, as a second Lennie was born in 1888. The 1900 census has three sons living at home: HC, seventeen; Joseph E., sixteen; and Jon L., thirteen. (He appears nowhere else, but his birthdate is too far off for him to have been Zona's child.) The family is not listed in the 1910 census. The absence of any child born in or near 1895 indicates that Zona's illegitimate child was raised by someone else. He could have died in infancy, but if so, his death is not recorded. All efforts to discover anything at all about him have led nowhere. There are today Woolridges living in the area (no Woldridges or Waldridges), but they know of no Georges among the family names. That he is called Heaster in the birth book would seem to indicate that he would be accepted and raised by them. But apparently that was not the case.

p. 11: Information about Dick Watts and Lewis Stuart being sent to tell Zona's family, and Mrs. Heaster's reaction to the news of Zona's death is from interviews with Nelle Watts, sister-in-law of Dick Watts, May 12, 1983, Lewisburg, West Virginia, and Edwin Coffman, now of Pompano Beach, Florida. Although the comment appears ambiguous (did she mean that Shue or the Devil killed Zona?), the understanding of both respondents is that she meant Shue killed her daughter.

p. 13: The *Greenbrier Independent*, July 8, 1897, details the queerness of Shue's manner at the time of his wife's death. Some information came from an interview with Lonnie Miles on March 8, 1983, Renick, West Virginia, and from an interview with Pauline Sheppard, April 6, 1983, Fairlea, West Virginia.

p. 14: An interview with Mrs. E. R. Hawkins of Alderson, West Virginia on February 3, 1984, yielded the information about Zona wishing to be buried in the scarf.

p. 15: The three "voices" are the idle gossip on the tongues of the community, sounds "in the air" of composite characters who, like the chorus in a Greek play, echo the sentiments of the populace. All accounts concur on the strange padding around the corpse's head. Obviously Zona's death was from the very beginning widely discussed, and all sorts of wild rumors flew about Greenbrier County. The accounts invariably refer to Shue's fanatic deathwatch, and his refusal to leave the side of the coffin as long as it was open.

p. 15: Zona is widely reported to have been very popular with the boys, and had already had an illegitimate child; thus Mrs. Heaster would likely have been nervous about Trout Shue.

p. 16: The sheet business is detailed in the McWhorter letter, which has already been cited, and appears in Appendix V. The ring incident is from the part of the trial transcript that Thomas Dennis printed in the *Greenbrier Independent* the following July.

p. 17: In an interview, Zona Carr Osborne, daughter of Albert Carr, averred that her father had been in love with Zona, but had lost out upon Trout's arrival, when she "fell for him like a ton of bricks." In later years when he married and sired a daughter, he named her for his slain sweetheart.

p. 17: The rumor about horse thieving was true, and anyone might have dug up this piece of "true dirt" on Shue. It is mentioned in the *Greenbrier Independent*, July 8, 1897, and the *Pocahontas Times*, December 20, 1887. It will be discussed in Part Three.

p. 17: A characteristic of Trout Shue that is frequently mentioned is his penchant for bragging. Even the newspapers reported that Shue was a braggart: the *Pocahontas Times*, March 12, 1897.

p. 19: The scene in which Zona and Trout meet is of course pure invention.

p. 21: Gossips never think they are gossips. Miz Dawkins is invented, a Greenbrier Everywoman. George Woldridge is, as has been seen, listed as "the supposed father" of Zona's illegitimate son. Lucy Tritt Shue died on February 11, 1895, which was within recent memory, about two years prior. Estie was from farther away, and it might have been harder to learn what happened to her, since she and Shue had been married November 24, 1885, or more than a decade before all this occurred. Estie did not die at Shue's hands, but accuracy has never been a trait of gossips. The McWhorter letter has already been cited, and is printed in Appendix V.

p. 22: The idea of Trout corresponding with another woman came from interviews with Lonnie Miles, Renick, West Virginia, March 9, 1983, and Edwin Ott, Ronceverte, West Virginia, a month later.

p. 22: I heard versions of the shoe purchase several times in my interviewing. When a man goes wrong, all his past sins, no matter how insignificant, are likely to be dredged up into the light. The present owners of Leef's Store in Meadow Bluff confirm that the store existed in 1897, and sold shoes.

p. 22: The voice echoes the common folklore that the young married couple seemed so happy together.

p. 24: Actually, Emery would have been at most under two years old, too early for childhood memories.

p. 25: What entertainment young people in Greenbrier had at the turn of the century they fashioned for themselves. Singing and story-telling were popular pastimes. Barnraisings, cornhuskings, and housewarmings were all useful occasions to socialize. Neighbors visited each other and chatted, exchanging local gossip, sitting on porches when the weather permitted, and around the fireplaces when it did not. Religious meetings were also social occasions, including funerals. A common entertainment among the young people of Greenbrier in the 1890s was what they called "playing." It meant, loosely, acting out in play form some story with which they were all familiar, like a Bible story, or a folktale, or a silly play like "Sister Feeby," or sometimes even the plot of a play by William Shakespeare. At times they read parts from prepared scripts, but often they played the parts extempore. The characters would shift as the players grew tired or bored, and a new Juliet or King David might move in and take over from a previous one.

p. 25: The encounter between the young people in the blacksmith shop is imagined, but I trust it is not implausible. All sources say Zona and Trout had a "whirlwind courtship," that she "fell for him like a ton of bricks," and "never looked at another boy again." Both had had previous sexual experience. And finally, rural people then seem to have enjoyed a more personal freedom than is possible most places today. They could be alone by themselves, away from others.

For example, Daisy Hume rode alone three miles to church on horseback, day or night, even as a child of ten or eleven. She shakes her head, remembering herself as a girl who "would try anything—twice," reflecting that it would be dangerous to do such a thing today. "If you passed someone," she says, "you couldn't see his face." Yet she vows that she was never frightened while roaming the sparsely populated hills of Greenbrier, on foot or on horseback. Although the entire scene is invention, Zonie had borne an illegitimate child, Trout Shue had been twice married, their courtship had to have been extremely short, and young people had a great deal of freedom.

p. 27: John Alfred Preston, the prosecuting attorney, born in 1847, was the son of a Presbyterian minister, a graduate of Washington College in Lexington, Virginia, and a long-time trustee of his alma mater, now Washington and Lee University. Preston, a

Civil War veteran and a Democrat, was elected to six terms as prosecuting attorney for Greenbrier County, two terms in the state legislature, and a term in the state senate. According to Cole's *History of Greenbrier County*, few men in the history of West Virginia have attained a reputation comparable to his for "insight, integrity, and nobility of purpose." He was a long-time elder in the Presbyterian Church. As prosecuting attorney of Greenbrier, it was his job to investigate any suspected foul play. He was a small man, very neatly turned out, with a bald head and ramrod posture.

p. 28: Shue bragged openly that he would outlive seven wives, and was described by all as magnetic and attractive. He was characterized in March of 1897 by his hometown newspaper, the *Pocahontas Times*, as "a bad man." Even if this was only neighborhood opinion, Shue was no doubt able to justify the errors of his life, at least to himself.

p. 29: Zona must have died at every supper table in the neighborhood. From January 30, when the death was reported in the official register, any citizen could have looked in the book and seen what the nosy Miz Dawkins saw. Her final quotation here is a return to the motifs of the section. Miz Dawkins represents the community's concerns, and brings us back to the "refrains" of the bloody sheet, the unpaid-for shoes. In the course of my research, I turned up twelve slightly different versions of the sheet detail, ranging from "the sheet turned pink," to "the sheets turnt to blood . . . ," and three reportings about the shoes.

p. 29: Most versions of the story tell that Mary Jane Robinson Heaster persuaded her brother-in-law Johnston Heaster to go with her to visit the prosecuting attorney, and took along "young Joe Heaster" as a scribe. There was a younger Heaster son named Joseph, but his granddaughter believed it was not he who went along, as he told the story of Aunt Zona all his life without claiming a part in it. Joe might also have been a nephew, the child of one of Hedges's brothers.

It is not known why Hedges, Zona's father, never figures in the story at all. Some say he was ill at the time; most just don't know. He lived until 1917. Johnston Heaster was his brother.

p. 30: Mrs. Heaster must have told Preston something like this. Her idiom, like that of her contemporaries, would have been informed by the Gothic stories so prevalent in the papers at the time.

Part Two
LET NOT
STRANGERS

Over on that golden shore, forms unseen are chanting low
Strains we loved in days of yore, memories of long ago.
Voices now are hushed forever, tears and flowers strew their
*   graves,*
And time's mighty rushing river buries all beneath its waves.

"Gently Down the Stream of Time," Major J. Barton, 1869

In the weeks following Zona Heaster Shue's death, the ghostly visits, and the decision to reopen the case, much came to light about Trout Shue. Zona had been his third wife. His first marriage, to Allie Estelline Cutlip, in 1885, had produced a child, Girta, and ended in a divorce four years later, while Shue was serving time in prison for horse stealing. In 1894 he was married again, this time to Lucy Ann Tritt, who died less than eight months later under mysterious circumstances. In the autumn of 1896 he moved to Greenbrier and married Zona.

Nonie Shue McNeal:

"Trout was the fifth of nine children, and his name in the family Bible is Erasmus Stribbling Trout Shue. My grandmother, Josie—that was John Patrick Bruffey Shue's wife—told me all about him. In one place his name is written Erastus. He was probably born in 1861 in Augusta County, Virginia. After the Civil War his parents, Jacob and Elizah, moved to West Virginia, to Droop Mountain, near the border of Greenbrier and Pocahontas counties. His next brother, John Patrick Bruffey Shue, was my grandfather. Uncle Trout was a big man, tall, powerfully built, strikingly handsome, dark, artistic. The Shues had money and owned most of Droop Mountain. Trout was only eleven when he carved a butter paddle for his oldest sister Susan for a wedding present. I have a pie cutter he made. When he was nineteen he hewed the logs for Mt. Olivet Church on Droop. He made furniture and could build anything. He made things out of iron and was a good blacksmith. He

41

was an artist; he drew in pen and charcoal. And he could sew and cook as good as any woman."

 ## The Reverend R.R. Little:

"Listen. I knew Trout Shue more than ten years ago. I remember the exact date. It was two days before Thanksgiving of 1885. A Tuesday. It stands out in my mind. Some things tell you a lot about a man. I had been called there, to the Shue home on top of Droop Mountain, you know, to perform the marriage of one of the Shue children. The Shues were previously not known to me, yet I knew that they were people of considerable holdings, the patriarch a good blacksmith and, I had heard one time, an itinerant teacher of music. I believe he had nine children. I was somewhat surprised to learn that the child to be married was a son.

"It was a cold bright day late in November, and I went there gladly, as a marriage generally affords a bit of food and drink, and sometimes a little music. It is a joy to join in matrimony two children of God, and surely one of the most welcome duties for a man of the cloth, called so often to soberer obligations, such as the closing of the eyes of some dead loved one, and the comforting of those left behind, or the administering of Communion to those thirsty and hungry for God's Grace, or the visiting of the ill.

"At any rate, I arrived at the house early in the afternoon, in frank anticipation of a few hours filled with warmth and joy, which are rare enough in the life of a Methodist circuit rider. At least, the Lord be praised, we worship God with song.

"At once I saw there was no joy here, but an atmosphere of tension such as one sees at weddings for which the reason is the imminent arrival of a child. Yet if that was the case, the girl, the bride-elect, Estie they called her, was not far along. I could perceive no swelling of that narrow waist, nor the pallor of those first sick weeks. But her eyes were not restful, their glances darting from spot to spot as a nervous bird's might. In addition she looked alarmingly young; at first I would have supposed her to be twelve or thirteen, her hair still down her back and clasped with a big bow at the back of her head, her frock a dark blue schoolgirl's dress. Then I saw that she was merely a very small person; I learned somewhat later that she was actually seventeen. For the major part of the afternoon she sat, rocking slowly, in a chair in the sitting room, rubbing her hands upon her knees as if anxious, while the others came and went, talking uneasily, going about their usual chores, the children generally quiet in the atmosphere strained by the presence of strangers, the small ones hiding behind their mother's skirts to peer at me or the girl.

"For it was clear that Estie was a stranger, and, I gathered, not an especially welcome one. Only Mrs. Sam Good, called Sue, was solicitous of her. The child, for truly she was, refused cider, and did not offer to help with the supper or the fire or the feeding of the livestock. Perhaps she feared criticism from her future family, or perhaps she was saving her clothing which, though shabby, may have been her best. She was from Spring Creek, some twenty miles away, but her uncle, her father's brother, was a neighbor of the Shues.

"Her intended husband, the middle son of the family, whom they called Trout, was absent, having gone to Marlinton for the marriage license. Many hours passed as we waited for him. As dark fell, we sat rather crowded together at the plain pine table to a supper of beans and pone and winter cresses boiled in sowbelly, so dark green they appeared black by the candlelight. The women had fried pies and made cottage cheese.

"There was also a great gingerbread prepared for the wedding party, and set over upon the chifforobe, but we, the assembled company, were allowed only the perfume of that, and still the groom did not appear.

"Yet strangely it was he that was the main subject of our talk. I became aware as the day drew on that he seemed to exert some peculiar power over the rest of them. In his absence there was more presence than many people ever command in person.

"After supper and clean-up, in which the girl Estie again did not offer to help, we returned to the sitting room and the fire, which should have afforded us pleasure and contentment. Several of the women and men smoked pipes. Coffee was served to us. I admired a bear's head, which was mounted over the fireplace. Of course Trout had killed the beast, inspiring more conversation on their remarkable progeny. A carved butter paddle I remarked upon was also reported as his handiwork, and again we must sing his praises. I noticed that the girl Estie smiled when we did.

"The father, Jacob, a tall silent man with a great beard and a high cerebral forehead, led us at my request in singing some sacred music, and for an hour or more the tension seemed to lift a bit. Then Jacob Shue treated us to a rendition of 'Lorena' and his deep voice brought tears to my eyes. Some of the family joined in the chorus, and their singing blended into a lovely harmony. I had heard that they sang for socials and gospel meetings. When he sang, 'We loved each other then, Lorena, / Far more than we ever dared to tell; / And what we might have been, Lorena, / Had our lovings prospered well—' I glanced at Estie, whose eyes were unreadable, staring into the firelight, and sighed for all the world's lovings that go awry. Jacob then sang 'Good Ole Rebel' at Sam Good's request, and that brightened our spirits considerably. Again cider was passed around, and Estie took a cup this time, but seemed to dislike the taste, and I noticed that she put it down again after only one sip. To my way of thinking, it was an excellent cider. My own thoughts kept gravitating towards that gingerbread.

"In the kitchen I believe some of the men were drinking a bit of whiskey. From time to time one or two would withdraw from the company, disappear, then return in a few moments. I was, quite properly, not invited to indulge, although I would have been tempted.

"Again and again one would say, 'What is keeping him?' or, 'He ought to be back by now.' I offered to leave them and return the following week, but that emphatically would not do; they all seemed to fear the groom's anger should he return and find me gone. So I continued to wait along with them, reminding myself that patience is a godly virtue. Once one of the little girls, Allie, fell, cutting her lip against a chair; she was given to her grand-mother's mountainous lap, where she could enjoy all attention for a time and have a wet cloth held to her wound. Directly she fell asleep, only to be awakened by her sister's vigorous efforts to join her or oust her from Mrs. Shue's lap. Mrs. Good, their mother, intervened, disappearing upstairs with both of them.

"From time to time we spoke of things: the fine autumn weather and good harvest, the smallpox in the neighborhood, the astonishing mad-stone advertised in the newspaper and guaran-teed to cure snakebite, mad-dog bite, and in addition nearly any other ailment known to man. Time moved slowly. Sue's little girls Maggie and Allie were long asleep. Minnie, who was eleven, then Charlie, just in the first flush of young manhood, were sent upstairs then. And we waited some more. Generally, the Shues seemed a silent lot. Estie held her hands as a winding-rack for some wool that Maggie sought to untangle, but they did not chatter much, as two girls together on one task are apt to do.

"Finally, around midnight, Shue burst in with the license, shedding chilly air and exclaiming about the coldness and the beauty of the night. His eyes fairly flashed with excitement. He kissed the girl briefly. At once her face changed, as if with hope. In fact, his presence seemed to have an electric effect on everyone in the room. Though by then some were dozing, when he came in, all of them got up stretching and began moving around with more energy than had been apparent in all the long hours.

"He was an impressive man, filling the room with his pres-ence. All hung on his pronouncements, and when he spoke, all the others fell silent. He had slick dark hair, eyes that positively danced, and a mouth that one had to call sensual. His upper body looked very powerful, though his legs seemed slightly ban-died. He was, they had told me, twenty-four. His voice was more amazing, however, than anything else about him: it was absolutely full, resonant, stunning, commanding, a singer's or an orator's voice. It was clear that he was the energy for this fam-ily. He took charge at once, greeting me emphatically, then immediately directing the others where to stand, what to do, as if it were the most natural thing in the world for a wedding to take place at a quarter after midnight. All the while he rubbed his hands briskly to warm them. The girl's eyes followed him with solemn adoration.

"Before I could perform the ceremony, of course I had to examine the license to ascertain that it was in order. Upon doing so, I discovered that the license had been issued in Greenbrier County, not in Marlinton, which explained why he had taken so long to obtain it, because Lewisburg is several miles farther away. His age was listed as twenty-four, his birthplace Augusta County, Virginia, his residence Pocahontas County. E. S. Shue, it said. When I questioned him, he replied it stood for Erasmus Stribbling, that 'Trout' was his third name, and that all the male children in the family had four names.

"The girl he had listed as Ellen E. Cutlip. 'Estelline' was her middle name, he said somewhat impatiently. Could we not get on with it?

"'This girl is twenty-two?' I asked, for so her age was written. He explained he had been in a hurry; he reckoned he could have been mistaken. There was something in the fierceness of the look he gave that caused my heart to fail; I cleared my throat and nodded, under some spell of fear. Perhaps, I told myself, she merely appeared very young.

"Looking back and forth between them, feeling especially sorry for the dark-eyed girl who seemed so far from her home, and simultaneously quite anxious for myself, I said, 'I am sorry, sir, but this license was issued in Greenbrier County, and this home is, if I am not mistaken, in Pocahontas County. I cannot legally perform a marriage ceremony in Pocahontas on a license issued in Greenbrier.' As I said it, I confess I felt a regretful pang for that gingerbread.

"A general confusion followed, while I stood feeling vaguely relieved that something had intervened in this peculiar event. I could not sense God's nearness in any of this. It did not feel right.

"Shue suddenly snapped his fingers high in the air: as all

listened, he reminded me that it was a moonlit night, the eve of the full moon in fact, and that less than a mile would put us across the county line into Greenbrier. With a reluctant heart, I nodded, unable to think how to refuse. Then, weakly, I protested that the children ought not to be left sleeping unattended. But it was agreed among them that since we would be gone for only a short time, they would simply awaken the thirteen-year-old, tell him of our plans, and put him in charge of the three little girls, his sister and two nieces.

"It was bitterly cold, and crisp, with frost stiff upon the grass and dry leaves in the weeds there at the edge of the road. The moon was as yellow as new-churned butter, and the land was almost as light as if it were day. Silver pumpkins still lay in the fields, and cornstalks stood like bony figures in one field where some Droop farmer had been slow to plough them under.

"I was still of two minds about the thing. Everyone was tramping along behind, talking intermittently among themselves, every now and then laughing softly as if all the waiting were over and all were right. Thanksgiving was but two days off. The bride never said a blessed thing that my ears heard, but the groom sang out that this was a fine night to marry, and bragged how he had 'got them after all to marry us, Estie!' He wore only a sheep-skin vest over his day-shirt, his shirtsleeves and collar showing brightest white in the light of the moon.

"'Trout, where is your greatcoat?' Mrs. Good asked at some point on the brief journey.

"'Oh, on a walk this short, I won't freeze,' he retorted boldly.

"'But tonight you might,' his sister chid him. 'Look how all the countryside is frosted!' She pulled her own coat around her, then said affectionately, as if to soften the chiding, 'It would be a dreadful thing to have the groom to die before the wedding.'

"'Ah, Sue, don't be foolish,' he replied. 'You know I'll live to bury seven wives!'

"Up to now, I had not heard the bride-to-be laugh. But she did a little at that, along with the rest. Good, thought I, she will be in need of laughter. Yet I thought to myself that those were strange words for a man on his wedding eve.

"I glanced up at the star-sprinkled sky. The air was as clean and sharp as Heaven. I could hear the grass crunch as we walked, and feel that my nose was nearly frozen by the way I could not feel it anymore, and smell woodsmoke from a nearby house, the Sydenstrickers', as I recall.

"My misgivings grew. There was some banter between the groom and his brother about a girl named Annie whom he apparently was 'leaving behind' to marry this one, and more and more the bride appeared to me a brave and tragic little slip. I was moved to fall back beside her in our walk and ask her privately were her parents living.

"'They are,' she responded briefly. Were they apprised of these events?

"'What events?' she asked innocently.

"'Why, this wedding, of course. Why are they not present?' And she at once grew agitated, her hands fluttering up towards her face, and flung me a frightened look out of her big eyes.

"Before she could gather an answer, behind us Trout Shue boomed out that we were there, quicker than I could have thought possible, at the sign marker on the Greenbrier County line, and the bridegroom then said very lively to me, 'One more yard, Brother Little, and we shall be on Schusler's land and can proceed with this wedding before daylight!'

"I drew myself up, looking again at that innocent-seeming girl, all dark and quiet and big-eyed and some father's loved daughter. I drew in my breath and said firmly to him, 'Does this lady's father know of this proposed union?'

"His answer rolled out so easily I was calmed. Indicating the small procession coming up on us now with a sweep of his white arm, he said simply, 'Does this appear to you to be a secret elopement, sir?'

"And I, anxious to have my anxiety put to rest, arranged them before me again, she small in her dark frock and woolen cloak, he in his working clothes. The rest made a sort of half-circle around them, facing me.

"'Dearly beloved,' I began, the words sounding strange to me out of doors and under the clear sky of Heaven, past midnight. I read on, continuing until I had read the part which states, 'If any man can show just cause why they may not lawfully be joined together, let him now speak, or else hereafter forever hold his peace.'

"Then I waited, hoping for some intervention in this wrong thing. As I paused, I looked around me at each of them: his mother Eliza, too old too soon, her body shapeless from all the children; his sister Susan Good, the spunky one, who had already taken over from her mother a good many of the homely matriarchal duties. Sue's husband Samuel, easy-going and red-faced, stood next to her, then the boy John, near Trout's age, and by him his sister Maggie, scarred from smallpox and fat, about eighteen. Finally there was the old man himself, the dignified bearded patriarch of the lot. I looked then at the couple before me, the frail girl with dark hair, the strange frightening man himself, whose name on the marriage license was written E. S. Shue, whose willfulness had brought all of them to this— had brought here, in fact, all of us, as I too had come, and possibly no less willingly than any of the others. All the company stood by and there was no human help in all this madness: I must do what must be done alone.

"It was at that moment that God spoke, a calm voice deep within my soul. You must do what you know to be right. The certainty of afterlife affirms that you will be known by what you do in this moment. Will you choose Right or Wrong?

"By now all the company were moving nervously, shifting slightly, clearing throats, arranging wraps, shuffling feet. They had begun to look around at each other. The bridegroom darted looks out of the sides of his eyes at the girl; she in turn swallowed as though she had something obstructing her throat, and reached up with fluttering fingers to scratch her neck. Trout cleared his throat, finally, as if reminding me to go on, when I said loudly, 'Then I object.'

"At once Trout Shue startled, and stared at me with his mouth open, apparently disbelieving. A small uncertain smile crossed his lips; then he frowned, and demanded to know why I objected. There was a general milling about, and several taut whispers.

"So I said, 'This girl whom you propose to marry is only a child, and none of her people are present. It is now one o'clock in the morning and we are all here in the county road. A marriage ceremony is a sacred rite and should at least be performed under ordinary circumstances. I cannot help but think there is something not right in this case, and I will go no farther. So there will be no wedding so far as I am concerned.'

"And I stuck to it, and departed forthwith, and arrived at my boarding house as the sun came up, without ever the first taste of that sweet gingerbread."

The Reverend R. R. Little later learned that Shue had persuaded the girl to visit her uncle Luther Cutlip on Droop Mountain, who was courting Trout's sister Maggie at the time, and was soon to marry her. Once Shue had got Estie away from the influence of her parents, he had persuaded her to marry him. But Little's refusal counted for naught, for they were married next morning by the Reverend William McMiller in Frankford.

As the Reverend Little had feared, Estie and Trout's lovings did not prosper. From the Greenbrier records we know that they were married November 24, 1885, the day after the bizarre midnight assembly, at Frankford in Greenbrier County, and were legally divorced four years later, on November 5, 1889. According to information in the divorce decree, after their marriage they went to live on Spring Creek with Estie's parents, Mr. and Mrs. James Cutlip. They lived "some six months" with the Cutlips, then moved, according to Shue family information, into a log cabin on Estie's family's property, and on February 22, 1887, Estie and Trout's daughter Girta Lucretia Shue was born.

Wenona Shue McNeal:

"I'll tell you this because you'll find out about it anyway. Trout had an illegitimate child. My grandmother told me. During the winter Uncle Trout and Estie lived at Spring Creek, he was one snowy night mobbed for fathering a child on a girl named Annie Williams, who was my grandfather's sister. Annie's brothers, the Willliams boys, kidnapped Shue from the house where he was living with Estie, took him to a deep spot in a nearby river, probably the Greenbrier, called Manning Hole, where they ducked him in the icy water, chanting, 'In the name of the Father Jacob, and brothers John and Joe, into this hole you go.' They did it because he had wronged their sister."

A Renick man:

"I think he was kind of crazy. They had a baby. That was Girtie. She lived with the Cutlips—Emily and Jim."

An elderly resident of Spring Creek:

"I wouldn't know nothing about their trouble. I don't think he would work."

Shirley Donnelly, a Beckley preacher who took an interest in the case:

"Estie one night found a razor under Trout's pillow, assumed it was intended as a murder weapon to be used on her, and left him."

A Spring Creek man:

"Shue told Estie he was gonna kill her. She asked him what he was doing and he said he was digging her grave, and she followed him and he was digging a hole, so she left him."

Frieda Hendricks King:

"Trout was my grandfather. When he and Estie stopped living together, Trout took baby Girta with him, for at least a while. My mother often talked fondly of her time with her father, which I think lasted a couple of years.

"All her life, Girta kept a little card he sent her in January 1889, that said, 'I love you,' and passed it on to me, her daughter. I recall her talking often about her father. I always heard that he was a good man, very handsome, with brown hair. Girta, my mother, told me how good he had been to her, how he rocked her, and talked to her. My grandfather took his little daughter often with him on horseback when he went places. I don't know how it was that the separation and divorce came about: I think, though, that when Girta was little, her father, Trout, came one day to his in-laws' house, where she, Girtie, was living, and mopped up the floor. Grandpa Cutlip figured that Trout had done it to make the rest of them sick, and chased him off. I don't know any more about it than that."

Wenona Shue McNeal:

"My grandma Josie told me about what happened with Estie. She abandoned Trout and Girtie. Trout had to take care of Girtie all alone. I've always thought she was mixed up with another man. Then, when she decided she wanted Girtie back, she wrote Uncle Trout a letter telling him to come see her and bring their daughter along. Trout was trusting and brought Girta to visit her mother. But when he got to where the appointed meeting was to be, Estie was standing on a stile. There was brush all around. Her father and brothers stepped out of hiding, took Girta away from Trout at gunpoint, and told Trout to leave and not come back. And then Estie never even raised Girtie. Just gave her to her parents to raise, never paid the least attention to her."

From the divorce decree in the Greenbrier County Courthouse:

"He without any cause abandoned and deserted me. He said he wanted me to leave him. I said to him that I was not going to do any such thing, and he took his property away and threw what I have out of the house. He moved out when Girtie was about a year old, on or about the first to the middle of March 1888 . . ."

A Renick man:

"Oh, I know about him. He was a horse thief. And I'll tell you, any man who would steal a horse or a dog is automatically a son-of-a-bitch."

Henry Gilmer:

"Well, now, being assistant prosecuting attorney is sure a more inneresting job than writing wills or disputing property lines. And I reckon you can't ask much more of life than that it be inneresting.

"But you do come up on some ornery ones. You take this Shue fellow. He don't come home, don't write to his folks, stole a horse from a colored man up on Droop, name of Wilson, landed himself up there in Moundsville. Man like that, if he was to fall in the river, you'd go upstream to try and get him out. It was while he was in the cage his wife divorced him. Couldn't find Nathan Wilson, but I ran into a fellow today named McKeever, Giles McKeever, knew Shue, said he was a rascal. I asked on what grounds he said it, and he said Shue was a wife-beater. Said he moved around from job to job, wouldn't settle down. Said he reckoned every family had a black sheep, and he was theirs. I asked him how he knew about Shue beating his wife, and he told me."

Giles McKeever:

"In the winter of 1886–1887, there was a young teacher at
Leonard, in the Spring Creek district, named M. W. Walton,
who had attending his school not only the younger children of
the area but also about eighteen lads from the surrounding community, including myself. We were all around seventeen or eighteen. During this winter Shue and his first wife Estie lived in a
cabin on Rock Camp Run, a tributary of Spring Creek, on land
belonging to Trout's father-in-law, Jim Cutlip.

"Shue was a young man of rather fine physique, apparently of
great strength. He delighted in singing sacred music, and had a
good singing voice, but he was a braggart, a great boaster of his
strength. I would go so far as to call him a bully. He hung out at
the local store, and was always bragging about what a man he
was. This did not set too well with the youths of the area.

"Every few days, the news would be circulated in the community that Shue had whipped his wife again. This went on for
some time. After a while, we, the young men of Walton's group,
decided to do something to put a stop to this cruel treatment. It
was deep winter, and our plan consisted of ganging up on Shue
some night and giving him an ice-cold bath in a deep hole of
water a short distance from his house.

"The ones who went were the schoolteacher Mr. Walton, Jim
Walton, Doc Brown, Amos Williams, Jack Hannah, my best
friend Doak B. Rapp, and myself. We cast lots to determine who
would do what, and it fell to me, Doak, and Jack Hannah to do
the bathing. Doak Rapp volunteered, as I recall, to go up on the
porch of the cabin, and to call Shue to the door and catch him.

"There are some moments that live in your mind, and this was
that kind of a moment. There was the silent winter night, and
the biting, stinging air in our faces. The snow creaked and
crumbled under our feet as we approached Shue's cabin.

"When we reached the cabin, Hannah and I hid behind a
rock bench just in front of the porch, and Doak stopped at the
edge of the porch and called out.

"Shue came to the door in his nightclothes, which consisted
of nothing but a shirt.

"Doak engaged him in conversation to lure him out into the open where we could grab him.

"'Can you show me the way to Nathan McMillan's?'

"Shue replied with the question, 'What is your name?'

"Doak Rapp said, 'My name is Raymond.'

"And Shue asked, 'Where do you live?'

"Doak said, 'I live near Alderson.'

"And Shue said, 'I believe I know you.'

"Doak Rapp, working his way up close during this brief exchange, finally reached Shue and jumped on him, and caught him around the waist. Hannah and I leapt in, and pounced on Shue like wildcats on a rabbit. Before we got hold of him, Shue had succeeded in pulling my friend Doak into the house and getting a firm grip on the door facing with his left hand. The three of us seized him and gave a surge. The door, during our struggle, came off its facing.

"Surprisingly, Shue fell into our arms as limp as a rag at that point, never making another struggle but begging for mercy like a child. At that point, Mrs. Shue came out on the porch and went to her husband's aid by picking up an old axe handle, and hurling it at Rapp. It missed Doak's head, glancing off his shoulder, at which she retreated into the house, begging us to let her husband go.

"We dragged Shue through the wintry woods down to the water hole, broke through the ice and threw him in. Standing around the edge, we told him why we had done it. The rest of the group stood by, not far away, witnessing the event. We performed a sort of farcical baptism, chanting, 'In the name of your father and his son John, we baptize thee, and into this hole of water you go.'

"Shue's attempt to even the score misfired. He went the next day before Squire Scott at Renick Valley, and swore out a warrant for the four of us that he could identify: Doak Rapp, Jack Hannah, and me, Giles McKeever, of course, as we had been the actual perpetrators—and Doc Brown, who had been part of the watching group. Jack Hannah dealt with the problem by moving his place of residence, probably to another county out of the jurisdiction of the summons. In short, he fled.

"The warrant was placed in the hands of Constable Billy Mike Gillian, who served it on Brown and me. Cleverly, when the state had presented its case, Brown, who had stood on the sidelines, took the stand and testified that he had not been on Jim Cutlip's land that night. Three of the others came forward to swear that he was telling the truth. Fortunately, Brown was not asked how close to Cutlip's land he had been! Mr. Walton, the teacher, then made a motion that the warrants be set aside, Brown was released, and none of the others of us was ever asked to testify."

Giles McKeever:

"The only consolation the writer has ever had for participating in the bathing of Shue is that he has felt for a long, long time that the three school boys, totally ignorant of the fact that they were violating the law, took Shue from his home one winter night when the thermometer was registering ten degrees below zero, broke the ice and performed the rites of baptism, without having been first ordained, by immersing him in a deep hole of water, prolonged a good woman's life for many years." [*sic*]

On December 20, 1888, the *Pocahontas Times* reported that "Trout Shoe [*sic*], who was some time ago committed to jail charged with horse stealing, was last Saturday taken to Hillsboro and given a preliminary examination before Justice Kennison. In default of bail he was recommitted to await the action of the grand jury." There followed a regular court session in January, but his case did not come up.

The February 1, 1889, *Pocahontas Times* announced, "We had four trials in town last Saturday. I tell you, a man has to walk straight while he stays in town now." But Shue languished on in jail, to await the next session, still three months away.

His trial was on April 3; he pled guilty and was convicted of horse stealing. The *Greenbrier Independent* reported on April 11 under Pocahontas Circuit Court: "There was but little business in the Court. Shue, who stole the horse from a colored man on Droop mountain, confessed his guilt and was sentenced to serve a two-years' term in the Penitentiary."

Shue arrived in Moundsville and was admitted to the West Virginia Penitentiary on April 11, 1889. He was listed as a farmer, born in Virginia. He was assigned prison number 1817, meaning he was the 1,817th prisoner to be lodged there since the opening of the prison in 1865. He was of course listed as having been sent up from Pocahontas, and his age was given as twenty-eight. (This is an instance in which his birthday seems to have been 1861 instead of 1863.) On his record, next to "education" there is merely a "yes." Other vital statistics given are that he was a white man with a dark complexion, eyes of dark blue, hair of dark brown, that he was five feet seven and a half inches tall, and had a scar where his left ankle had sometime before been broken.

Given that people tended to be somewhat shorter in those days than we are today, still it is very interesting to see that this man, whom all invariably remembered as tall, big, and powerful, was in fact only about five feet seven inches, short even by nineteenth-century standards, or at least certainly not above average.

On December 20, 1890, Shue was discharged from the penitentiary, having served four months less than the designated two years. It seems likely that he was released in time to spend Christmas at home with his family, and perhaps it is fair to read into his early release that he had behaved in an exemplary manner while in prison.

Wenona Shue McNeal:

"He never stole the horse. He borrowed it. As Uncle Trout was walking home through Hillsboro in the snow, his feet got cold and he was tired. Over in a snowy field there was a horse grazing. Trout went over and got on the horse and rode home, then turned the horse loose. The horse, which belonged to Nathan Williams, went on home, as Trout knew it would. For that he got two years!"

A neighbor:

"Stole a horse, as I said. I'd have to say it don't surprise me none. That's about the same as crippling a man. If I was to learn I come down from a horse thief, I couldn't hold up my head."

Photographs from the time show us that, among men, short haircuts were the style, and dark, elaborately cut wool suits with vests. Work clothes were bibbed overalls and blue-gray chambray or striped "hickory" shirts. White shirts with suits were reserved for Sundays, unless a man had a profession, like medicine, ministering, or the law. Mustaches were common. Trout Shue apparently had one at least at some time in his life. Beards were less common than they had been during the Civil War era, but apparently among veterans they were a sort of badge of identity.

Although girls when young wore their hair long and flowing, bunched back with a ribbon, or braided, and dresses that revealed their lisle-stockinged legs, when they grew up they pulled their locks up into knots or braids atop their heads, and donned dresses that hour-glassed their figures and had fancy skirts reaching to the floor. Such fashions symbolized the prevalent ambivalence about the body: long hair was sexually attractive, yet the hair was worn knotted up, hiding its beauty; the dresses, while covering ladies' "limbs," as legs were called, emphasized the curves of breasts and buttocks, the narrowness of waists. Plumpness was fashionable, as thinness was associated with tuberculosis, and therefore thought to be unhealthy. Boys donned long pants instead of knickers at around fourteen or fifteen to symbolize that they had grown from the innocence of childhood to responsible manhood. No concept of "teenage" existed yet.

Most people played one or more musical instruments, and most could "tell a skillful story." Trout Shue, by all accounts, sang well, and the stories he told were famous in the area.

Four years after his release from prison, Trout Shue reappears. According to the Greenbrier marriage record (Book 1), E. S.

Shue married Lucy A. Tritt on June 23, 1894. She was born in Greenbrier County, according to this record, and was "24 and 2 months"; he was born in Augusta County, Virginia, and was thirty-two. The *Greenbrier Independent* announced their marriage in the July 5, 1894, issue, stating that G. O. Homan performed the ceremony.

Jess Stanley:

"I can tell you about Lucy. She was my blood aunt. My mother, Amanda Tritt Stanley, was her sister. And her grandfather, the original Tritt settler in Greenbrier, was a lawyer who rode an ox from Fayetteville to Lewisburg to open his law office. One time as he was traveling, he stopped to ask directions of a man on the road. 'Mister, can you tell me where this road goes?' The man replied, 'I been here fifty years and it ain't went nowhere yet.' Well, about Lucy? She was supposed to be an awful good-lookin' woman.

"The family always said that Lucy and Trout had not been married long, it was winter, and Shue was supposed to be building or fixing a chimney on the house where they lived, between Alderson and Rupert, out there at a place called Kenny's Knob, and he asked Lucy for a drink of water. She went and got it, and when she brought it back, he dropped or threw a brick on her and killed her—brained her. People felt that he did it intentionally.

"I remember being a kid the day my uncle Bob, one of Amanda and Lucy's brothers, rode up to the house on a huge shiny black horse to tell the family that Lucy had been killed. Some of the neighbors chased Shue, who ran and hid in an outbuilding, a barn. They were going to kill him just like he had killed Lucy. They shot at him many times through a door, but Shue jumped out a hole or window and took off across a field. They caught him, and tried him, and put him in the penitentiary and he never got out 'til he died.

"That door, full of bullet holes, was took by a gunsmith who made gunstocks out of it. I used to own one of them, but I can't find it anymore. I believe Shue wrote a book while he was in prison—an autobiography. Who's got it? Well, I wouldn't know. But I think the law has it. That's right—the law. Probably over in East Virginia somewhere."

"Let's see now—the brothers and sisters: Lena, Amanda, Lucy, Ellen, the one who married 'Bud' Clay, Sam, Betty, Bob—I think that was the lot of them."

Wenona Shue McNeal:

"That's wrong. I know exactly what happened to Lucy. After their marriage, Lucy and Trout, and his next brother John Patrick Bruffey Shue (that was my granddaddy) and his wife Josie, were all living together with my great-grandparents Jacob and Elizah, in the family house on Droop Mountain. When winter came, Trout went to work at Knob Logging Camp in Greenbrier County. My grandmother, Josie, told me, and she never told a lie in her life. One day while Uncle Trout was away from home, Lucy, heavy with child, slipped and fell on the ice while going to the toilet, which was up around the garden, and hurt herself. She was just young and naive, so she didn't tell anyone she'd begun to bleed. She bled for two days before telling anyone. They sent for Susan Good (that's Trout's sister, she was married to Sam Good) and her daughter Annie, who was with Lucy when she died. The way to the outhouse was just an icy path tramped out in the snow. I remember grandmother's telling the story many times. Trout's brother John, once they realized the seriousness of Lucy's condition, went to Renick for the doctor, but the snow was so deep, and there was a blizzard so fierce, that by the time the doctor got to her she was beyond human help. Brother John then walked for eight hours through the snow to the lumber camp to tell Trout that his beloved Lucy was dead. They buried her in Whiting Cemetery."

Greetha Morten Childress:

"My grandfather was John Robinson, Mary Jane Robinson Heaster's brother. He said after the trial some of Lucy's people told them that Lucy Tritt Shue died of laurel poison. Shue poisoned her by making her drink mountain laurel tea. I don't even know what that is."

Shirley Donnelly:

"No. Trout and his second wife were haying, and he yanked, or pulled, her off the haystack, causing her to fall and break her neck."

Today, people in Greenbrier still know who Trout Shue was. It does not seem as if nearly a century has gone by.

At the time of the events under discussion shoes sold for two or three dollars a pair, and well-built seven-room houses on big tracts of land for two or three thousand. The wealthy rode in horse-drawn carriages, called surreys, or hacks, which sold for around forty dollars. Ordinary men traveled by horseback or on foot. The nearest railroad station was almost twenty miles south of Livesay's Mill, at Ronceverte, so there was little contact with the outside world. Only twenty miles away, to the east, in White Sulphur Springs, was the palatial Grand Central Hotel, also known as the "Old White." The spot had attracted wealthy and even royal patrons since 1832, when the first summer residence was erected there. In 1868, the Chesapeake and Ohio Railway Company put its westbound line through White Sulphur Springs, thus making the resort more accessible. But to the people at Livesay's Mill, the magnificent Georgian hotel with one of the finest and largest ballrooms in the world was as foreign as the Arabian Nights, and probably seemed just as far away.

"Education" in those days in rural West Virginia meant reading, perhaps writing, and a little dab of arithmetic, which they called "ciphering." Three to six years of schooling gave a person all the education that he would ordinarily need or ever use. People drove nails into apple and cherry trees and pulled them out again when the trees bloomed, in the belief that the tree would yield more fruit, and that the fruit itself would be more healthful.

The state of scientific knowledge, especially medical knowledge in rural areas, as evidenced in the weekly newspapers, the only mass medium at the time, was appalling. It was commonly accepted that tobacco smoking was beneficial to health, because it killed microbes. Tobacco was raised as a garden crop, along with rhubarb and greens and root vegetables of many varieties. Smallpox still took its toll in the mountains of West Virginia. People probably feared vaccination, not understanding its concept of a little illness to prevent a greater one. Or perhaps smallpox vaccine was merely unavailable to people in the rural reaches of the nation. Tuberculosis (known by such names as hectic fever, phthisis, and scrofula, depending on how it was manifested in the body), diphtheria, and pneumonia appear to have been the leading causes of death. Influenza, "La Grippe," and bronchitis usually led to pneumonia, and frequently were considered to be synonymous with it. Ads for magical cures of many sorts appeared in the papers from time to time throughout the last two decades of the century, promising to cure anything. A waggish remedy for headlice, from 1890, calls for the patient to "rub the head with alcohol, and roll in sand, then let the drunken cooties kill each other in rock battles." Fleshwounds were treated with pine resin or with turpentine. Sore throats and colds were soothed with "sugar melted into kerosene in a spoon over a candle flame." Tea made from the roots of sassafras was drunk as a spring tonic. Medicines were given to cure nocturnal emissions, which were believed to be enervating and threatening to the health. Pulverized dried Russian cockroaches were administered as a cure for dropsy, or fluid retention. Scott's Emulsion was hailed as a cure-all, and it is clear from the multitude of laxative advertisements that a clear bowel was considered the basis for health.

In Greenbrier County a hundred years ago, for any and every bodily ill, physicians regularly prescribed spiritus frumenti, a fancy name for plain old whiskey with a little bit of other stuff, like wheat germ, added. Daisy Hume recalls a story about the same Dr. Knapp who figures in this story and took care of her family when she was a child: once, when one of her little brothers was sick, Knapp suggested a "little whiskey" every few hours, but Daisy's mother refused to administer the prescribed medicine, saying that "if the child should grow up and one day fill a drunkard's grave, she would ever more feel responsible."

Into the well-established rural society of Greenbrier County, a new blacksmith arrived in the autumn of 1896, resolved to make his way in a new place among new folks. He said he came from up on Droop, in Pocahontas, the next county north of Greenbrier. He attracted immediate attention, as any newcomer might, and within a few weeks married pretty Zona Heaster, a young woman who lived across the county from Livesay's Mill.

People living in small towns, despite the neighborliness and sense of safety that come from knowing those around them, eventually learn that all their business is certain to be known, that their affairs are apt to be picked over as vultures will pick over the remains of a dead animal—in short, that all kinds of people will be interested in all kinds of things that are not necessarily any of their business. Everyone had something to say about the death of young Zona Heaster Shue.

In the nineteenth century people were well acquainted with death and far less squeamish than we are. Every child grew up having seen death and dead bodies for as long as he or she could remember. The viewing of a corpse in an open coffin was one of the rare occasions to socialize. It was common then to have dead children especially photographed in their coffins, for "memory" pictures. When a healthy young woman died, childbirth was usually the presumed cause. A lot of people went by to speak to the Heasters and express their sympathy to the bereaved husband and to look at Zona Heaster Shue in her coffin. In the days following her death, the loose head, the discolorations on her right cheek, the high-necked dress and scarf, Shue's fanatic deathwatch over his wife's remains—all these things were noticed, discussed, and duly recorded in the memories of Mrs. Heaster's neighbors.

In Zona's case, although Dr. Knapp examined her after her body was discovered, no attending physician's name appears in the official death book, only the name of Handley Undertaking Establishment. However, we know that Zona's body was never taken to the undertaker, and Trout dressed her himself, so apparently the undertakers' role was limited to providing the casket. A clerk recorded all the deaths that Handley's had taken care of in the past week (they are all in the same hand) and next to Zona's name wrote as cause of death "childbirth." Dr. Knapp had been treating Zona for some time prior to her death, yet as we have seen was unable to make a complete examination at the time of death. This would seem to imply that she was pregnant at the time of his treatment of her, and that fact doubtless led to the cause of death being listed as "childbirth."

Winter closed in on Greenbrier County after Zona's funeral, but it did not freeze the tongues in folks' heads:

"They said he did terrible things to Zona. Things—it's hard to tell a lady. They said he stuck red-hot pokers into her, that's what. That's the kind of man he was."

Nonie Shue McNeal:

"My grandfather, Trout's brother, John Patrick Bruffey Shue, went down to the funeral, and returned home to tell the family that there was a baby girl in the coffin with Zona, fully formed, with blond hair."

Nelle Watts:

"Well, naturally Mrs. Heaster was against him. He was older than Zonie by some, don't you know, and he already had two wives before her. Folks around here didn't know him from a sack of salt."

NOTES

p. 41: The Jacob Shue family had a rather large house, more elegant than most dwellings in the neighborhood where they lived, a blacksmith shop, and store, and a considerable amount of land on Droop Mountain, near Hillsboro, not so much a mountain as a high plateau, 3,060 feet above sea level, where a Civil War battle had taken place. Today Route 219 runs over that battleground, connecting Marlinton and Lewisburg, following the same Indian trail along the spine of the ridge that Shue must have taken in the fall of 1896 to get to his new home. A highway marker on the battle site reads: "Here, November 6, 1863, Union troops commanded by Gen. W. W. Averell, defeated Confederate forces under Gen. John Echols. This has been considered the most extensive engagement in this State and the site was made a State Park in 1929."

p. 41: Details of Trout's early life are from Nonie Shue McNeal. I have tried to confirm any part of it: but Mt. Olivet has no records dating back to the nineteenth century; one pencil drawing survives that Trout most probably drew; his height turns out to have been about 5'7"; the family Bible that Nonie refers to has disappeared; there is no record of Trout's birth in Augusta County, though two of his siblings' births are recorded there; and finally, there are no certain extant portraits of Trout Shue, and in fact only one that is alleged to be of him.

p. 42: Information in the long episode by the Rev. R. R. Little, the circuit rider, comes from an article printed in the *Greenbrier Dispatch* in 1944; from the *Pocahontas Times*, May 1897; from the West Virginia State Penitentiary; and from conversations with Nina Shue Cutlip and Wenona Shue McNeal, as well as from a personal tour of the old Shue house on Droop.

A Methodist circuit rider might cover an area of several hundred miles, making his full circuit no more than six times a year, especially in parts of the country not yet served by the railroad. In inaccessible areas, weddings were held up, as well as funerals, and sometimes even burials, until the circuit rider should come again. Thirty to forty congregations were not considered an excessive number in thinly populated areas. In fact, one old-timer told me of a spring when he was a lad, when his community was snowed in for several weeks, and there was a lot of pneumonia. Many folks died, he said. As a grown man he can still see that pile of coffins when the circuit rider finally got around to them to officiate at the burying. In the end, this method of covering every part of the country served the church well by increasing its rolls, and of course it served the people living in outlying areas where there were no churches. The preacher's thoughts are imaginary, though his observations about the scene reflect his stated sentiments.

Shue's name appears once, in the 1880 census of Greenbrier County, as R. Trout, reflecting, one supposes, a scenario that went something like this: Census worker: "What's the next boy's name?" Informer: "Well, his real name is 'Rasmus, only we call him Trout . . ." The banter about Annie referred to in the midnight walk is explained in the first note for p. 51.

p. 48: Pearl S. (for Sydenstricker) Buck grew up less than a mile from the Shue home on Droop Mountain.

p. 50: Frieda Hendricks King told me the birthday of her mother, Girta Lucretia Shue Hendricks.

p. 51: The "dunking" story came from Wenona Shue McNeal. The family story is that Miss Williams went to the Greenbrier Poor Farm as an unwed mother, and in good time brought forth a son who took the name Shue. His kinfolk do not know the boy's first name, or with whom he lived. Beyond this, the family says that the boy "at the age of fourteen visited Trout's brother Joseph Wilson Queenie Shue, who was then living in Virginia." Since then, they say, they have lost track of him. In attempting to correlate dates, I conclude that this visit to Joe, if it was real, if the child ever existed at all, could have coincided with the boy's father's death in 1900.

There was indeed a Poor Farm outside Lewisburg in the nineteenth century, though all traces of records from it seem to have disappeared. It seems odd that the Shue family does not know the name of the boy, since they know the rest of the story so well. This boy's birth apparently is not recorded in the Greenbrier County records any time in the 1880s.

p. 51: The quotes following came from old-timers in the Spring Creek area, including Lonnie Miles, Mrs. Neil Tharp, and Shelby Lewis, and are intended to represent community concerns and gossip.

p. 51: The razor story is from Shirley Donnelly, and he was not given to citing sources.

p. 51: The hole-digging story is from Shelby Lewis, and is oddly reminiscent of the old folk song popular all over Appalachia, called "Pretty Polly." The story has many variants, but in many of them, Polly discovers, by following her husband or lover when he goes out at night, that he is digging her grave.

Pretty Polly

Pretty Polly, Pretty Polly
Over yonder she stands
With rings on her fingers,
And her lily-white hands

He led her over hollows
And valleys so deep,
At last Pretty Polly
Began for to weep.

Oh come along, Pretty Polly,
Come take a walk with me,
Before we get married
Some pleasure to see.

Sweet William, Sweet William
I doubted your way,
You torment my body
All into the grave.

p. 52: I interviewed Mrs. King by telephone in the spring of 1983. It is clear from her point of view as Trout's granddaughter and Girta Lucretia Shue's daughter, that he was a man much maligned.

p. 52: The story about "mopping up the floor" on one level of meaning makes no sense. But there is a common idiom "wiping up the ground with" someone, meaning to bawl that person out. The child Frieda, hearing the story about how Girtie's father came to the house one day and "wiped up the ground with them" could remember that statement in later life as it is told above, having formed a mental picture at the time of someone literally mopping a floor.

p. 52: Estie's subsequent marriage to T. A. McMillion did not occur until a week before Trout married Zona, or until about eight years had elapsed, which pretty much indicates that she did not divorce Shue to marry someone else. It is on record that Alice E. Cutlip, twenty-eight, married T. A. McMillion, twenty-two, on October 14, 1896, in Greenbrier County. They had seven children together. A neighbor who remembers McMillion describes him as "a slow, easy-going sort of fellow," and Estie is variously recalled as "black-haired, pretty—a jolly and good-natured person whom everyone loved," extremely shy, becoming reclusive in her old age, and as "a large silent woman."

p. 53: Gilmer was notorious for acting the backwoodsman.

p. 53: On August 7, 1889, Estie, or Allis, as she was then calling herself, instituted divorce proceedings. On September 2, she summoned Trout Shue to appear for a hearing.

To Erasmus S. Shue

You will take notice that on the 2nd day of September 1889 at the residence of James B. Cutlip, Falling Spring District, Greenbrier

County, West Virginia, I shall take the depositions of said James B. Cutlip and others to be used in evidence on my behalf in a certain suit in chancery now pending in the Circuit Court of Greenbrier County in which I am plaintiff and you are defendant; and if from any cause said deposition be not commenced or concluded in that day the taking of the same will be continued from day to day at the same place until completed.

That he was in prison at the time is never mentioned. Of course he could not appear, and on November 5, 1889, Estie was decreed divorced from her first husband. The decree is titled *Allie Estelline Shue* v. *Erasmus S. Shue*. It is on record at the Greenbrier Courthouse that he "without any cause abandoned and deserted her," for which she sought "a divorce a vinculo matrimonii." She testified in part: "He said he wanted me to leave him. I said to him that I was not going to do any such thing, and he took his property away and threw what I have out of the House." The divorce document is signed Allis Estaline Shue, and cost her $1.50. Estie remarried and, according to relatives, kept her counsel about Shue in later years, declining to discuss her first marriage at all.

p. 54: The wife-beating story from which Giles McKeever's recollection was taken was first printed on June 2, 1944, in a now-defunct newspaper called the *Greenbrier Dispatch*, but it was referred to in the *Pocahontas Times* on March 12, 1897, at the time Trout Shue was in jail awaiting trial. ". . . He has always declared he would have seven wives, and his third wife being dead and he only thirty-five would indicate that he was getting along fairly well. Shue was visited one time while he lived here by a vigilance committee and roughly handled for abusing his wife." It may be possible to detect the shadow of his future acts in this episode.

If the dates of McKeever's recollection are accurate, then Estie was pregnant at the time of the alleged beatings. Shue's beatings must have been excessive, for the neighbors to know about them, and especially to cause them to band together in Estie's behalf, violating the sacrosanct privacy of marriage. Pregnancy appears to be a condition in marriage that can sometimes bring on wife-abuse.

I spoke with two of Giles McKeever's sons, and the daughter of Doak Rapp. All confirmed the story as printed, and said that their fathers had added other items, such as the detail of the flung axe handle, and that their fathers had disliked Shue for "coming into the small country store near Spring Creek and bragging about what a man he was." All said that Shue was a very strong, vigorous man.

p. 56: It is interesting that, if his family were well-to-do, as Nonie claims they were, they did not put up bail for him.

p. 57: West Virginia law in 1883 stated under "Offenses Against Property": "If a person commit simple larceny of goods or chattels, he shall, if they be of the value of $20 or more, be deemed guilty of grand larceny and be confined in the penitentiary not less than two nor more than ten years . . ." Thus two years was the prescribed punishment for a first offense of grand larceny at that time. A horse was worth more than twenty dollars.

A horse was a farm labor machine, a man's transportation, even a family's safety, if, for example, someone needed to get the doctor quickly. So serious a crime was horse thieving that during the Civil War it was punished by hanging the thief on the spot; and it was accepted that to steal the enemy's horses was perhaps the most damaging thing that could be done to undermine him. Towards the end of the century a story in the *Pocahontas Times* informs its readers that in Radford, Virginia, a man named Gregory was arrested for stealing horses, and in twenty-four hours he had been indicted, tried, and sentenced to eight years in the penitentiary. The same paper mentions that the only woman ever convicted of horse stealing in Missouri was "a beautiful girl of fifteen years, on May 7, 1889." The jury (benevolently, we are assured), gave her only two years in prison. West Virginia newspapers picked up the story. And near the end of the century the *Moundsville Echo* relates the tale of one Peter Zimmerman, who had the longest prison record in the entire state of West Virginia. He was then seventy-three, and had spent forty years of his life in seven penitentiaries. Every conviction was for horse stealing, for which Mr. Zimmerman had apparently quite a penchant, if not a great deal of ability. "His appearance has anything but a criminal cast," notes the article. "He is well-preserved for a man of his years, and looks more like the average well-to-do farmer than the graduated criminal."

p. 57: The examination in the subsequent divorce decree names the "colored" man as "Nathan Willsin."

p. 59: The story about Lucy came from an interview with her nephew, Jess Stanley, Alderson, West Virginia, March 21, 1984. The 1880 census for Greenbrier County lists the following children of Isaac and Elizabeth Tritt: Elizabeth, twelve; Madeline, eleven; Lucy A., nine; Isaac R. L., seven; Amanda J., four (mother of Jess and Margaret Stanley); Ruth E., two (perhaps the girl wrongly named Lucy E. in the Greenbrier marriage records who married Thomas G. Clay). Isaac's will mentions sons Samuel and Robert. Apparently Samuel was not born by 1880, and apparently Isaac R. L. is "Uncle Bob" as a Robert Tritt died in 1899 at age twenty-six of "stomach trouble." Near neighbors (next on the census list) were Clays, who had a son Thomas G., aged 16 in 1880.

Lucy had an illegitimate son when she married Shue. Lonnie A. Tritt's birth is recorded in Greenbrier as Lucy's illegitimate child, and he appears in the Greenbrier death register—married, a laborer, who died "sudden, mashed by a falling tree on October 16, 1928, at the age of 37, 4 mo., and 18 da." An Alderson man recalls that he was "big and mean, a street-fighter." Brack Campbell of Rainelle, who knew him, believed him to have been Lucy Tritt Shue's younger brother, and recalls him as a big, gentle, man, though subject to severe epileptic fits. He says Lonnie's mother's death was "known to have occurred when her husband dropped a rock on her head off a chimney," but says Lonnie himself did not tell him that.

p. 60: The Shue family version of Lucy's death is from an interview with Wenona Shue McNeal, Lewisburg, West Virginia, May 30, 1983, and a letter from Darleigh Shue of Droop, West Virginia, dated December 26, 1983.

p. 60: The laurel tea quotation is from a letter written by Greetha Morten Childress in May 1984. Her grandfather was John Robinson, brother of Mary Jane Robinson Heaster. The poison in mountain laurel, rhododendron, and other Ericaceae, was first isolated in 1883 by a German chemist, Plugge. Soluble in cold water, it was named Andromedotoxin (also spelled "Andrometoxin") and yields a solution of an alkaline reaction. It is not precipitated by ordinary alkaloidal reagents or by solution of metallic salts. Mountain laurel was known to be poisonous: the Delaware Indians were said to have used it to commit suicide, and sometimes animals died from eating the plants containing it if there was nothing else to eat. Hard to detect, the poison causes excessive tearing of the eyes and nasal secretions, as if the sufferer had a bad cold. It causes severe drops in blood pressure, increasing lack of coordination, and eventually convulsions, paralysis, and death.

p. 61: Shirley Donnelly changed his stories from time to time. A preacher and newspaper columnist, he had little interest in accuracy. Another of his columns claims that the second wife (that was Lucy) died when the rock fell and hurt her.

In the face of such contradictory stories, is it possible to sort out truth from fiction? There are no records on Lucy Shue's death in either Pocahontas or Greenbrier, and her death as reported in the *Pocahontas Times* on February 15, 1895, is of little help: "Mrs. E. S. Shue, wife of 'Trout' Shue, died very suddenly at her home near here on last Monday morning the 11th. We haven't been able to learn the particulars of her death." This news item sounds like an unfinished story, yet it is never followed up.

Though we can never know for sure, perhaps there is some indirect evidence that can help to clarify the story. To begin with, "near here" gives us a clue that Lucy did die on Droop, near Marlinton (where the paper is published), and not near Alderson, as Stanley said, which is about fifty miles to the southwest. Second, for several months leading up to the time of Lucy's death, the newspapers are full of predictions for a particularly harsh winter. In November of the previous year (1894) the *Pocahontas Times* had warned: "Those who study the signs, say another long winter, filled with storms, is ahead of us. The goosebone is nearly all white, and snow, so they say, will lie on the ground from early in December on til April, or perhaps later. Cornbanks are more than usually thick."

The woodchucks and chipmunks were in November "already fat enough to kill," with dense, fine, soft fur, a sure sign of a cold winter coming. The corn was said to have thicker husks than usual, and all signs were for an unusually severe winter.

It is interesting how accurate those predictions were. In the same issue of the paper that reported Lucy's death, there is much about the fearsome cold: "We have weathered a good many storms, but that of last Thursday, Friday, and Saturday for whirling snow, cold cutting winds and general disagreement, capped the climax. All day Friday the mercury remained from 4 to 6 degrees below zero, and complaints of frozen ears, fingers, and toes, were quite numerous. Cows' feet were swollen, windows broken from gusts of winds, and streets completely blocked . . ."

The *Greenbrier Independent* of the same week describes how scores of baby lambs died in the temperatures that dropped to twenty-eight degrees below zero in Greenbrier County, and how the local residents were so hungry that they dug frozen hibernating woodchucks out of their dens for something to eat, and how ripe oranges froze on the trees in Pensacola, Florida. One elderly resident recalls hearing how poor folks in the county had to tie sacks or rags on their feet to keep them from freezing. The weather "recalled to many the winter of 1850, the worst on record, when . . . the tops of trees eighty feet tall were just visible in the deep hollows full of snow . . ." In the same issue of the *Pocahontas Times*, on the same page on which Lucy's death is noted, there is a tirade against the "mail service on Trotter's line," which of course along with everything else, came to a halt in the face of the extreme weather. Finally, when the postal authorities in Washington, "failing to realize the extent of the blockade," persisted in railing at Mr. Trotter about his failure to deliver the mail across the mountain from Staunton, Virginia, to Pocahontas County, Trotter responded with an outburst of a letter to the Post Office Department: "If you were to knock out the gable end of h——! and turn it loose on Cheat Mountain, it wouldn't generate steam enough in six months to open up the snow drifts."

On the day Lucy died, February 11, 1895, the new Street Commission was out with "a force of hands tunneling through the snow drifts on Nicholas Street" in Hillsboro.

In light of the weather, certainly the haystack story cannot be accurate. Chimney repair in such weather sounds like an impossibility—but if there were a broken chimney that had to be repaired, then it does not seem unlikely that an accident might occur in all the ice and snow. When Lucy died the entire East Coast was in the grip of a hard freeze.

Furthermore, the local papers report a great deal of sickness, "La Grippe" and pneumonia. If Lucy died of some respiratory illness, her symptoms might in retrospect—say, when Trout was accused of murder—have struck observers as the symptoms of laurel poisoning. Or, conversely, laurel poisoning would have appeared to be a respiratory illness.

The Shue family's story in this case has the virtue of checking out with verifiable facts. Lucy's grave, if it is in the tiny, beautiful Whiting Cemetery, as Nonie claims her grandmother said it was, is not marked—but of course many graves at the time either went unmarked, or were indicated by wooden slabs, which soon yielded to the elements.

p. 61: Prices of things come from perusing newspapers from the area at the time. Daisy Hume is the source for most of the homely details. I poked around in some medical and pharmaceutical texts from the end of the last century, and Harper's Weekly

Magazine, 1896–1900 passim. The "headlice remedy" is from a notebook that my grandfather, Greenlee D. Letcher, kept as a young lawyer. It is dated 1895. Pharmacists Jack Mills of Owensboro, Kentucky, Patrick Macnamara of Buena Vista, Virginia, and Andrew Johnson of Lexington, Virginia, provided me with some information for this part.

p. 64: One particularly vicious rumor tells that Shue tortured Zona by sticking red-hot pokers into her. A tale like this may not be the truth, but may hide another truth. This story may hint at an abortion, or an attempted one. Inserting sharp objects into the uterus to try to dislodge the fetus is a very ancient practice. Of course the story may well be utter invention. But we must recall that Zona's death is officially listed as caused by childbirth.

p. 64: As we have seen, Book 1, p. 230, l. 310, of the Greenbrier birth records reveals that on November 29, 1895, E. Zona Heaster delivered a male child, her firstborn, the supposed father being George Woldridge. A local doctor named Rupert attended the child's birth. This child is not mentioned in Hedges Heaster's will, though another illegitimate son (by one of the boys) is. The official record says Zona died of childbirth. Nonie Shue McNeal, granddaughter of Trout's next brother, Patrick Bruffey Shue, tells of the baby in the coffin. It is an interesting possibility, and had it been the case, would have provided Shue with a motive, if not an excuse, for killing Zona: the realization that the baby could not have been his.

p. 64: The "sack of salt" quotation is from Nelle Watts of Lewisburg.

Part Three

FEBRUARY 1897

We all within our graves will sleep,
A hundred years to come;
No living soul for us will weep
A hundred years to come;
But other men our land shall till,
And others, then, these streets shall fill,
And other birds will sing as gay,
And bright the sun shine as today,
A hundred years to come.

"A Hundred Years to Come," Anonymous, 19th century

By all accounts, John Alfred Preston, the prosecutor of Greenbrier County, was at first merely polite—gentlemanly and sympathetic to the distressed Mrs. Heaster, who said that the ghost of her daughter had visited her four times.

It is reported many places that Mrs. Heaster, Johnston Heaster, and Preston spoke together "for several hours." Whatever conversation passed among them, by the end of the meeting, Preston had agreed to dispatch deputies to talk to Knapp, Anderson Jones, Aunt Martha Jones, and perhaps even Shue himself.

Newspaper accounts say it was "certain citizens" who grew suspicious, which does not, of course, preclude Mary Jane Robinson Heaster, but would seem to include others also. The *Greenbrier Independent* and the *Pocahontas Times* say that the postmortem investigation was ordered because of "rumors in the community" which must certainly refer to people beyond family members. "We hear . . . that Shue's conduct at the time of his wife's death and when she lay a corpse in his house was very suspicious," reported the *Pocahontas Times*. Preston, as his job required, began his investigation.

 ## John Alfred Preston:

"The prosecutor's lot is a peculiar one: I will only be able to be fair in this if I can lay aside my own disbelief in what this woman claims. How must I deal with her? I have no doubt that the woman is deranged, though she appears sane if not remarkably intelligent.

"The comfort of the law is logic. I am prepared, as prosecuting attorney of Greenbrier County, to mediate in a property dispute; disposed, as a legal man, to trace a deed; eager, as a citizen and attorney, to prosecute a criminal for the good of us all. But this is no ordinary domestic disagreement. The sea of suspicion has no shore, and they who set sail upon it are without rudder. This woman: they say she is pious, she appears to be pious, and it seems that she truly believes she has been visited by the ghost, for God's sakes, of her daughter. Four times, she would have it (though the conventional story would have had the ghost visit three times), the girl returned in the night, in the flesh (but cold), to say that her husband had brought about her demise. Dressed she was, but in the clothing she supposedly was killed in, not the dress in which she was buried. Her brother-in-law quickly denied, when I asked, that he, or anyone else, had been paid a visit by the apparition. And the child, writing carefully the whole time, shook his head slowly and solemnly no when I asked him if he had ever seen a ghost.

"For several days after the funeral, Mrs. Heaster told me, she prayed constantly. It was during this time that she washed the sheet that had been left with her after the burial. It would seem that on Monday, when the coffin was to be sealed and Mrs. Shue buried, Mrs. Heaster had attempted to return the bereaved husband's sheet to him. He refused, telling her to keep it. Thinking that it smelled peculiar, though it appeared clean, she tried to wash it. The water, she says, turned red, causing her to think at first that she had ruined her other wash, but when she scooped up the water, it was clear. She even boiled the sheet and hung it out and froze it for three or four days, but still the red color remained. It was this sheet that first aroused her suspicions: she saw it as a 'sign' that something was not right about her daughter's death.

"For a few nights, she prayed to know how it was that her beloved daughter had died. She could not, did not, believe it was from natural causes. In her own words, 'I prayed that she would come back and tell on him,' quite specifically suspicious of Shue.

"And naturally it did not surprise me to hear that her daughter obligingly came back and told on him.

"But four times! Each time, she insisted, her daughter spoke more freely, eventually revealing the entire scene of the crime: an argument, his violent and deadly reaction.

"After the fourth time, the woman 'decided to tell someone.'

"And apparently lost no time doing so. The neighbors at first scoffed, doubting the stories and belittling them as merely the delusions of a mother's grieved mind . . .

"My grandmother used to swear that the chair in her parlor rocked of its own volition every time that a family member was about to die! I came to believe, as I grew in the law, that that belief amounted to nothing more than a piece of hindsight, a vain and mistaken effort to control the future by 'reading' the past, so that in effect, one says, 'Surely in a thing so momentous as death, there was a sign, a warning. What was it?' And before long, the searching mind falls upon a recollection that the rocker apparently rocked alone at some recent moment. And the same mind fixes on that rocking as an omen, where in truth there is none. What are forgotten are all the other occasions when the chair was rocked by wind, or a slight earth tremor, or a skirt caught up on a wood projection, or a cat's sudden quiet departure—a thousand natural reasons argue against a super-natural one!

"I first heard of this ghostly visitations business in the courthouse a week ago, the story supposed to have come from a servant in one of the houses in town—and I was amused at a story as tawdry as any printed each week in our own *Independent* for the confusion and moral weakening of its readers. It is irony that now, a week later, I am called into it.

"One can see how the bereaved mother craves explanation, and dreams of her daughter's appearance. And because some noticed the corpse's head to be loose upon the neck, the mind brings that to her notice in the dream, and the waking mind concludes that the dead woman is the victim of murder.

"People at the wake, she reported, remarked the looseness of the head upon the neck. They also thought Shue was acting strangely. Mrs. Heaster admits to praying 'that she would come back and tell on him.' The brother-in-law, Johnston Heaster, then rode over and talked with the blacksmith, who apparently could say nothing that allayed anyone's suspicions.

"Of course there is something else. The woman admits to never having liked the man her daughter married. And now jealousy and suspicion have determined her to find mischief in the girl's death. Perhaps the girl fell down the steps. Knapp is no sawbones, and he believed her death a sudden heart failure. He admitted that there were bruises on her cheek.

"Suspicions I can deal with: they are real, and perhaps reasonable; justifiable if not justified. The wife Lucy Tritt is too long dead for any examination. The first wife, Estelline Cutlip, may be alive. I reckon that I have no choice. Despite the fact that we shall undoubtedly lose the case, I must proceed with the investigation."

The Honorable John Alfred Preston went himself out to the Richlands to see Dr. Knapp, who admitted that his examination of the dead woman had been incomplete. The attorney must also have talked with some other folks in the area.

Preston and Knapp together agreed that an autopsy would clear things up, confirming or denying the suspicions Mrs. Heaster and others had voiced, and allowing Knapp to know better how Zona Heaster Shue had died. Of equal importance, an autopsy would lift suspicion from the shoulders of the new blacksmith, if indeed he was innocent. So Preston, somewhat reluctantly, one supposes, set the events in motion.

Obviously, haste was necessary. An exhumation was ordered, an inquest jury assembled, and the day appointed. For convenience, they chose to perform the autopsy in Nickell School House, just a few yards' distance from Soule Methodist Church. The log structure is now gone. It stood, according to local residents, "in back of Soule cemetery." The schoolchildren were let out for the day. Zona was buried roughly halfway between the two little buildings, church and schoolhouse. Three physicians were chosen to participate in the posthumous examination. The day, according to the local folks, was cold and raw. The temperatures during the month that Mrs. Shue was buried had rarely gotten higher than the teens and several times had dropped below zero.

And so, on February 22, 1897, thirty-one days after it had been buried, the body of Zona Heaster Shue was brought to light again, and a postmortem examination was performed. This was, incidentally and ironically, Girta Lucretia Shue's tenth birthday.

We can only imagine the scene: the perfectly understandable human reluctance to violate custom and reopen a grave and disturb its contents; the inescapable sense of horror all of them must have felt at this gruesome necessity; the raw February weather, with just a skift of snow over the Greenbrier landscape; finally, the sinking sick knowledge that what must be done must be done, though it was deeply ingrained in all of them that once a Christian burial had laid a body to rest, it was not supposed to be brought up again, like some dog-planted bone, or a squirrel's winter nut supply.

It was reported by the *Greenbrier Independent* that Shue "vigorously complained," but it was made clear to him that he would be forced to go to the inquest if he did not go agreeably. He said, on the way, that he knew he would come back under arrest. Then he added, "But they will not be able to prove I did it." Also brought in a buggy were Aunt Martha and Anderson Jones. Preston probably came on the black mare that he rode everywhere.

And the scene itself:

Mrs. Heaster, in the bone-chilling cold, waits on the steps of the little log schoolhouse, staring out at the raw spot where her daughter's remains have rested for four and a half weeks, knowing it is her insistence that has brought into action this day's doings. She wishes there were grass over the grave, but none has grown, of course, in the month of freezing weather. She feels tired, edgy, and the gray in her hair has increased noticeably in the last month, at least it appears so to her in the tin mirror, the only one in the house. Her face is drawn and colorless, and her mouth is perpetually grim, and dry despite the fact that she rubs lard on it all the time. It is the time, for her, of the change: all things eventually dry up. . . . Tom Lewis comes up and nods, gives her hand a squeeze. She thinks how he would have made as good a human doctor as an animal one.

Everybody had something to say about how floppy Zona's head was in the coffin, even after he'd poked all those sheets and things in to keep it from dropping off to one side. And he would no more let anyone look under all that collar and bow arrangement than fly to the moon. Zona's face had looked red on the right side, but he said it was just that he put too much rouge on her. Then he'd joked about not being clever with rouge, as he was only a man.

She wanted to see what was wrong, couldn't remember that other corpses had heads that dauncy. She has talked and talked to Dr. Knapp, and more recently to Dr. Rupert. She has prayed and prayed.

She hears the buggy approach the schoolyard. Her world is still heavy and terrible from Zona's passing: there is no pleasure in any of life's joys. Her husband and the boys' needs suck out her strength, and sometimes she hates them each one for not being a girl, her daughter, someone to gossip and work with, the light of her days. Her days are now without light at all. Though she feels weary and aching and tired all the time, she cannot sleep a night through, and all food closes up her throat as if she were trying to swallow clods of dirt. Her head hurts. She rubs her forehead. Her eyes sting. Often she wishes she could die, too, just lie down and sleep forever, until Jesus wakes her up to some morning that is eternally June . . .

She knows they have moved two tables together to lay Zonie out upon, and brought blankets and extra lanterns, as the day is dark. Three small boys lurk at the edge of the cemetery, peering curiously, but they have been instructed to stay away. When they edge closer, Matthew Collison walks towards them and they scatter quickly, disappearing into the woods.

In the horsedrawn buggy ride the three doctors and Justice

Harlan McClung. All alight with their black medicine bags, in which Mary Jane Heaster knows there are knives and scalpels to open the flesh and find what truth has lain buried for four and a half weeks. Dr. Knapp treated Zona before death. Dr. Rupert knew Zonie all her life, and attended the birth of the little boy fourteen months ago. Dr. Houston McClung is unknown to her, and never saw Zonie alive.

So they have brought Shue along. Mary Jane gazes with distaste at the men: Preston in his fine clothes, his heavy cloak, sits proudly upright astride his fine black mare, who prances even after the long climb up the mountain. Then Constable Shawver on his red gelding, and that black devil of a blacksmith on a black horse. Shue sits loosely in the saddle, slumped forward. She sees he will not catch her scorn, will not look in her direction, and notes the stray lock of hair that always falls upon his forehead. It was one of the things Zonie once told her she loved.

And down the road come Mr. Osborne and Mr. Burns, two neighbors. They glance apologetically at her as they begin to remove the dirt, first hacking at the frozen top with pickaxes, finally getting down to softer dirt, throwing spadefuls up on the mossy winter ground. William Graft joins them, with yet another shovel, standing by to take over when one of them tires.

She lifts up her eyes at the miserable colorless day, while around her hover like a protective band her kith and kin, all being soft-voiced, polite, careful, all their living breaths visible in the winter air. Judging from the dirty gray-yellow February sky, it is around noon. But time no longer matters. All of them speak gently, and politely, as they file past her. No one smiles. Tom Lewis comes up with one of the spades, and he nods his sympathy as he walks past her into the schoolhouse. He and four other men will make up the inquest jury, following the progress of the autopsy and making certain that its results are known.

At the last minute, when her son-in-law is close enough to touch if she had wanted to, he flings his head up and says loudly, "You're a pretty thing, having your daughter brought up and cut up like this." Even with these words, his voice is as vibrant as a musical instrument.

Shawver jerks his arm, and Trout Shue stumbles across the threshold going in, muttering a curse. Mrs. Heaster swallows, stares out over the quiet graves, afeared she will cry again. Has anyone ever hated as she hates him?

As he enters the dark schoolroom, Shue says, over his shoulder, "I don't know what they are taking her up for." Mary Jane doesn't know if he is speaking to her, or to anyone in particular. "They aren't going to find anything," he mumbles into the darkness. And she thinks, Dear God, they have got to find something. They have got to.

The piles of dirt are too high to have come out of that one little grave, and yet they have.

Then she feels nothing, concentrates on feeling nothing, and manages to keep the feeling until she hears the sound of the spade scrape upon wood.

On February 25, 1897, under the title "Foul Play Suspected," the *Independent* reported on the autopsy. Since Mrs. Shue's death and burial, according to the story, "rumors in the community" had caused the local authorities "to suspect that she may not have died from natural causes." The paper states that "her husband, E. S., commonly known as Trout Shue, was suspected of having brought about her death by violence or in some way unknown to her friends." The newspaper goes on to say that an "inquest was accordingly ordered and on Monday last, before Justice Harlan McClung and a jury of inquest assisted by Mr. Preston, state's attorney for the county, Mrs. Shue's body was exhumed and a post-mortem examination made, conducted by Drs. Knapp, Rupert, and Houston McClung, Shue being present and summoned as a witness."

Shue reportedly sat in the corner of the schoolhouse on a bale of hay, whittling nervously during the three hours that the autopsy took. The doctors worked in the uncertain light of kerosene lamps. The little black boy, Anderson Jones, was there, too, and recalled in later years watching Shue carefully. His hands were trembling, Jones said, as the doctors worked. His whittling reportedly increased to a frantic pace as the doctors, after finding nothing amiss with the vital organs, or, apparently, the reproductive organs, finally got around to examining the head and neck. This detail seems puzzling: would Shue, regarded already as a potential murderer, have been allowed any kind of knife at all, which at any instant might have turned into a weapon? This story seems to have originated with Anderson Jones, who in certain other details later proved unreliable. Shue was not, of course, under arrest until after the examination, but certainly he would have been carefully watched.

The body of the dead woman was reported to be "in a near-perfect state of preservation," owing to the low temperatures during the month of its interment.

The autopsy did not take three days and three nights, as Anderson Jones was later to claim. And the body was exhumed not because of any ghostly visitations, but for absolutely earthly doubts about the cause of Zona's death. A jury of five men watched the proceedings. It is not reasonable to believe that the newspapers withheld information, or gave reasons other than the true ones for the exhumation.

Most versions of the folktale tell that first the doctors looked for signs that Shue had poisoned his wife. This detail does not jibe with the fact that the ghost supposedly told specifically of the broken neck. If the physicians suspected a broken neck, surely they would have investigated that possibility first, sparing themselves a great deal of unnecessary and obviously unpleasant work.

But the newspaper accounts explain this odd detail in the usual versions of the folktale which state that the autopsy began with "examination of the contents of the stomach in search of poison." The physicians did not know what they were going to find. Even if Mrs. Heaster claimed that the ghost had revealed the manner of death, apparently nobody took her story seriously.

One report asserts that the physicians performing the autopsy "nearly ruined their hands with carbolic acid." There were no rubber gloves in those days, so there was no avoiding contact with the body. The doctors, not knowing what Mrs. Shue had died of, used the only disinfectant available to them, the very strong carbolic acid, to avoid "catching" anything from the corpse.

It may seem odd that the broken neck was not immediately and externally evident, but physicians say that this is one of the most difficult conditions to detect, as all corpses have floppy heads, and a human head is extremely heavy in relation to the rest of the body, and particularly so in a corpse, as all the muscles are absolutely relaxed. A mortician and a pathologist report that it is not uncommon to break a corpse's neck merely by moving the body without supporting the head. Further, the first vertebra is buried deeply in the neck directly under the skull. Recall also that these nineteenth-century rural physicians simply did not know what they were looking for.

In fact, an autopsy then, as today, was probably done in accordance with a standard procedure, and the folktales, which always mention that "they first checked the stomach for poison," retain this truth. An incision is first made in the front of the body to examine the vital organs of the chest and abdomen for signs of disease or damage. Today samples of the organs are often taken for microscopic examination, but modern physicians doubt that the microscopes available in 1897 could have revealed very much. The most likely poisons to have been used in 1897 were heavy metals, arsenic or strychnine. Arsenic was a common treatment for syphilis at the time, and doctors and pharmacies stocked it, so it was easily obtainable. Strychnine was widely used on farms and in households to eradicate pests. Crows and gophers were controlled by soaking corn in strychnine and putting it out for the birds to eat, or pouring it down gopher holes. Metal would precipitate out when either one of these was mixed with an acid. Probably the doctors tested for other poisons by odor, as most other poisons available to laymen at that time, like cyanide, had characteristic smells. Therefore, since Zona Shue had been ill for a month previous to her death, they perhaps suspected that her husband had poisoned her. Not knowing what they were looking for, they checked the stomach contents for indications of poison.

Meanwhile they would have noted what the woman had eaten prior to being killed, and found traces in her stomach of bread, butter, various fruit preserves—but no meat. The stomach contents would have revealed fairly accurately the time of death, as all digestion halts at the moment of death. The accounts printed did not address themselves to the time of death.

Following the examination of vital organs, an incision is usually made in the back of the skull along the hairline so that the brain can be removed if necessary for examination. Probably this step was not taken in the case of Mrs. Shue, because of what they found before they got to that point.

Shue's whittling reportedly grew more erratic and more rapid, as the physicians moved the focus of their attention from the body cavity to the neck and head of the dead woman.

Newspapers reported that at the end, the doctors, working around the head and neck, suddenly began to whisper together, then one of them turned to the man on the bale of hay and said, "Well, Shue, we have found your wife's neck to have been broken."

It was later reported in the *Nicholas County News* that "then Shue's head drooped, and all observers noted [that] a change of expression came over his face." The *Pocahontas Times* account on March 9 was most specific: ". . . the discovery was made that the neck was broken and the windpipe mashed. On the throat were the marks of fingers indicating that she had been choken [*sic*]." The examination disclosed "that the neck was dislocated between the first and second vertebrae. The ligaments were torn and ruptured. The windpipe had been crushed at a point in front of the neck." Trout Shue was heard to say then, as he would many other times, "They cannot prove that I did it."

The results of the autopsy were made public at once, printed in considerable detail in at least the two local papers at the end of February. Thus everyone who was interested knew from then on that Zona had died of a broken neck, dislocated between the first and second vertebrae. Had Mrs. Heaster come to Preston with an accurate story, and had the exhumation confirmed that story, the newspapers would have been quick to print such a story.

The physicians and the public also knew what was in the woman's stomach when she died, so presumably anyone could have found that out. The autopsy report was anything but secret. The account in the *Greenbrier Independent* stated, "From one of the doctors we learn that the examination clearly disclosed the fact that Mrs. Shue's neck had been broken. The jury found in accordance with the facts above stated, [and] charged Shue with murder . . ."

It seems unlikely that any written report of the autopsy's findings was ever put on file anywhere. The difference in wording of the printed articles argues that there was no standard written account from which reporters were quoting, but suggests instead that they were interviewing the various doctors and writing their own stories. The West Virginia Department of Vital Statistics has no report of an autopsy from that date, nor has the Greenbrier County Health Department. Today most autopsies are performed at hospitals and become a part of their records departments. An autopsy performed anyplace else, as this one was, entailed no obligation to file a report.

Since the articles tell us frankly the autopsy results, it is not reasonable to believe that the physicians selectively chose not to reveal parts of their findings. Yet it is curious that the physicians did not address themselves to the problem of Zona's illness prior to her death, or to the "death from childbirth" entry in the death book.

William B. Collison:

"Oh, I was only a small boy at the time, living eight miles from the Shue home. My mother was kin to Zona. I remember that the neighbors talked of little else for days. I think I remember that Mrs. Shue's clothing was found under a lumber pile not far from the house."

An autopsy can be requested by a lawyer simply to determine the manner of death, but since it is a medical, rather than legal, procedure, it is not entered into any legal record. To have the autopsy performed, Prosecuting Attorney John Alfred Preston would have had to go to the justice of the peace and get a warrant to disturb a buried body. And since Shue was taken on suspicion before the indictment, he had to have been arrested on a second warrant. Sheriff Hill Nickell served Shue the warrant, which was the legal method for "binding him over" or allowing him to be held in jail to await the grand jury hearing.

Following the exhumation and inquest on February 22, 1897, E. S. Shue was placed under arrest by Sheriff Hill Nickell and, after a preliminary hearing, jailed pending his arraignment, which could not take place until the April term of the Circuit Court.

The newspaper says that E. S. Shue was allowed to return to his house one last time. Obviously Trout Shue was under guard on this trip back to Livesay's Mill. It is recorded that, while there, he cooked a meal for Constable James Shawver, John N. McClung, and Estill McClung, in whose custody he was. The newspapers tell us he "acted in a cheerful manner." And he continued to say, "They cannot prove that I did it."

Trout Shue is strangely cheerful the whole way, and entertains them with stories of the girls he has known, the places he has been, his adventures in the logging camps in Pocahontas where he has worked so many winters: of the cold so sharp that old Cal Tharpe's feet had to be amputated after freezing. And how Mr. C. W. Workman was frozen to death—he had bent down to pick up something; that was how he was found in the snow. He tells them that both of these things happened during the same snowstorm that took away his dear wife Lucy.

But then, he continues, the next summer, the one just past, on August 10 it was 106 in the shade as he chopped trees for the Cherry River Lumber Company. Each hour, he said, they stopped, drenched themselves in the river for ten minutes, and returned to chop down more pine trees . . . He brags of how only he, of all the men, could balance on a log and unjam the river with a peavy, such was his strength! This reminds him of a horse race he had one time with a friend up on Droop. He bet the fellow seventy cents that he could win a race into Hillsboro on his old crippled horse. Once his friend had got a head start, whipping his horse to a lather, Shue merely turned around, and made his way back home in a leisurely fashion. Next day he asked his friend, "Where were you? I got to town, and waited and waited, and when I got tired of waiting, I rode on home." Shue laughs loudly when he tells them this. It is as if all is settled, and there is a great load off his shoulders. And he tells them about all the girls who came by the blacksmith shop with pies and cakes and jellies when he first arrived, and how some of them left with tears in their eyes . . .

Once back at the house, the men see that things are in need of a woman's hand. The hens are scraggly, rags and jars lie about in the yard, and dried mud is tracked up on the porch. Fences are broken and unrepaired. A big dog with matted fur greets Shue by banging his tail on the ground, but he doesn't get up. The yard is almost entirely dirt, with a few patches of old snow here and there.

But melting snow drips from the eaves, and the sun has come out finally, a pale gold light at the end of a colorless day. On the way into the house, he calls their attention to a few snowdrops just growing out of one of the islands of dirty snow, and a bit of hardy periwinkle's dark green. He remarks that Zonie would have loved that, that she just loved flowers. He speaks of her just as if she wasn't dead at all . . .

They move and shift uncomfortably, looking around uneasily, perhaps trying to imagine the scene of the murder. For all their badges of office, they are still a tad skittish at being where it all happened, wondering when and how he did it. Inside, flour is spilled on the floor, and plates and pots are piled everywhere. A cabinet door hangs open, and the smell of rancid fat and rotting food permeates the room. Mice droppings are everywhere, and several of the varmints scatter for shelter as the men enter the house. Shue seems to find it amusing that he cannot find any clean clothes. Very well, he will take them in dirty, and the black woman in town can wash them for him! Looking about, he suddenly suggests that they must all be hungry, and that they must eat. McClung and Shawver glance uneasily at each other, and begin to protest. But Shue is insistent, and expansive, so that any refusal seems impolite, and before they can make excuses, out come a slab of bacon, eggs, bread, jam, butter. His high spirits seem strange. He is acting as if they are just here on a social visit. Though they watch him warily, they are tired and hungry, and he, apparently oblivious, moves about the kitchen slicing, putting jars on the table, stoking up the banked fire he had left early that morning, comfortable performing the tasks of a housewife. As he fixes food, he tells them of coming here, of the good harvest in Greenbrier, of the green of the land. He regales them with the story of how, as he attempted to find directions to Tuckwiller's farm at Livesay's Mill where he had heard tell they needed a smith, an old man, trying to think, asked, "Do you know where they laid the old railroad bed?" He says he shook his head, said he did not. "Do you know where the Livesay's store is at?" asked the old fellow. Again he said he did not. "Well," the man said, "I can't tell you nothing if you don't know nothing."

Though at first his guards glance shyly at each other, and rub their noses in embarrassment, at this man who talks endlessly and cooks like a woman, soon the smell of bacon frying has them all eagerly anticipating the meal. He produces coffee, steaming and pungent. They sit around the wooden table, the plates they are eating from still wet from a hasty washing, and the food and hot drink revive them. Shue leans back, balancing his chair on two legs, and says, "Ah, I won't eat this good in jail." And several times he says, "But I'll be out soon. They will not be able to prove I did it." They all dip snuff when they are finished, though Shue tells them he does not ordinarily use tobacco.

When they are ready to go, Shawver follows Shue upstairs to watch him as he collects what clothing he will need, a razor, a toothbrush and a tin cup, a pad of paper for writing or sketching, and a Bible. Shawver reminds him of the cold, and he rolls everything up in a dark blanket for his sojourn in the Lewisburg jail.

Shue was locked up in the little stone county jail still standing on Washington Street, just a block from the center of Lewisburg. He obviously was still under the impression that a man could not be convicted on circumstantial evidence alone.

Grand jury proceedings are under seal; the items in an indictment are separate and distinct charges against the accused. In this case, the state would have presented what evidence it already had: autopsy findings, the testimony of neighbors, the suspicions of various people. The grand jury decided there was reason enough to try the case; that is, that there was reason to believe that Shue had probably killed his wife. That being so, the grand jury brought back a true bill, and an indictment was made up, showing what the state was accusing Shue of.

Subsequent to the grand jury proceedings, a law order was written into the record, on Thursday, April 22, 1897, in Greenbrier County Courthouse, which reads in part, ". . . E. S. Shue, being arraigned in his own proper person, pleaded not guilty and put himself upon the County, and the attorney for the State doth the like, and issue was theron [sic] joined. Whereupon motion of the defendant, this cause is continued untill [sic] the 2nd day of the June term, 1897." Shue, in effect, said to the Greenbrier grand jury, "You prove I did it." There was no motion for a bond.

In a crime for which capital punishment is a possibility, the state has to prove the corpus delecti, or the mass of the crime; that is, it must prove that the victim is dead, and that the victim died as a result of criminal agency. The possibility that death occurred as the result of an accident or natural causes must also be considered. In this case, obviously the victim was dead, and the question was, did she die by criminal agency? Anderson Jones, according to Judge McWhorter, said later that Shue had "dragged" her body over to the bottom of the stairs so it looked as if she'd fallen. Could she not, in fact, have fainted, fallen, and broken her neck? But the autopsy had addressed this issue, reporting that her body was not bruised or injured, and there was "no evidence that she had hurt herself." Thus accident and natural causes were ruled out by the autopsy. It seems, too, that abortion, natural or induced, can also be ruled out, as the *Independent* account stated, "There was no mark upon her person to suggest, or other evidence to show that she had subjected herself to any sort of violence," and the *Pocahontas Times* reported, on March 9, 1897, that "All other portions and organs of the body were apparently in a perfectly healthy state."

Of John Alfred Preston, the *History of Greenbrier County* has this to say: "As a lawyer, he was clear and earnest; as an advocate, forceful and eloquent, and as a man, frank, conscientious, and sincere, without ostentation, yet with the courage of his convictions, never being swayed where principle was involved. His kindness, gentleness, and generosity endeared him to all people. His high sense of honor and integrity of character have earned him a reputation seldom attained and his influence for truth and right have been and will continue to be felt throughout this section for many years."

People in the area say that the reason Mary Jane Heaster and Johnston Heaster took along one of Zona's cousins or brothers, "young Joe," as scribe, when they went to see Prosecuting Attorney Preston, was that neither Mary Jane nor Johnston could write, and that this same Joe accompanied them in later months as they traversed the area collecting evidence for the trial.

Together with his assistant Henry Gilmer, Preston, as the state's agent, now had to begin work in earnest, to try to build a case against Shue as the murderer of his wife.

 John Alfred Preston:

"We must at all costs find other facts. Prosecute I will, but we must not permit any weight to be placed on the revelation of the ghost. It will make all of us look like fools.

"Rucker and Gardner will of course seek to discredit her sanity. Therefore, though we must call her to the witness stand, I will question her only about her suspicions and those of others, and instruct her to avoid mention of her dreams.

"In Mrs. Heaster's behalf, we must be passionate with detachment, and convincing without belief. I am forced to regard anyone who traffics with revenants as unbalanced, though I admit she tells her tale well. Nonetheless, she must be made to understand that the ghost business must not be brought into the courtroom."

Trout Shue:

"What were those flowers she said? Those lilies, the flowers white, glowing in the black shade as bright as candles almost, their heads nodding so graceful and a perfume to them like roses and lemons and spices and every good smell you ever imagined rolled into one, and you'd give a thousand dollars to be able to keep that smell around you all the year? That grow only a day or two a year, in full spring, in pine woods far away from everything else, on the inward-sloping edge of hollows where the ground is a bed of fallen pine needles, so fragrant and soft you'd never want to get up and go back to the world . . . What were their names?"

The assistant prosecuting attorney, Henry Gilmer, is recalled as careless of appearance and grooming, and, in the words of Daisy Hume, "a great big old fat dirty thing." A woman who remembers him described him as "a big, red-faced countrified fellow who wore farmers' clothes instead of proper lawyers' attire," and another who as a child knew him says he "practiced law in his undershirt." One admirer praised him as a free spirit, saying he was "practically an outlaw"—that he and his wife lived together without benefit of matrimony for several years and through the births of several children before deciding to tie the knot. Yet all who speak of him say he was a bright and shrewd attorney.

Henry Gilmer:

"I'll tell you the world is full of truth and lies. You hear something from two different people, and it is two different stories entirely and both of them swearing on a stack of Bibles it is his version that is true.

"You have to consider every possibility, some of them maybe so ridiculous you're ashamed to entertain them. But you have to think of them anyway. Take this Shue case. You have to consider that the girl maybe did come back from the dead. Not likely, see, but there are a lot of unexplained things in the world. They say Jesus did.

"Could be the mother broke the neck herself, after the body came to her house. Why, you say? Well, this woman seems to harbor more than a usual animosity towards the blacksmith. And why might that be? If he killed her girl, of course. But wait: the mother's an attractive woman herself; maybe she wanted the blacksmith and maybe he spurned her.

"It may be that Knapp was trying to get rid of a baby for her, and that they broke the neck later to cover that up. And it may be that the black boy killed her.

"Ah, well. No hurry. I'll watch the fellow, and I'll watch her. Sooner or later I'll know."

While Shue was in jail awaiting trial for Zona's murder, he obtained, or was assigned, the services of two lawyers, each of whom was, in his own way, a maverick. It is not clear how they were chosen to defend the accused murderer. They were William Parkes Rucker and James P. D. Gardner. In a serious case, the court will often appoint an older experienced lawyer and a young "green" lawyer, as they want to be sure the defendant gets full and complete legal representation. Rucker, who during the War had been an active Unionist, was an old hand; Gardner was brand-new in Greenbrier County, and was black. In the years after the Civil War pro-Union attorneys in the South—to which Greenbrier County belonged in spirit—often volunteered to defend criminals in capital cases, in a sort of Robin Hood gesture, to make themselves representatives of the poor and downtrodden. A guess, in the absence of evidence, is that Rucker volunteered to defend Shue, and that Gardner was appointed to assist Rucker. It would seem a particularly self-defeating act on Shue's part voluntarily to take on a Yankee-lover and a Negro to defend him before a Greenbrier jury.

During the next four months, while Shue was incarcerated in the Lewisburg jail, Preston and his assistant Henry Gilmer went about seeking evidence to convict the man they now believed had murdered his bride of three months. At the same time, Rucker and Gardner undoubtedly tried to establish their client's innocence, and sought out character witnesses, but perhaps they urged him to confess and explain mitigating circumstances, which could have resulted in a lighter sentence than a conviction on a charge of first-degree murder.

 Jim Gardner:

"I know enough of ignorance and superstition to know that we can make the woman look foolish enough to get this man freed for lack of evidence. Yet I believe he is guilty.

"But what am I projecting? He is, unlike my people, innocent until proven guilty. There is suspicion enough, yet all they know about him appears to be inadmissible. Still, I could wish he had chosen to steal the horse from a white man."

Wenona Shue McNeal:

"Uncle Trout's choice of Rucker and Gardner was an act of self-sacrifice. As you know, the death records list the cause of Zona's death as 'childbirth.' Trout's hiring of Rucker and Gardner was an act he knew would lead to his conviction—a fate he chose to embrace in order to save Zonie's reputation, since the child, the one in the coffin, obviously was not his."

Jim Gardner:

"Today, I said to him again, 'Mr. Shue, I am your counsel. If you could offer me some explanation, or provide yourself with even a shred of a motive, I could help you. I believe that no man kills without reason.'

"And he replied, not addressing me by name then or ever, 'In this jail, in broad daylight, I can look up through that grill in the window—there, up high—and see the stars. In broad daylight!'

"I thought a bit, and said to him, 'Mr. Shue, you may be able to see stars, but you cannot see the light, and you may never see Heaven. Think about it.'

"Then he frowned and stared through me with his angry blue gaze, and said it again, 'How can a nigger help me? In court, I will speak for myself.'

"I rose quickly at that and said, 'Then I hope you hang.'

"And he said haughtily, 'They will not be able to prove that I did it.'"

Shue's efforts to gather witnesses, alibis, or other evidence of his innocence, must have been discouraging, for on May 20, 1897, the *Greenbrier Independent* reported that "Trout Shue, who is now in jail awaiting trial for the murder of his wife, has threatened to kill himself."

Trout Shue:

"A nigger and a backwoodsman. They are always at me: proof, proof, they ask. They want proofs of my innocence. Or they want a confession. A motive. If I will confess, they say, my sentence won't be so hard.

"I can escape. I'll think of a way. I can go somewhere, change as the weather changes—my form, my clothes, my work, can be as different as I want. I can be what I will. I have grown a beard and gone unshaven, and even dressed as a dandy. My mother, for all her endless nattering, showed me the way, by calling me first Erastus, then changing it to Erasmus on a whim, because of some picture in the rotogravure.

"She liked long one-sided discussions—would put aside her book and lay her pince-nez upon it, in the dim winter evenings, and talk on and on. Father Jacob would occasionally utter a sound to indicate his attention, but it was Mother whose word was made flesh. She wanted all of us to be educated. But I liked working outdoors, stressing my body to the breaking point. Mostly I liked doing what I liked doing.

"I can kill myself. I can rob them of that pleasure."

On June 3, the *Greenbrier Independent* reported that Judge McWhorter was "quite sick," so ill that he had been unable to hold court in Monroe County that week. Would he recover in time to preside at the trial of *State* v. *Shue*?

And on June 17, under "Pickups" in the *Greenbrier Independent*, it was reported that "the trial of Trout Shue is set for Wednesday next [June 23]. It is said that Shue has had 120 witnesses summoned." These would have been mainly people Shue had worked for, or with, who could supposedly testify to his good character: perhaps they included family members, preachers and teachers who had known him, people like the blacksmith he had been working with at Livesay's Mill, Jim Crookshanks. A law order exists for the summoning of only one of these, J. P. Shue of Webster County. Presumably this was his brother, John Patrick Bruffey Shue. In fact, a deputy was paid $37.50 later for expenses incurred while fetching this witness from, not Webster, but Braxton County, rather than allow a continuance of the trial on account of his absence. Apparently Mr. Ludington, the deputy, had to so some traveling to track down J. P. Shue. Trout must have regarded his brother as a key witness.

On June 25, 1897, the *Pocahontas Times* remarked, "On the issue of this trial depends the question of whether Shue, who is a Droop citizen, will reach his seventh wife, as he has boasted he would have seven. The passing of the third endangers his neck or is liable to send him to the penitentiary where there is no marrying or giving in marriage."

Mrs. Heaster came to Lewisburg and rented a room in a boarding house for the duration of the trial. She brought with her the stained sheet.

 Trout Shue:

"I have the memory of a dream that comes back to me all the time; or maybe I have the dream of a memory. It don't matter. I was thirteen.

"It was summer, with the smell of grain and grass. Where the afternoon sunlight come through the hayloft door dust hung in the air, suspended, moving only slightly, it was that still. Outside the barn I could hear the sounds of summer—the songs of birds, a cow lowing a quarter mile away on the next hilly rise, a door slamming back at the house. That's how it was when I fell asleep.

"I was waked up by a soft, low chattering sound. There, in the sunshaft was perched a bird—a golden bird, shining in the afternoon as bright as the sun itself.

"As I rose up to have a better look, it soared out towards the woods. I hurried down the slick wood ladder to the barn floor below, and without thinking about it, I followed it.

"I was used to being in the woods alone. I thought that the bird must be a Carolina parakeet, which I had heard the old-timers tell about, though I wasn't ever sure. Folks around Droop Mountain called them kelinkies.

"The bird kept watching me. It seemed like it was tame, stayed close by, not a bit afeared of me, but always just out of reach, calling back to me as it led the way into deep and deeper woods on the back of Droop.

"I couldn't let it get away: it seemed to me like a creature out of another world. I followed it for hours, bewitched by its grace, its rainbow colors, its coy manner. At first, I just loved it, just wanted to watch it, it was so pretty. But after a while, I decided I must have it. Finally, I felt love turn to anger as the bird eluded me, leading me ever deeper into the woods after those flashing colors. It even began to sound like it was talking to me, calling me on, and laughing at me. I stumbled and fell down, bruised myself on rocks, and tore my flesh on tree branches. But then I was too mad to turn back. Eventually, I became tangled in berry vines, devoured by buzzing biting insects, and dizzy with the heat.

"Finally, I realized that I was lost, and had no idea which way to go. The bird still perched, out of reach, in a patch of sunlight that fell through the dark trees. Just like it knew it looked beautiful there. A cat'll do the same thing.

"I tried to find my way back by the sun, and then the bird followed me. I knew I had to have it. It seemed to me that only if I could have the bird, would I be safe, I would be calm again, and I would never want anything else as long as I lived. Meanwhile the bird began flirting with me as sure as I saw girls do when I watched my brothers with them. It seemed to belong to me, and to let it go then would have seemed like cutting off my arm, or tearing out my heart. Yet of course I knew all along that birds are supposed to be free, and that boys cannot under normal circumstances capture them. The parrot perched just above where I was, cocking its head to look down on me in my misery. It seemed curious to know what I would do.

"I said under my breath I would show it what I would do. I made my way to a nearby creek, kneeled down and splashed water on my face. I drank out of my hands, my heart pounding and spider webs still clinging to my eyes, as I looked up to see if the bird was still there. It was, perched up above on a branch, its feathers apparently wrought of sunup and rainbows and autumn leaves and spring grass, all those colors and more. From its perch it watched me, with a large solemn eye. Looking back down into the cool gold water, I saw my weapon: a rock washed round by the flowing water.

"Even then my aim was good, and I hit the bird in the breast with the rock, knocking it to the ground, where it flapped around, wounded. A panic seized me. Looking about, I found a fallen branch, and beat the bird to death.

"When I was done, I stared at the shattered bloody thing at my feet, and could not believe what I had done. There in the woods, the shadows lengthening, I burst out weeping. I had killed it even knowing how rare a kelinky was.

"And yet, unbelievable as it may be, looking about, I immediately caught sight of a landmark, a burnt-out stump of a tree where we always found morchella mushrooms in the spring. Then I knew how to get home. I wiped my eyes and left the woods without looking anymore at the bright ribbons of feathers and blood on the ground. I was going to take it home to show, but I knew I would catch heat for that. I don't know why I did it, but the bird deserved it.

"That night, I couldn't sleep for the pictures in my head. After many hours, as I tossed in my bed suddenly the room became light, as if dawn was coming. I leaned up on my elbows, and I saw standing by my bed a beautiful girl, or woman. She was like a magnolia blossom, or a mountain waterfall, her arms stretched out to me as white as new snow. Her hair was golden, and smooth like a bird's wing. But as she stood there, I could see that her breast was bloody and dark. Without speaking, she smiled sadly and said, 'Didn't you know that I was your true love? You will never see me again.'

"And when I sat up in bed, the room was like it always was, and outside was blackest night. Either she was gone, or had never really been there. I learned then that desire that comes before ability and must outlive it! No other woman was ever so perfect, but many have been as desirable, at least in the beginning . . . I know it may have been a dream, and yet I would swear that it really happened.

"From then on I knew that the heart never gets finished with wanting, and that the heart can never match its wanting. In the years after that, when my luck ran out and things went wrong, and I decided to change, to leave, to come here, and start a new life, my mother turned her back to me when I went to tell her good-bye, and would not speak to me. So I changed my name too, this time to Edward, and it seemed to signify that things were going to be different, better."

NOTES

p. 77: Preston's thinking is of course only my own reasoning about the ghost. The sheet business, again, comes from the Mc-Whorter letter and testimony printed in the *Greenbrier Independent* at the time of the trial in July. Preston's thoughts offer a good reason why he never brought up the ghost in the trial.

p. 81: All names of persons at the postmortem are real, collected from letters, newspaper accounts, and interviews with people whose antecedents were involved in the exhumation.

p. 84: The "pretty thing" quotation is from Nelle Watts and Edwin Coffman.

p. 86: Information about the difficulty of diagnosing a broken neck is from Dr. William W. Old III, M.D., Dr. Michael Cunningham, M.D., and William B. Lomax, a mortician.

p. 86: According to Dr. Jules Karpas, M.D., medical examiner from Southold, New York, a cross-section of the uterus would have revealed a recent birth or miscarriage. But the outward appearance of the uterus returns to normal very quickly after such an event, and might have been missed by the three physicians who were, after all, only local doctors and not pathologists, and perhaps had not examined cadavers recently.

p. 88: The Collison quote, a voice in the community, is from a letter about the Shue case printed in the *Beckley Herald* in the mid-fifties.

p. 89: The stories Shue tells the men on the trip back to Livesay's all came from items in the *Pocahontas Times*, February 15, 1895. Stories about Shue's bragging are many. My own father fooled a friend in a horse race once like the one described. The story of the man wanting directions was told to me by Robin Williams of Middlebrook, Virginia, about his grandfather. The messy house is invention, but it seems likely that if Shue had been living there alone for a month, rather distracted, to say the least, that things would reflect his personal chaos. Edwin Ott claims that Shue had a dog named Perk.

p. 94: Roger Groot of the Washington and Lee University law faculty provided information suggesting how Shue happened to obtain Gardner and Rucker for his lawyers.

p. 95: William Parkes Rucker, lawyer and physician, blood-kin to George Washington, was a staunch Unionist throughout the Civil War, during which he was arrested and released seven times. Robert H. "Hal" Walls, in an article in the *Greenbrier Historical Society Journal* of 1978, vol. III, no. 4, tells a story of his sheer bravery on an occasion early in the war:

Finally on July 21, 1861, he was taken before a military committee of representative secessionists who threatened to shoot and hang him. He defended his loyalty to the U.S. eloquently and was let go, only to be confronted by a violent mob. The leader, one Michael Soice, "charged that the language used by Rucker in the courthouse was treasonable." Rucker replied, "You shall not tell me that I use treasonable language."

The leader replied: "What would you do if I were to tell you that you are a damned traitor?"

"I would cut the heart out of you as soon as the words came from your traitor mouth," replied Rucker.

"You are a God damned traitor," shouted the leader, simultaneously striking, or attempting to strike Rucker with his loaded stick, while Rucker at the same time dealt him a fatal blow with his bowie knife and he fell dead at the doctor's feet.

Rucker then held the mob at bay for over two hours while the magistrate, for whom he himself sent, came to accept his surrender. Jailed for a month, he mustered his own legal defense in both the murder trial and the treason trial, and was acquitted in both. He went about business as usual after this, though his life was clearly in danger. The man that emerges from Walls's excellent article is a fighter, a man of fearsome integrity who commanded respect for his courage and position even while living among people who violently disagreed with him. That he took Shue's case is very interesting: in America, of course, a man is innocent until proven guilty, and Rucker was apparently determined to protect his client's rights to a fair trial.

p. 95: James P. D. Gardner was the first Negro lawyer to practice in Greenbrier County, and the only one to this day. He usually practiced in Bluefield, sixty miles to the south. This was his only case in Greenbrier. Harry Fields, caretaker of the Greenbrier County Courthouse in Lewisburg, who knew him well, says Jim Gardner was a man of medium height, and a sharp dresser, who normally practiced coalfield law. How was he regarded? "Well," says Mr. Fields, "he made a living as a lawyer." He had received his license to practice law in Greenbrier only a month previous to Shue's grand jury hearing. Gardner's soliloquies are fiction, but we know Trout Shue stole a horse from a Negro, we know what nineteenth-century white sentiments about black professionals were generally, and we know that Shue took the stand himself to argue his own case.

p. 97: Trout Shue's irrational soliloquy is that of a desperate, cornered man. Of course he had not the courage to go through with his threat.

p. 98: The large number of witnesses called by Shue does not indicate that he had given up and wanted to be found guilty, as Nonie suggests.

p. 99: The dream-memory deals with the themes of the unobtainable woman (Shue had tried already three times), and the idea of freedom. Also the transformed lover, or the tale of the disappearing lovely perfect woman who of course in real life does not exist, is a frequent theme in British and American folklore, and common in Appalachian tales. Of course it is also symbolic of his behavior. Shue seems to have been a man lacking in the self-confidence to give a woman her freedom—he beat one wife, killed one, and the third may also have died violently at his hands. Finally, it must be the case that freedom becomes a theme both in the daytime thoughts and the nighttime dreams of a man imprisoned. Carolina parakeets, once numerous and destructive in orchards and forests in the eastern United States, were going extinct at the end of the century, and were then quite rare. They were about thirteen inches long, with plumage of yellow, orange, red, and lime green: skins still exist in old bird collections.

p. 101: Apparently such spelling variations and name changes were fairly common in that place and time; for example, we have seen already that Trout Shue changed his name from Erasmus to Edward. In 1885 Estie was named Ellen Estaline Cutlip, and then four years later was calling herself Allie Estelline Shue, and later signed the divorce order Allis E. Shue.

Part Four
JUNE 1897

In the gloaming, oh my darling! when the lights are dim and low—
And the quiet shadows falling, softly come and softly go—
When the winds are sobbing faintly with a gentle unknown woe—
Will you think of me and love me, as you did once long ago?

"In the Gloaming," Annie Fortescue Harrison, 1866

The circuit court of Greenbrier County opened on June 22, 1897, and two cases were heard that day.

As promised in the newspaper, Shue's case began the next day, on Wednesday, June 23. Entered in the Law Order Book No. 14 in the Greenbrier Courthouse, in spidery handwriting, are maddeningly vague notes for each day of the trial. They name no witnesses, but note for each day that E. S. Shue was that day led to the bar in custody of the jailer, and that the jury, "having heard the evidence in part," were at the end of the day once more committed to the "care and custody" of the sheriff of this county and his deputies . . ."

Let us try to imagine them.

The Greenbrier folks come crowding in at the double oak doors, jostling like cattle before a storm. Here, for a few moments, while it is quiet and empty, the courtroom feels as cool as a church. The white walls and high white ceiling above costly walnut paneling and somber maroon carpeting compel those entering to awed silence. As strangers arrive, the local residents stare, wondering if they are Shue's kin.

The men are in their white Sunday-go-to-meeting shirts, without the collars. It is very hot, the temperature hovering around ninety-five degrees outside. It's a spell and they know it, being watchers of weather; everyone knows there'll be no relief for probably a week. They talk in nervous, whispery voices: "I heard he was supposed to be corresponding with another woman . . ." "No, it was a letter from Zonie to her mother, behind some

cellar boards . . ." They talk of the heat, of the death the week
before of one of them, a young woman with childbed fever, of the
dryness—their corn is shriveling up. Over in Wheeling the temperature yesterday was 100, while in St. Louis, they heard, it
had reached 108!

The flags of the United States and West Virginia hang limply
on either side of the judge's chair. The benches, reminiscent of
church pews, begin to fill, and people crowd in to fill the back
and side aisles. "Didn't they find her bloody clothes in the cellar?" "I don't know. I heard they got everybody in the county as
witnesses."

A man cranes to see over or in between the heads of the
others; his face and neck are bright red, as if from a recent
scrubbing. You can tell it is hot as the hinges of Hell. Everyone
is sweating; only a man standing aside with his thumbs hooked
under his galluses looks cool. Even the ladies have come to this
trial, to fan themselves with palm-leaf fans, and to gawk at the
riffraff. Quick rustles can be heard throughout the room. Here
and there, a well-dressed lady flutters an inlaid Chinese fan
made of brightly painted silk. They already know there is no
direct evidence. Other hands could have killed Zona. "Looks
like if they can't prove he did it, they'll have to let him go." A
man in leather britches gives a quick grin and a fast nudge to a
fat man with an apoplectic face and wispy red hair turning to
white. "Hot enough for you?" The fat man hitches his pants and
nods back, quick and solemn. "It's hot. I ain't gonna lie to you."
They have heard that Trout Shue has had 120 witnesses summoned. "Said it right in the paper!"

Around the room men newly deputized for this trial appear to
swagger a little, eyeing everyone, loaded for bear or a shoot-out,
fingering their Colts and shotguns. Some of them are double-
armed, holding their shotguns across their chests while their
pistols wait in stained darkened holsters pointing down from
their hips.

In April, under "The Circuit Court," the *Pocahontas Times*
had commented that "It is believed that the Grand Jury will have

business of unusual importance . . . questions respecting the peace and dignity of the commonwealth are to be addressed . . ." —and they have all been talking, talking, and talking more for over two months now. They are all interested in watching the lawyers assemble up front, curious to try to predict the outcome.

At one end of the long table is the Honorable John Alfred Preston, straight as a ramrod, light glancing off his bald head; he appears quite a contrast to his assistant, Henry Gilmer, large and disheveled-looking, his overalls ill-fitting and his blue shirt wrinkled, yet a man who just makes you want to trust him, whose face always looks as if he knows some terrific joke that's just about to bust out of him. All wool and a yard wide—that's Henry Gilmer! Preston and Gilmer sit together, going over some notes.

At the other end of the table is Rucker, bearded and forbidding, a big, fierce-looking man; and Gardner, slight, dark-skinned, suited in immaculate black, painfully well groomed.

Wenona Shue McNeal:

"My great-grandfather, Jacob Shue, and my grandfather, John Patrick Bruffey Shue, attended the trial, along with other family members who rallied in support of their kinsman and came to testify in his behalf, and all Trout Shue's relatives were handcuffed before they'd let them into the courtroom.

"I believe that Trout himself held little hope for a fair trial since he had a prison record."

 One of the deputies waves people back from the front row; that will be needed for the witnesses, who are sequestered elsewhere in the courthouse. There are no flies buzzing today, which means that the temperature must be nearly 100. Flies won't move when it gets that hot.

Here comes the jury, filing in, twelve men from the surrounding countryside who have been instructed, judging from their chastened demeanor, in the seriousness of their task. Some of them glance nervously at the assembled spectators. Finally comes Shue, in shirtsleeves, his shoulders set defensively, led to the table where Rucker and Gardner are already seated. His arm is in the beefy grip of Sheriff Hill Nickell, with Deputy Dwyer following closely behind, his hand resting lightly on the butt of his pistol. The prisoner stares at the floor and takes his seat. A ripple like a breeze or a brushfire goes quickly through the room. Gone is the jauntiness from his shoulders, the wicked wild look from his eyes. The only sounds are the hiss of starched clothes and the whisper of fans.

The bailiff, acting as master of arms, announces that the court will come to order, requests that all rise, and announces that Judge Joseph Marcellus McWhorter will preside. Amid a great scraping of chairs and clearing of throats, they stand as the judge enters, clad in his black robe.

Judge McWhorter, described by J. R. Cole in *The History of Greenbrier County* as "a staunch Republican," spent most of his life in public office. He had served a term as mayor of Lewisburg from 1887 until 1893. At the time of Shue's trial, he was nearly seventy, bald, with a long white beard and a high, distinguished forehead, and had been elected in 1896 as judge of the judicial circuit of which Greenbrier County is a part. His law practice had at the time of the trial already been entrusted to the hands of his son, J. S. McWhorter. After his death, it was written of him, in *The History of Greenbrier County*, that "he filled out the full term of eight years, his decisions being marked by equity, justice, and impartiality."

When he had taken his seat in the courtroom that day, the judge announced that the case they were trying was *State* v. *Shue*. He asked if both the prosecution and the defense were ready.

The jury for the case of *State* v. *Shue*, elected, tried, and sworn within the first hour, is listed as follows in the Law Order Book No. 14: A. B. Gardner, D. S. Lockart, C. W. Dunbar, A. B. Stuart,

C. W. Hogsett, J. M. Hughart, T. W. McClung, J. A. Vaughn, C. M. Thomasson, J. A. Hartsook, Richard Blowfield, and J. R. Ridgway. McClung was elected foreman. According to the law orders, they were committed to the "care and custody" of the sheriff and his deputies, whose instructions were "to keep them together without communication with any other persons, and to cause them to appear again in court" each morning at nine until the trial was over. Each night, of course, Trout Shue was returned to jail, and, one assumes, carefully guarded.

In addition to the jury selection, other pertinent law orders on the first day, June 23, instructed one Minnie V. Grose under oath to take "full and complete stenographic notes in this case and to transcribe same when requested."

The trial began with the prosecuting attorney making an "opening statement." Attorney Preston, according to the *Greenbrier Independent*, which covered the trial, explained to the jury that the case against Shue was entirely circumstantial, but that the evidence was "such as had never been presented in any court before." It has since been assumed, in the absence of the actual transcript, that Preston referred to the ghost testimony. But that is not at all clear—in fact, the ghost story was never referred to in any of the summings-up at all, as we shall see. The opening statement was by way of explaining to the jury that the state intended to prove that Shue had murdered his third wife, Zona Heaster Shue. Quite likely, all Preston meant by the words which the paper quoted was that he had so great a wealth of circumstantial evidence against Shue that the blacksmith would be convicted on the basis of that evidence, lacking direct proof. Although not unheard of, this was certainly not usual. Following Preston's opening statement, defense attorney Rucker may have addressed the jury. He could have done so if he chose. Following this, the witnesses for the State were questioned, with the object being that they had to prove together beyond reasonable doubt that Shue was the murderer of his wife.

On Thursday, June 24, Friday, June 25, and Saturday, June 26, a steady stream of witnesses testified against Shue. We know who some of them were, and we know who some others must have been: the doctors Knapp, Rupert, and McClung, who assured the jury that murder had been committed; Anderson Jones, of course; Aunt Martha Jones, his mother; Charlie Tabscott, the schoolteacher whose horse Shue had been working on when the news came; Mr. Crookshanks, for whom Shue worked; Mr. Tuckwiller who owned the farm on which the shop where Shue worked stood; Johnston Heaster; Mary Jane Robinson Heaster; her brother John Robinson, and many other neighbors whose names are now lost to time.

Maud Dawkins:

"I said to Mr. Dawkins, I said, 'He is guilty as sin. I have thought so from the first. At the wake. I said it then. Guilty as sin. Don't you think so?'

"And Mr. Dawkins just spit. 'Aw, he never killed her. They're just out to get him. Jury's been agin him from the start.'

"So I say, 'How are you so sure? He was already a horse thief.'

"And Mr. Dawkins only said, 'Yes and no—' He is a stubborn man.

"So I said, 'Yes and no? What do you mean by that?'

"'Well, there's borrowin'. Some say he just borrowed that horse.'

"Now I am not the type to argue. But I believe he is wrong. So I say, 'But he went to the penitentiary for it.'

"And that man! All he will say is, 'Maybe so—maybe not.' And he spit again.

"'Maybe not?' I say. 'But the records—'

"'Listen. Shue was cocky. Cheeky. Good-lookin'. Moved around a lot. Women liked him. A man like that, he ain't got no friends.' I see I'm not getting anywheres. Just like a man, I'll tell you. Stubborn.

"But I am a tolerant woman. Lord knows I would have to be, putting up with that man lo these many. So I says, 'But he went to the penitentiary. A good man does not go to prison.'

"And Mr. Dawkins, he says, 'All I'm sayin': we are all thieves.

Horses, money, women. Time. You name it. There's not a one of us. But he's unlucky. That's all I'm sayin'.'

"But I told him. I says, 'I still say he is guilty.'"

According to the *Greenbrier Independent*, Dr. George W. Knapp, the physician who examined Zona's body after her death, was the first witness for the state. Presumably, after the autopsy, Knapp had to revise both his early conclusions. The first, "an everlasting faint," tells us only that he was baffled as to the cause of death. The recording of childbirth as the cause of death a week later would appear to point to a wrong but logical assumption based on what had ailed Zona for the last month of her life. If all of this confusion makes him appear to be an incompetent physician, apparently he was not thought to be so, as he later served a four-year term as president of the Greenbrier Board of Health, beginning in 1900. He told the jury that Shue had requested, "after he had resorted to the usual means of resuscitation, to make no further examination of the body." He surely told the jury what the autopsy had shown. Certainly Rupert and McClung, the other two doctors who had assisted at the autopsy, were called to testify also. The *Greenbrier Independent* reported, "The evidence of the medical experts, Dr. Knapp and others who conducted the postmortem examination, makes it quite clear that Mrs. Shue did not commit suicide. The postmortem made it clear that her neck had been dislocated but there was no mark upon her person to suggest or other evidence to show that she had subjected herself to any sort of violence."

Then Anderson Jones testified. Under some circumstances, he might have been a likely suspect himself. (In fact, one of Shue's relatives asked me, "Why didn't they suspect the Negro?") Shue may have hoped and even planned that suspicion would fall on the child. At the time of the trial Andy was only about eleven, and he undoubtedly told the truth then. For one thing, the events were clear because they were near in time; for another, he was under oath; third, he was a child; and fourth, he was a black boy in a white man's society. For all these reasons, he probably told the truth in 1897, though in later years he reportedly could not resist the impulse to embroider the story. On July 9, 1897, the *Pocahontas Times*, in reporting on the trial, described what Andy Jones found, and what he testified to:

Shue . . . went to the house of a negro woman and asked the son of this woman to go to his house and hunt the eggs and then go to Mrs. Shue and see if she wanted to send to the store for anything. This negro boy went to the house of Shue, and after looking for eggs and finding none, he went to the house, knocked and received no response, opened the door and went in. He found the dead body of Mrs. Shue lying upon the floor. The body was lying stretched out perfectly straight with feet together, one hand by the side and the other lying across the body, the head was slightly inclined to one side. The negro boy ran and told his mother that Mrs. Shue was dead . . .

Jones may have told of her mouth being open, as if in a laugh. In death, all muscles relax, including those that in life hold the mouth closed. (It was conventional at the time to wrap a rag or twine about the jaw and head of a corpse to keep the mouth closed.) Possibly Jones mentioned her cold, stiff body.

"Aunt" Martha Jones was called to the stand following her son's testimony: on the day of the discovery, she had been asked by Shue four times to send her son Andy to help his wife; she had seen Zona before she was dressed and afterwards, so she knew Shue had dressed the body himself, and "in doing so, put around the neck a huge collar and a large veil, some several times folded and tied in a large bow under the chin."

Other state's witnesses testified that Shue "was the only person seen or known to have been on [his] premises prior to finding Mrs. Shue dead." Many witnesses in the days to follow "observed the head to be very loose upon the neck, and would drop from side to side when not supported." Others still testified that "in his conversation and conduct after his wife's death he seemed in good spirits and showed no proper appreciation for the loss he had sustained." Some people may have reported on Shue's stated intention of having seven wives. Other bragging stories he had told around the community may have come back to haunt him. And close neighbors declared, according to the *Nicholas County Register*, "that they did not think Shue, from his actions and words, was regretful of the death of his young wife."

Some witnesses told the jury "that when summoned to the postmortem and inquest out at Soule he said . . . that he knew he would come back under arrest." And finally, it had been noted by several who testified that, in the preceding months, "in speaking to a number of witnesses on the subject, he always said he knew that they could not prove he did the killing." The newspaper account ends with "Etcetera," indicating that there were other damaging reports, but that these were the most important.

The question that is central to the story of the Greenbrier Ghost is whether it was in fact the ghost story that led to the jury's decision to find Trout Shue guilty of murdering his wife.

The law orders for each day of the trial say only that, pursuant to adjournment, "having heard the evidence in part," the jury were once more taken away. The order of witnesses and their names, on both sides, are missing, since the transcript is gone. But from the news accounts, we know some of the things they said.

From reading other transcripts, it is clear that most of the questioning at this or any other trial is of a trivial, boring, and repetitious nature. What is your name? What relationship did you have with the defendant? Were you at the wake? Did you notice anything odd about the corpse? Did you see Shue the morning of the murder? These questions would have been asked scores of times in the long hot days. From an 1893 transcript involving the same prosecutor, with Gilmer then too as his assistant, and Rucker defending the murderer, we can reconstruct how tediously the questioning doubtless went. (The witness is an imagined representative of those who testified.)

Q.—State your name.

A.—Robert Smith.

Q.—Have you been sworn?

A.—Not today.

Q.—But have you been sworn for this trial?

A.—Yes sir. Tuesday. Or Monday. I don't mind which.

Q.—Monday or Tuesday?

A.—Yes sir.

Q.—Do you know Mr. Shue?

A.—Yes sir. I know him when I see him.

Q.—Did you know Mrs. Shue?

A.—Yes sir. She was a neighbor.

Q.—Are you kin to Mr. Shue?

A.—Not as I know of.

Q.—Are you kin to the late Mrs. Shue?

A.—No sir.

Q.—What was your relationship to Mr. Shue?

A.—Neighbor is all.

Q.—Where do you live?

A.—Up Rock Run a piece.

Q.—How far is that from Livesay's?

A.—I call it a mile and a half.

Q.—Do you know Mr. Shue well?

A.—Well?

Q.—Yes. Is he a friend of yours?

A.—I wouldn't call him a friend.

Q.—Then what would you call him?

A.—What would I call him?

Q.—Yes.

A.—I'd call him an acquaintance.

And so it goes, establishing relationships, attitudes, propinquity to the criminal or his victim, reliability of the witness.

But all present had heard that a ghost was involved in this trial, and they assumed that Mrs. Heaster would tell about it. Thus when Mary Jane Robinson Heaster was called to the witness stand, there was undoubtedly a renewed interest among the observers, as well as the jury. She was a leading state witness; her suspicions were the seed that had grown into the murder trial of her former son-in-law. The newspaper editor knew it would make good copy.

What Thomas Dennis, editor of the *Greenbrier Independent*, chose to print is not her original testimony. We know this because at the end are three questions of "re-cross-examination."

Each time a witness is on the stand, he is first questioned directly, by the side that called him; then cross-examined by one of the lawyers on the other side of the case; then directly re-examined by his own lawyers; then re-cross-examined by the opposite side, always in that order. In fact, the newspaper account fails to distinguish among the Examination, Cross-examination, Re-examination, and Re-cross-examination, which is the order of the court. Although what Dennis printed may have been Mrs. Heaster's entire testimony on the subject of the ghost, it was certainly not her entire testimony.

Both Thomas Dennis, in 1897, and Judge McWhorter, in 1903, assert that the testimony about the ghost was brought out by the defense. Surely it would seem strange for the defense to have voluntarily called up a hostile witness, the mother of the dead girl, who had the most compelling reasons of all for hating their client! Yet it was indeed the defense that through questioning brought out the testimony that Dennis printed, and which perhaps actually destroyed Shue.

What we can assume is that Prosecutor Preston, not the defense, first called Mrs. Heaster to the witness stand, as the mother of the dead girl and the first person to call his attention to the fact that there were reasons to believe that Zona's death had not been natural. But all Preston would have questioned her about was what she had first taken to him—her suspicions of foul play. It was the suspicions entertained by her and others, and not the tale of the spectral appearance of the dead girl, that had led to the autopsy. The *Independent* of the previous March had stated, as the reason for the exhumation and autopsy, "that her husband, E. S., commonly known as Trout Shue, was suspected of having brought about her death by violence or in some way unknown to her friends." Preston no doubt called Mary Jane Heaster as a witness because he wished to demonstrate to the jury that she was sane and reliable, and had not set a trap for her son-in-law. He would have skirted the ghost story for at least two obvious reasons: one, it would have made his witness appear to be irrational, and, two, it was basically in the area of inadmissible evidence, as it was hearsay, secondhand evidence. The actual teller of the story, Zona, could obviously not be cross-examined, and therefore her testimony must be considered unusable under American law. So Preston would have avoided asking Mrs. Heaster about the ghost.

The defense attorney Rucker also knew that the ghost story was inadmissible as evidence, yet he set out to bring it out anyway. It seems obvious that in so doing he was trying to make Mrs. Heaster look ridiculous to the jury, to discredit what Preston had been trying to establish: her good and sane character.

Her testimony, as printed in the *Independent*, follows, the questions being asked by Dr. Rucker.

Q.—I have heard that you had some dream or vision which led to this postmortem examination.

A.—They saw enough theirselves without me telling them. It was no dream—she came back and told me that he was mad that she didn't have no meat cooked for supper. But she said she had plenty and she said that she had butter and apple butter, apples and named over two or three kinds of jellies, pears and cherries and raspberry jelly, and she says she had plenty; and she says don't you think that he was mad and just took down all my nice things and packed them away and just ruined them. And she told me where I could look down back of Aunt Martha Jones', in the meadow, in a rocky place; that I could look in a cellar behind some loose plank and see. It was a square log house, and it was hewed up to the square, and she said for me to look right at the right-hand side of the door as you go in and at the right-hand corner as you go in. Well, I saw the place just exactly as she told me, and I saw blood right there where she told me; and she told me something about that meat every night she came, just as she did the first night. She came four times and four nights; but the second night she told me that her neck was squeezed off at the first joint, and it was just as she told me.

Q.—Now, Mrs. Heaster, this sad affair was very particularly impressed upon your mind and there was not a moment during your waking hours that you did not dwell upon it?

A.—No, sir; and there is not yet either.

Q.—And was this not a dream founded upon your distressed condition of mind?

A.—No, sir. It was no dream, for I was as wide awake as I ever was.

Q.—Then, if not a dream or dreams, what do you call it?

A.—I prayed to the Lord that she might come back and tell me what had happened; and I prayed that she might come herself and tell on him.

Q.—Do you think that you actually saw her in flesh and blood?

A.—Yes, sir, I do. I told them the very dress that she was killed in, and when she went to leave me she turned her head completely around and looked at me like she wanted me to know all about it. And the very next time she came back to me she told me all about it. The first time she came, she seemed that she did not want to tell me as much about it as she did afterwards. The last night she was there she told me that she did everything she could do, and I am satisfied that she did do all that, too.

Q.—Now, Mrs. Heaster, don't you know that these visions, as you term them or describe them, were nothing more or less than four dreams founded upon your distress?

A.—No, I don't know it. The Lord sent her to tell it. I was the only friend that she knew she could tell and put any confidence in. I was the nearest one to her. He gave me a ring that he pretended she wanted me to have; but I don't know what dead woman he might have taken it off of. I wanted her own ring and he would not let me have it.

Q.—Mrs. Heaster, are you positively sure that these are not four dreams?

A.—Yes, sir. They were not a dream. I don't dream when I am wide awake, to be sure; and I know I saw her right there with me.

Q.—Are you not considerably superstitious?

A.—No, sir, I'm not. I was never that way before and am not now.

Q.—Do you believe the scripture?

A.—Yes, sir. I have no reason not to believe it.

Q.—And do you believe the scriptures contain the words of God and his Son?

A.—Yes, sir, I do. Don't you believe it. [sic]

Q.—Now, I would like if I could to get you to say that these were four dreams and not four visions or appearances of your daughter in flesh and blood?

A.—I am not going to say that; for I am not going to lie.

Q.—Then you insist that she actually appeared in flesh and blood to you upon four different occasions?

A.—Yes, sir.

Q.—Did she not have any other conversation with you other than upon the matter of her death?

A.—Yes, sir, some other little things. Some things I have forgotten— just a few words. I just wanted the particulars about her death, and I got them.

Q.—When she came did you touch her?

A.—Yes, sir, I got up on my elbows and reached out a little further, as I wanted to see if people came in their coffins, and I sat up and leaned on my elbows and it was light in the house. It was not a lamp light. I wanted to see if there was a coffin, but there was not. She was just like she was when she left this world. It was just after I went to bed, and I wanted her to come and talk to me, and she did. That was before the inquest and I told my neighbors. They said she was exactly as I told them she was.

Q.—Had you ever seen the premises where your daughter lived?

A.—No, sir, I had not; but I found them just exactly as she told me it was, and I never laid eyes on that house until since her death. She told me this before I knew anything of the building at all.

Q.—How long was it after this when you had these interviews with your daughter until you did see the buildings?

A.—It was a month or more after the examination. It has [*sic*] been a little over a month since I saw her.

The *Nicholas County News Leader* and the *Monroe Watchman* both added three questions and answers of *re-cross-examination*:

Q.—You said your daughter told you that down by the fence in a rocky place you would find some things?

A.—She said for me to look there. She didn't say I would find some things, but for me to look there.

Q.—Did she tell you what to look for?

A.—No, she did not. I was so glad to see her I forgot to ask her.

Q.—Have you ever examined that place since?

A.—Yes sir. We looked at the fence a little but didn't find anything.

We must recall that the autopsy had ascertained what was in Zona's stomach. In addition, the information that her neck had been "squeezed off at the first joint" could only have come from the autopsy. Even in the area of ghostly behavior that was a bit much; although Zona might have known she was choked, she would not have been able to tell, any more than anyone else, that her neck had been "broken at the first joint."

Mrs. Heaster's testimony shows prejudgment against Shue when she admits that she "prayed that she might come herself and tell on him." In other words, Mrs. Heaster had already decided he was guilty.

Several people—Andy, "Aunt" Martha, Dr. Knapp, presumably Charlie Tabscott, and possibly others—had seen Zona before Trout got her dressed up for the burial, and any one of them could have described to Mrs. Heaster how Zona looked when she died, or when she was found—at any time in the intervening months. She could very easily have heard what the house at Livesay's looked like from neighbors coming to the funeral, or from her efforts to justify her suspicions that Shue killed Zona, and by June she had visited there herself. Rucker could have followed up on what might have been behind the loose planks in the cellar, but he didn't. Given the questions of re-cross-examination printed in the *Nicholas County News Leader* and other papers, but not in the *Independent*, we know that the testimony printed was not her original testimony. Rucker did not follow up on any of these obvious lines of questioning, probably because he saw he was not going to move her from her story.

Rucker quite sensibly characterized Mary Heaster's visions as a mother's ravings, and sought to discredit them by bringing them to the jurors' attention as foolishness that had led to the entire county's turning against Shue. He continued his line of questioning, trying to get her to admit that she could have been, at the very least, mistaken. And Mary Jane Robinson Heaster, of course, turned the tables on them. Her mentioning "a ring he must have taken off some other dead woman" seems significant, yet no further examination of this point was made. Rucker might well have pursued the "several little things . . ." she claimed to have discussed with Zona, but he did not bother. Rucker seems to have been satisfying his own curiosity to see how far she would carry the story when he asked, "When she came, did you touch her?" Her fanciful answer, about the ghostly light in the house, and wondering "if people came in their coffins" when she had not previously mentioned seeing a coffin, would have borne further examination. But Rucker saw that the testimony was not going his way and stopped.

Just as there are rules governing most formal contests, there are rules regarding evidence during a trial. Most of what is admissible as evidence is clear to judges and lawyers, provided it involves common matters. The main reason for excluding hearsay evidence is that it prevents the opposing side from cross-examining the person who made the statement, which is its right to do. It generally involves the testimony of persons not present in the court, often because they are dead.

Judge McWhorter wrote in 1903 that the sheet that had been in the coffin "was brought into court at my request as an exhibit," and that "it was a decidedly reddish color." There are of course numerous readily available agents that added to water will turn a white cloth pink.

Dennis printed Mrs. Heaster's portion of the testimony because as a newspaper editor he had a nose for sensationalism. People, the community at large, apparently believed Mrs. Heaster had seen the ghost of her daughter. It is clear that the jurors were not supposed to take into consideration her testimony. The lawyers did not mention it in the summing up. Yet her story may have swayed the jury. Even if the jury had been instructed to discount her evidence, as it was hearsay, secondhand, and highly il-logical—even if they were told to disregard all she said, that story of the brave young bride valiantly doing her best, Shue's irrational anger at finding no meat on the table, and his sudden, violent, and unfair fury, was the only scenario they had for the murder. The fact that ten of the jury wanted to hang Shue may well reflect the fact that Mrs. Heaster was a talented and convincing witness.

It seems significant that as a part of her story Mrs. Heaster had Shue packing away Zonie's clothes. This detail is almost identical to Estie's testimony, recorded eight years before, and on file at that time in the Pocahontas courthouse. It is quite likely that, in the months of searching for evidence against Shue, one of the state's lawyers might have uncovered his divorce decree, and that Mrs. Heaster had been told about it.

What then was the prosecution's role in the use of the ghost story in court? Were they prompting Mrs. Heaster? Did Mrs. Heaster really believe in the ghostly visits?

All bits of incoming information, one assumes, stay in the mind, little piles of facts like tiny squares of colored glass, stone, or tile of which mosaics are made. And sometimes, out of the junkheaps of images, passing remarks, random observations, and all the half-noted events and words of any day, or week, a mosaic will fall together so that it appears we have in fact "intuited" a new piece of information, when in reality the subconscious mind has merely "assembled" many tiny pieces into a reasonable whole. Mrs. Heaster undoubtedly knew that her son-in-law's previous wife had died "mysteriously." She would have known from talking to neighbors what dress Zona had died in, what her house looked like, and other small details. Considering that the lady did not approve the marriage in the first place; considering that she knew her previously healthy daughter had been ailing before her death;

considering that she was suspicious enough of Shue to have said, "The devil killed her"; considering that folks at the wake talked about how floppy Zona's head was; and considering that Mrs. Heaster had "prayed that she would come back and tell on him," is it difficult to suppose that she might have dreamed of Zona's return and accusation, even perhaps of Zona's neck being broken?

Once the autopsy had been performed, and the word of its findings had gotten out, Mrs. Heaster could have filled in the details, and made her "ghost story" very specific.

Dennis printed the cross-examination testimony by itself, in a column separate from the trial report, knowing it was what his readers would find most fascinating. He introduced the column by writing, "The following very remarkable testimony was given by Mrs. Heaster on the pending trial of E. S. Shue for the murder of his wife her daughter, and led to the inquest and postmortem examination which resulted in Shue's arrest and trial. It was brought out by counsel for the accused." Now we see why Rucker got her to tell about the ghost. He and Gardner thought they were going to expose her as insane. The lawyers for the prosecution anticipated that, and let her go on. Although the "testimony" was inadmissible, Rucker, the defense lawyer, would not have had it stricken from the record because he had brought it up. Gilmer, for the prosecution, would not have had it stricken because it had worked so well.

The state, when it had finished with all its witnesses and exhibits, rested. Then the defense presented its case.

In their opening arguments, Rucker and Gardner would have painted Shue in the best light possible, probably emphasizing his status as a stranger in the community, his popularity with everyone, his industry, his grief at finding his dear wife dead. They surely pointed out that he had made no attempt to leave the area following Mrs. Shue's death. They would have instructed the jury that this trial represented an opportunity for them to put an end to the cumbrance of suspicion that had been laid on this innocent man by idle gossip, irrational stories, and careless or vicious tongues—to relieve the poor man's sufferings and let him get on with his life.

The newspaper says nothing about the 120 witnesses earlier predicted for Shue, though there may well have been people testifying to his good character, blameless behavior, and warm nature. We know of only one witness, his brother John Patrick Bruffey, and he had to be forced to come to testify. Though Deputy Ludington went to look for him first in Webster County, just northwest of Pocahontas, he had either moved to Braxton, the next county northwest of Webster, without leaving a forwarding address, or fled there in an attempt to avoid having to testify. Either way, the conclusion does not support Nonie's story that the family came and rallied to Trout's support. The newspaper does not report whether John Patrick Bruffey Shue ever actually testified. Perhaps some others came without incident to testify in Shue's behalf.

When the defense had finished with its other witnesses on Tuesday afternoon, six days into the trial, Trout Shue himself took the witness stand. In a criminal trial, the defendant testifies last. It used to be, in early American law, that the defendant could not testify at all, as no "interested witness" was allowed to testify, meaning anyone with an obvious bias, such as a mother or a wife or the accused himself. In the early nineteenth century, however, the defendant was deemed "competent" to testify in his own behalf. He was put on the stand and allowed to make a statement. In some places, it was optional for him to swear or not. If he swore, then he could be cross-examined.

In general, where the defendant is either required or permitted to make an unsworn statement, the jury is given special instructions that the defense cannot be cross-examined, and to give only such weight to the testimony as they, the jury, think it deserves. In West Virginia, according to the Hennings Statutes of 1863, a defense lawyer could either put his client on the stand or not— but if called, he had to be sworn.

Shue obviously chose to testify, because no one then or now could be forced to testify against himself. Why would Shue have chosen to speak? How could he have felt that his own testimony could further his cause? One answer may lie in his bragging nature. Shue had a remarkably attractive, resonant voice, which he and his lawyers must have been aware of and probably banked on using. He was a big talker and no doubt figured to talk his way out of this. Another answer may be that Shue was smart, and had already spent two years in prison, quite conceivably "studying the law" with other inmates who were trying to obtain appeals and new trials. After all, Shue seemed very confident during the pretrial time, and told many people, "They will not be able to prove I did the killing." Rucker and Gardner doubtless underestimated in advance of the trial the importance of Mrs. Heaster's testimony, and may have assured Shue that there would be no conviction. Finally, his lawyers must have realized belatedly how damaging the effects of Mrs. Heaster's testimony had been, and must have felt that their only hope was to give Shue a chance to give a convincing account of his side of things. It is well known to criminal lawyers that a defendant has the edge with juries, as in general people would rather act benignly than otherwise.

At any rate, the *Greenbrier Independent* on July 1, 1897, reported that ". . . Shue was on the stand all Tuesday afternoon, that he was given free rein and talked at great length, and was very minute and particular in describing unimportant incidents, denied pretty much everything said by the other witnesses, said the prosecution was all spite work, entered a positive denial of the charges against him, vehemently protested his innocence, calling God to witness, admitted he had served a term in the penitentiary, declared that he dearly loved his wife, and appealed to the jury to look into his face and then say if he was guilty." The *Greenbrier Independent* then informs its readers that "His testimony, manner, and so forth, made an unfavorable impression on the spectators." So, in the end, Trout Shue's natural charm appears to have abandoned him.

Mention of his earlier conviction would not have been admissible unless his lawyers or he himself brought it up. Rucker and Gardner must have believed it was in his best interest to come clean about it. Probably this was because there were rumors about that Shue had been in prison previously. The *Greenbrier Independent* further observed that "The prisoner's statement amounted, for the most part, to a denial in detail of the state's evidence."

Without the transcript we cannot know for certain what people said, but the concluding arguments summed up in the *Greenbrier Independent* at the time of the trial are very important: "There was no witness to the crime charged against Shue, and the state rests its case for conviction wholly on the circumstances connecting the accused with the murder charge."

In concluding, the *Independent* carefully repeats, "So the connection of the accused with the crime depends entirely upon the strength of the circumstantial evidence introduced by the state." (The state did not introduce the ghost story.) The *Independent* also reported, "There is no middle ground for the jury to take. The verdict inevitably and logically must be for murder in the first degree or for acquittal."

On Wednesday, June 30, the evidence was concluded in the morning, and the concluding arguments, called "elaborate on both sides" by the press, were begun in the afternoon.

The *Monroe Watchman*, a nearby newspaper, reported the next day, July 1, that "the defense had finished most of its evidence Tuesday evening but had proved little to show the innocence of the prisoner."

Finally, Rucker had no recourse but to state to the judge, "Your Honor, the defense rests."

The prosecutor, in his closing arguments, reminded the jury of all the circumstantial evidence against the defendant, and suggested to them that they bring back a verdict of guilty as charged. Mr. Gilmer in his argument showed that "Shue was all the time laboring under the impression that he could not be convicted on circumstantial evidence, and felt secure in knowing there was no witness but himself to the crime." This, Mr. Gilmer argued, "showed not a lack of sense, but information, and accounts for Shue's presence at the inquest and his oft-repeated remark that they could not show he did it." It was printed in March in the same papers that Shue was more or less forced to go to the inquest, so one assumes this statement at the time of the trial means that "lack of information" about the law accounts for the fact that Shue stayed put after the murder instead of hightailing it for parts unknown.

Apparently the defense lawyers had argued in their closing that, had Shue been guilty, he had certainly had plenty of time, the entire month before the autopsy, to make an escape. That he had not argued for his innocence, they said. This was a weak argument, as the previous paragraph shows. The newspaper story concludes, "The case probably went to the jury yesterday evening, June 30."

During the jury's deliberation, the prisoner was taken to a room and guarded. In the courtroom, people rose, stretched, and milled around, talking in low voices. No one had any idea how long the jury's deliberations would take. The judge retired to his chambers, to await the announcement that the jury was ready. From the papers we learn that the gentlemen of the jury deliberated for an hour and ten minutes only. In the closing moments of the trial, the judge reappeared, having been informed that the jury had reached a decision. The court rose, and the foreman handed a slip of paper to the judge, who then asked the defendant to rise to hear the verdict.

Thursday, July 1, the law orders for the day read in part:

. . . E. S. Shue, who stands indicted for a felony, was this day led to the bar in custody of the jailer of this County, and the jury sworn on a former day of this term appeared in Court pursuant to their adjournment, and having heard all the evidence and arguments of counsel, retired to consider of their verdict, and after sometime [sic] returned into Court, and on their oath do say, "We the jury find the prisoner Erasmus S. alias E. S. Shue guilty of murder of the first degree as charged in the within indictment, and we further find that he be punished by confinement in the penitentiary." Thereupon the prisoner, by counsel, gave notice that he would move the court to set aside the verdict, and grant him a new trial. And said prisoner is remanded to jail.

The judge then asked the court if there were other motions. Rucker and Gardner, after consulting with Shue, entered a motion for a new trial. The law orders do not tell on what grounds. The motion was withdrawn the next morning.

It is almost automatic in the case of a conviction for a capital crime to seek a retrial.

The *Monroe Watchman* reported that ten of the jurors wanted Shue sentenced to death by hanging, but two would not go along with the others, so a compromise had to be made, probably because he was convicted on purely circumstantial evidence, evidence "beyond reasonable doubt" but still unwitnessed by a single living soul.

A week later, on July 8, the *Greenbrier Independent* published its final news story on the sensational trial, headed "Shue Convicted of Murder." It ended: "Taking the verdict of the jury as ascertaining the truth, then we must conclude that Shue deliberately broke his wife's neck, probably with his strong hands, and with no other motive than to be rid of her that he might get another more to his liking. And if so, his crime is one of the most horrible, cruel, and revolting ever known in the history of this county. Mr. Preston deserves the thanks of the people for his diligence in hunting up the evidence and for his admirable management of the case before the jury."

In the law orders for that day is the following note: "It appearing in evidence that the prisoner has in his possession a small penknife and gold ring the property of the murdered woman Zona Shue. It is ordered that the Sheriff procure the said articles and turn them over to the father of the deceased woman." Another law order allows Miss Minnie Grose $75 for services as stenographer in the case of *State* v. *Shue*. And $37.50 was paid to the deputy who fetched J. P. Shue from Webster County. And finally, the law orders record Rucker's withdrawal of the motion for a new trial, and Shue's sentencing.

The *Pocahontas Times*, reporting on the trial the next day, July 9, 1897, declared that Mary Heaster's "visions" story was instrumental in bringing about the autopsy and inquest, by saying that the daughter's visits led to the postmortem examination and the arraignment of Shue for murder:

Trout Shue, formerly of Droop Mountain, was found guilty of murder in the first degree, in the Greenbrier court, the jury recommending a life sentence. The evidence was convincing that Shue had murdered his wife by breaking her neck, and the case presented this aspect, that the woman died of a broken neck, and that it was impossible for her to break it herself, and that no one could have done it except her husband. What was the closing scene of the woman's life will probably never be known, but the explanation of the "vision" of the woman's mother gives a very striking suggestion of the last quarrel which ended in the death of the woman. She said that her daughter appeared to her and said that on the last evening she had gotten a good supper except there was no meat on the table, and that her husband had become enraged on account of it. Shue is a bad man and he has no sympathy from the neighborhood in which he was raised.

A Frankford man:

"My daddy, who attended the trial every day, told me in later years that his conclusion was that the blacksmith was a lunatic—insane."

A man from Renick:

"I remember Andy Jones—a big, slew-footed Negro, real black, with a strange patch of white skin under his chin. He worked for the Cherry River Lumber Company. One time, when I was helping a friend collect up a load of coal, we ran into him. He told me, pointing at his throat, 'See this? When I found Zona Heaster, I turned white and this spot is all that's left.' He told me further that Shue had laid Zona at the foot of the stairs to make it look like she'd fallen."

An Alderson woman:

"When he killed her he wrapped her up in a sheet and hid it, and the ghost told the mother to go look, and she found the bloody sheet right out under the woodpile."

NOTES

p. 107: The Greenbrier Law Order Book No. 14 is the source of each day's report.

p. 109: If it was true that Shue's relatives were all handcuffed in the courtroom, it is very odd that the newspapers never mentioned this highly irregular action.

p. 109: The temperatures for Lewisburg, St. Louis, and other places are from the *Greenbrier Independent*.

p. 109: If Trout Shue was resigned to his fate, then why did he call such a huge number of witnesses?

p. 110: According to the *Greenbrier Independent* of April 1, 1897, only three months prior to Shue's trial, in the court of appeals in Charleston, in the case of *McManus* v. *Masons*, McWhorter's judgment was reversed, and a new trial ordered, proving, one supposes, that he was not infallible. According to local historian Blanche Humphreys, McWhorter came from the northern part of the state after the Civil War, and was considered by many local people a "carpetbagger." She says he was appointed judge despite his Republican politics, and was not very popular among the Confederate sympathizers of the environs of Lewisburg, who were overwhelmingly Democrats. Until 1863 West Virginia had slavery in the eastern panhandle and the area around Greenbrier.

p. 112: Miz Dawkins was the sort who would have attended every day of the trial, and had plenty of opinions about the testimony, as she had about everything else.

p. 115: The trial of Kenos Douglas in June 1894 for the killing of Thomas Reed was similar to Shue's trial in many ways, and the transcript of it (from which these questions were taken) was useful to me in informing me what trials were like in that place, at that time. Both trials were in Greenbrier, as both murders occurred there; the same judge presided, the same attorneys prosecuted, and Rucker defended the alleged murderer. Both murders occurred in winter, and both trials were the following summers. In the case of *State* v. *Douglas*, the body of the murdered man was also exhumed, that time a week after burial, with the purpose of finding a lost bullet. Only three years apart in time, the speech patterns would have been similar. Douglas's first trial ended with a hung jury, but he was convicted of first-degree murder in a second trial.

p. 129: The quotations at the end of the trial are voices remembering the event and its aftermath. The first is from Edwin Coffman, whose father took a great interest in this case all his life. The quote about Andy Jones is from Lonnie Miles of Renick, West Virginia, on March 3, 1983. The typically garbled quotation about the bloody sheet is from an Alderson woman, who claimed to "know all about" the case. It is placed here to show how easily the truth gets distorted.

Part Five
JULY 1897

This time late tomorrow, I know where I'll be,
Down in some lonesome holler, swinging from a high oak tree.
And the limb it being oak, and the rope it being strong,
Neither one'll get broke, my time will not be long . . .
"Tom Dula," Appalachian folk song, 19th century

The last public hanging in the state of West Virginia occurred in the year of Shue's trial, 1897, when John F. Morgan was hanged in Jackson County. Thus hanging was a real possibility for Shue when he was convicted of murdering his wife the same year.

The trial proceedings had stirred up enormous local indignation against the blacksmith, and although the verdict had satisfied the indignation, the sentence had not. Because Shue had pleaded innocent, he could not then offer any kind of explanation, motive, or excuse, for what he had done. No doubt the bereaved mother's testimony fired the public ire, as it was clearly intended to, although there is no evidence that her story had swayed the jury. Quite the contrary: the *Greenbrier Independent* stated clearly that the basis of the guilty verdict was the circumstantial evidence against Shue, not including any reference to the ghost.

Indignation grew; the days continued hot and dry, with no relief. People felt cheated by the sentence which robbed them of their revenge against the stranger who had killed one of their young women, in what the *Greenbrier Independent* had characterized as "one of the most horrible, cruel, and revolting [crimes] ever known in the history of this country." The *Independent* further editorialized, "Ever since the termination of the trial of E. S. Shue for the murder of his wife and his conviction for murder in the first degree with a recommendation by the jury that his punishment be imprisonment, there have been whisperings and rumors that mob violence might be a possibility . . ." Men grouped together, dominated by their common aim, originating from fear of and hatred for Shue, combined with affection for Zona, both leading to a compelling need for revenge. Their individuality disappeared, and their responsibility was given over to the mob, with the result that they lost self-control and acted impulsively, taking the law into their own hands.

George Harrah, a quiet man, was full of chicken, biscuits, early pole beans, and a blackberry cobbler. On his front porch there was just the merest suggestion of a breeze, so he eased back in the ladderback chair, still in his Sunday-go-to-meeting clothes. He raised his feet up onto the porch railing, and picked blackcap seeds out of his teeth. After a while, he perceived that the air was moving in a slightly different direction, and so shifted his chair over towards the corner of the porch by a foot or so. From inside the house came the sounds of clearing away dinner. The girls laughed and chatted . . .

Presently, Harrah fell asleep, with the rhythm of hoofbeats in his ears, along with the swish of oak leaves high in the branches of the big tree that shaded the house, and the song of a mockingbird imitating the creak of the gate.

He awoke abruptly to the strange impression that a lot of horses had ridden by in the few minutes he dozed. Curious, he lowered the chair back down onto four legs, and rose stiffly. He would just wander out to the road and see what he could see.

Almost at once, Otey Arbaugh appeared. George called to him, inquiring where he was going.

Otey drew up the reins reluctantly, but didn't say anything for a moment. "Jus'—a little meeting," he mumbled.

"What meeting is that?" But even before he finished the question, George knew. In town yesterday, Saturday, all the talk was of the trial, and its outcome. And his wife had heard there might be a lynching.

"Who told you that?" he had demanded of her.

She named the names to him. And told him Maud Dawkins had said, "The only way to destroy the venom of a rattlesnake is to cut off his tail—right up close to his head." And all the ladies had laughed nervously.

"Woman-talk," he had snorted. But it wasn't just that. It was in the air. He'd heard someone he didn't know say it in the feed and seed store: "Bible says an Eye for an Eye." The pronouncement had a strangely menacing sound.

And in front of the bank, several men clustered together had split apart quickly when he approached. Now it all added up.

He wouldn't be sorry to see the man hang, out of the way once and for all. Once more he worked his teeth with the ivory pick.

But this was not the way. They were wrong. Revenge is mine, saith the Lord. Justice still belonged to God. The law had been carried out. And he for one was proud of how it had gone, with all the threats of violence, all the lies told in the trial—and yet the law of the land had stood up. The state of West Virginia was going to be all right. At least it looked that way up to now. And he wasn't going to let them do anything to change that. Anything other than letting things be would be breaking the law, and risking a wrath higher than the law to boot. He walked purposefully into the cool house that still smelled of the savory fruit pie. "Emma," he said, "I got to ride over to Meadow Bluff. I'll be back just as soon as I can. You tell your ma when she gets up."

On Sunday night, July 11, 1897, a citizens' group variously estimated to number fifteen to thirty men organized at Brushy Ridge campground about eight miles west of Lewisburg on what is now Route 60, with the object of forming a lynching party, taking Shue by force from jail, and hanging him. They had procured a new rope, and were heavily armed, "with Winchesters and revolvers," and, in the words of the *Pocahontas Times*, "they meant business." But a nearby resident, George M. Harrah, got wind of the plan early Sunday afternoon. Apparently a reasonable and law-abiding man, he decided that his neighbors were wrong and must be stopped from this unwise and unlawful act of violence. So he rode immediately to Sheriff Nickell's house at Meadow Bluff, six miles farther west, and together they rode back towards Lewisburg to protect Shue.

The jail authorities had also been notified of the plans by a fishing party coming in from Clear Creek, who in passing the campground heard the plans and became alarmed. They went into Lewisburg and informed Deputy Sheriff Dwyer. It was reported in the *Nicholas County News* that Trout Shue, when he learned of this threat to his life, was "greatly agitated" to the extent that he could not put on his shoes by himself, and that he was "on the point of making a confession, and thus be prepared for extremities."

Deputy Sheriff Dwyer at once took Shue to "a place of refuge in the woods" a mile or so outside of town, at around sundown. Legend has it that the prisoner was secreted in a remote cornfield outside of Lewisburg, and some people say it was a "cornshock."

On their way back into Lewisburg from Meadow Bluff, Nickell and Harrah also had to pass the campground. At around nine, as they went by, they were recognized by the would-be lynchers, who guessed at their mission, and they were pursued and held at gunpoint, "after an exciting chase." Sheriff Nickell, fearless in regard to his own life, drew his gun and was about to fire, despite the overwhelming odds. Then, in the darkness, he recognized his assailant as a neighbor. Realizing he could not bring himself to shoot a friend, even at the cost of his own life, the sheriff called upon his powers of rhetoric, persuading the four mob leaders to retire with him to the nearby home of D. A. Dwyer to discuss the matter further. "After considerable parlaying" he persuaded them to hand over to him "the stout new rope" with which they had planned to hang Shue. The mob disbanded, returning to their homes. By then it must have been quite late at night. Later steps were taken to round up the twenty to thirty would-be lynchers, and "most of them," predicted the *Greenbrier Independent*, "will soon be in the coils of the law."

Bench warrants were issued for the six men that Nickell was able to identify in the dark. A black man, Charley Lewis, was detained, as it was believed that he had seen everyone earlier in the day, and could name all the participants. It was later reported that he refused to name a single person, and was eventually released. Four people were later indicted for the attempted lynching: C. G. Martin, J. L. Nary, Robert Hunter, and Otey Arbaugh.

On Tuesday, July 13, 1897, the *Greenbrier Independent* tells us, the prisoner was taken to Moundsville, West Virginia, where the state penitentiary is located. They arrived there the next day, July 14, according to the prison records.

They wake him in the blackness before dawn. Before anyone else is abroad, they have hauled him out. It is five miles to Ronceverte, where they will catch the train. In the darkness he can smell cows, running water, mint, pigs. A buzz of cicadas accompanies them. The air is cool, and the sun is just beginning to streak the sky with copper. Slowly the sky turns the color of blood.

In the wooden wagon pulled by two horses, Trout Shue is handcuffed to Nickell during the bone-rattling journey down to Ronceverte. Both armed lawmen have to remain alert at every moment to any other possible attempts at lynching. They mark the passing miles with relief, as they move away from Lewisburg and the summer anger that has flared among the citizenry. The men of Greenbrier also know the route to the train. And they must still continue to watch for any quick movement, any effort at escape, on the part of a man who has little else to lose. They breakfast without stopping on ham biscuits, the two men still bound to each other, Dwyer covering them with his Winchester.

At Ronceverte, the train pulls in only a few moments after they do, the enormous Mountain engine 137, black as coal and trimmed in silver. The Pullman day car on Number 3 is gold and maroon on the outside, brilliant to see with gilt stripes and decor and lettering: FFV. As the sun hits its side, their eyes feel scorched with splendor.

Inside it is like a palace: mahogany wood as shiny as water, maroon plush seats, electric lights! Uneasily, they board, and then sit just inside the enclosed vestibule, Shue with his back to the rest of the car, Dwyer next to him, the two handcuffed together. Nickell sits directly across, in the facing seat. Presently a porter brings them a tray with silver pots of coffee, china cups.

On the trip, talk is sparse. Shue stares down at the wine carpet, then out at the passing countryside. At Hinton, the crew changes; Nickell and Dwyer talk about the famous engineer Billy Richardson, who will take the train through the treacherous New River Gorge to Huntington. Even at this early hour, when the train is not moving the heat of morning settles on them as heavy as a panther's breath.

The FFV goes fast, passing scenes as quickly as pictures in a book. Shue captures in his head the picture, in one town, of a dog slinking into a cool place under a porch, his long tongue lolling. Outside the July sun blazes down, but the Pullman car is cool and breezy, going at incredible speeds. In another town, Shue looks down to see, for a fleeting instance, the face of a beautiful young woman with a baby on her shoulder, staring longingly, it seems, right up at him.

When they stop, the car heats up within minutes. Sweat runs in rivulets down off their bodies, and their shirts all have large dark circles under the arms.

At noon they are deep in the canyon cut eons ago by the New River. Cool air comes in when they are under the trees. But cinders fly in the open windows, and the plush becomes irritating and scratchy. Shue says he needs to urinate; the men sigh in irritation; then Nickell, standing, leads him the length of the swaying car to the water closet, still chained to him. Other passengers stare curiously up at them, their mouths half open.

At a brief stop, when he can look up and see an abandoned cabin high on a hill overlooking the track, with forest behind it, Shue wishes with all his might that he could just go there, and stay, forever. He would not bother with them again. Perhaps, for a fleeting second, he wonders, where do the sinkhole pine lilies grow? He has never quite been able to ask anyone if they really exist. Maybe she tricked him.

Huntington. As they pull into the station, Dwyer takes out his big watch, checks the time, and remarks that Uncle Billy has done it again, that he is invariably right on time. It is 1:45. At Huntington, they walk across the tracks to sit in the sun by a sidetrack, waiting for the Northbound Accommodation that will take them to Parkersburg where they will stay overnight. Off in the distance they hear a rumble of thunder, then a puff of cool air carries to them the portent of rain on dry earth. They hope the storm is ahead of them, rather than behind.

At 3:05 they board the Ohio River train: much slower, and much hotter, with leather seats and cloth upholstery, dark wooden walls and wooden floors. On the swaying journey, they eat chicken out of a box, cake, and cabbage slaw, and they drink lukewarm tea.

When for a while the railroad follows a river, the temperature drops, affording them a little measure of relief. Along the track, dust and soot have settled heavily on all the leaves and growing things, turning them from green to dull gray. Dwyer and Nickell fight drowsiness and fatigue.

Shue must be experiencing acute emotional strain with the realization that he may never again be so close to the smells and sights and sounds of earthly summer as on this last, sad journey to that grim fortress at Moundsville. This time he tells no stories, just sits in a hangdog silence, broken only by the snickety-snack of the train along the rails. He makes no confessions, having regained his composure after Sunday's fright. Perhaps in a corner of his mind he holds off emotion by planning to make an appeal.

When the train stops, one of the deputies can walk out for a moment to break the monotony of the journey. Shue watches as Nickell saunters into the station and comes back in a moment wiping his mouth with the back of his hand, a free man irritated only by the cling of a bench catching at his trousers, and unaware of the sudden envy his easy and careless freedom has aroused.

In Parkersburg, Trout Shue is walked the short distance to the jail and locked in. Dwyer and Nickell will stay there also, and there will be a double guard tonight to see that the murderer does not escape.

Once again they drag him out, bone-tired in the early morning, and take him across the silent blocks to the train station again, where the train has stood waiting all night. They are the only ones who board. In three hours they will be in Moundsville. Someone has provided them with bread and butter and warm coffee, and they eat out of their laps on the creaking coach.

Finally, they see in the morning light the enormous castle-like fortress of gray stone right next to the strange flat hill on the otherwise flat river bottom. It is the mound that the town is named for: Moundsville.

They will walk the short distance from the station to the prison. Perhaps Shue stares down through the slats of a bridge they are crossing, sees the pebbles washed in gold water, and sees where birds gather and rays of light pierce through. For the last time, he looks around him at summer, more vivid than ever before: berries ripening, jewelweed glowing in the shade, the creek teeming with bass and bream, white-flowering watercress at its edge, the very air redolent with the adventure of living, the adventure of life now denied to him forever. Shue knows the way from the station to the prison, for of course he has already spent two years here. He knows already the gray stone, the gray faces of the guards, the hoarse horn that wakes the prisoners each morning from their dreams of freedom, the gray food served up twice each day in the long ugly refectory. The community has grown up more since he was last here, nearly a decade ago.

Trout Shue already knows how the circular steel-barred door will swing inward with ease to receive him.

When E. S. Shue went to the penitentiary in 1889 for stealing a man's horse, the prison records show that he had only one scar—where his left ankle had at some previous time sustained a fracture. This time, eight years later, Shue was assigned prison number 3255, and recorded as being a blacksmith, thirty-five years old, five feet six and a half inches tall, from Greenbrier, of fair complexion, with blue eyes and dark brown hair, and a great many more scars than he had had when entering the penitentiary the first time: four on the back of his head, one above his right ear, one above his left ear, one on his shin, and one on his abdomen. There was noted in addition that he had a mole on his left nipple. Sometime between 1889 and 1897 Shue seems to have collected an unusual number of scars. In the absence of provable information, this fact may give some credence to the strange story told by Jess Stanley of Trout's being chased and shot at repeatedly following Lucy's death.

Back home in the Meadowlands, Mary Jane Robinson Heaster slowly closes the door behind her. One can imagine that, for a second, her eyes cannot see in the dim interior. These ten days are the longest she has ever been away from her home. It has been a long, hot ride from Lewisburg, her neighbors pushing the horses all the way, and she can taste the grit of dust in her teeth, smell it in her nose, and feel it in her hair. Tonight she will take a bath, to wash off the long days of sweat and anxiety, of heat and tension. The undersides of her wrists are streaked with dirt. Tomorrow she will comb her hair in the sun until all the dirt is gone.

Things in the house, even the house itself, have a strange cast to them, seem almost to shimmer and change at the edges. There is a newness, a feeling of things being slightly out of scale. She stands still, letting the house settle around her again. The coolness and familiar starchy, yeasty odor of her own life enfold her, with a comfort and a sadness so deep she cannot tell which is the truer feeling. Zonie seems to be everywhere, and yet she is nowhere. Over at the window, the yellowed curtain sways ever so slightly, as if in answer to something Mary Jane has said or thought. Zonie? But no, it is only the breeze, and the deep green midsummer air, the late afternoon light suffused through the maple leaves.

Can it be over? She thinks back: only one brief year ago, Zonie and the boys were coming and going, the children's laughter light on the air as the summer, like this one, was rounding to autumn, already the leaves crisping, and *he* had never even come to Greenbrier yet.

She sits down in the rocking chair next to the desk, for just a moment, before going into the kitchen to start supper. The summer of the circus in Lewisburg comes to her, the enormity of the gray elephant, and the children late at night roaming the circus grounds for dropped pennies and even a nickel or two.

Soon enough, Hedges and the boys will begin to gather for supper, and she must return to the tasks she has neglected these two weeks as a guest in someone else's house, an eater of meals cooked by others. She supposes there will be an oversupply of eggs. She doesn't know what they have eaten while she has been gone. Neighbors have brought food, she knows. She doesn't know what she'll find in the kitchen. Maybe they will have eggs and biscuits for supper, and last summer's preserves. She can make a cream pie, though the boys will grumble if they have to drink bluejohn milk. This year no preserves have got made, not even the February syrup. There is no rest for the weary! Blackberries and huckleberries have still not come in.

Then she thinks of something. She will read it once again, before anyone comes. She opens the desk drawer and takes it out: the *Greenbrier Independent* dated January 28, 1897, now six months old, and worn as soft as tissue to her touch. Moving the wooden rocker to the window where the light will fall on the newspaper, she reads, first on page three, then on page one.

NOTES

p. 133: Harry Lynch, of the West Virginia News, provided the information about the Morgan hanging, on September 13, 1983.

p. 133: Information and quotations about the lynching attempt are from newspapers in the area, especially the *Greenbrier Independent* for July 15, 1897, and the *Pocahontas Times* for July 16, 1897.

p. 134: George Harrah is a real person, but this account of him is totally fictionalized. It is, however, not inconsistent with his reported deeds.

p. 137: E. Sterling "Tod" Hanger and Tom Dixon of the C & O Historical Society mapped out from 1897 train timetables and the likeliest route for the deputies to have taken to deliver Shue to the penitentiary. They also were kind enough to provide me with descriptions of the trains.

p. 140: John Massie, records keeper at the West Virginia State Penitentiary, provided me with physical details and photographs of the prison.

Part Six

AFTERWARDS

Tell me the tales that to me were so dear,
Long long ago, long ago.
Sing me the songs I delighted to hear
Long long ago, long ago.

"Long Long Ago," T. H. Bayley, 19th century

Greetha Morten Childress:

"My grandfather was John Robinson, Mary Jane Robinson Heaster's brother. Grandfather always said that one of Shue's sisters came to his sister Mary after the trial, and told her that Trout had killed his two other wives. The reason she had not admitted it before, she said, was that she was afraid of her brother and feared he might not be convicted."

A Rainelle woman:

"He was a great big mean man. There's a tree out on 60 yet—they call it the hangman tree?—it's the tree where they hung him. Yep, I can take you and show you."

In Greenbrier, men turned their thoughts and their conversations back again to the soil, the coming harvest, the summer heat, the smallpox up in Pocahontas, politics. Trout Shue, the murderer, the outsider, yet in a strange way their summer hero, was safely behind bars. Perhaps it would have suited them better if he'd met a more dramatic end, but he had afforded them some excitement, which had to be balanced over against the fact that he had robbed them of one of their own.

In Moundsville, at least once, Trout Shue asked for paper for sketching. Bored? repentant? lonely? hopeless? One can imagine that life in the West Virginia State Penitentiary during the years when the twentieth century was just approaching had little to offer in the way of stimulation for the minds or spirits of the hapless souls, social misfits who spun out their days behind its walls.

The drawing is intricate and interesting, and Trout Shue, the convicted murderer, was pleased enough with his artwork to send it along with a letter, no longer extant, to his former employer in Livesay's Mill, Charlie Tuckwiller, who owned the blacksmith shop where he had worked for less than five months in 1896–97.

Trout Shue's double portrait is an intricate, and extremely interesting, drawing, done on old yellowed school paper, the kind with lines, in soft lead, of Trout himself, on the viewer's left, looking a little like a mustachioed Burt Reynolds, and Zona, a dumpy double-chinned Mona Lisa with a funny little smile that raises more questions than it answers. Two coffins adorn the top of the drawing: hers, small, closed, floats in the air above his head, and his, open, floats in the air above her. He is sitting, and she is standing to his left. Entwined between them and over them are vines growing out of pots, among which flits an accurately drawn hummingbird. There is no signature to prove authorship.

Wenona Shue McNeal:

"In prison Uncle Trout taught Sunday school until the day he died. In early spring of 1900, when he realized that he was going to go, he wrote to his mother, Elizah, saying that he was dying, but not to worry, that he loved her, that he had never killed Zonie, and that soon they would all be together in Heaven. Elizah carried that letter in her bosom until it was worn to shreds."

And Trout Shue lies, in the early spring of 1900, on a narrow cot in a small whitewashed cell in the West Virginia State Penitentiary. He moves restlessly, still a young man, not quite forty, but drowning as his lungs fill up with fluid. It is pneumonia. They can do no more. Perhaps he thinks, as he falls asleep, "Sinkhole pine lilies. Just once, I would like to see one, or smell one."

Wenona Shue McNeal:

"Trout, not wanting to trouble his family needlessly, told the prison to give his remains to medical science that he might even in his death serve mankind. This I see as the final one of a long line of unselfish deeds. He died of a broken heart, betrayed and friendless. We've never found a grave for him. Trout Shue was a lover, not a killer."

Ervin Shue:

"I always heard that an ancestor who was a horse thief back in the nineteenth century was buried in Augusta County, Virginia, outside the walls of a small cemetery near Mint Springs. See, no horse thief could be buried in Christian ground."

The *Pocahontas Times* in March of 1900 notes: "There is a great deal of sickness in this part of the country, and more deaths than I ever knew in the same length of time. The suffering has been very severe among our people, with mumps, measles, and pneumonia."

The death toll was high, even for early spring, all over the state. His hometown newspaper did not, then or ever, report Trout Shue's death, though the West Virginia State Penitentiary recorded that he died March 13, 1900, around his fortieth birthday. At that time the penitentiary commonly buried unclaimed remains in the Tom's Run Cemetery, for which no records were kept until the 1930s. Wooden tomb markers were used prior to that, but a flood on Tom's Creek in 1927 washed most of them away. If, as Nonie claims, his body was given to medical research, this fact is nowhere recorded. All but the barest of the old prison records have been spirited away to the state archives in Charleston. The numbers of prisoners no longer jibe with the number system on the files; archivists for the state of West Virginia believe, after a thorough search, that all records on Shue have disappeared or were destroyed long ago. There is no trace left of E. S. Shue, prisoner #1817, and prisoner #3255, except for the bare information on the filing card. The FBI has no records on anyone by any of his various names, even though it does maintain files on nineteenth-century criminals.

The *Greenbrier Independent* in March 1900 reported plenty of rain and mud, bad roads, some maple sugar being made, but little plowing. Corn was getting scarce after a long hard winter. Jacob Shue, father of Trout, died on December 12, 1901; his obituary spoke of him as "a man worthy of the respect of his fellow men." In addition to losing his son the year before, he had lost a daughter. Fannie had died at thirty-five.

Life continued. The Reverend R. R. Little, who had tried to prevent Shue's first marriage, went on to serve the area for several years, conducting services, and at least once giving the address at the commencement of the Bluff School in Peterstown. Estie Cutlip Shue McMillion bore eight children in all, and lived to a ripe old age. Her children say that she declined to ever discuss her first marriage with any of them.

In 1902 Miss Minnie Grose, the clerk who transcribed the trial testimony, married a German named Scherr and moved to Kanawha County. Whatever personal papers she may have had are now gone. Her grandson was surprised to learn that his grandmother had been a court reporter.

Dr. Knapp was seriously injured in a fall from a horse later in 1897, but recovered to complete a term as head of the Greenbrier Medical Association. He died of Bright's disease in 1909. Judge McWhorter died in 1913. Mr. Gardner, the black lawyer, returned to Bluefield to practice coalfield law.

Mary Jane Robinson Heaster lived to tell her tale to those who would listen, and died in September 1916, without ever, apparently, recanting her story. Jacob Hedges Heaster, her husband and Zona's father, died about a year later, and no one recalls that he ever spoke of his daughter's death. Judge John Alfred Preston died the same year, 1917.

Andy Jones, the Negro boy who found Mrs. Shue's body, could not resist the impulse to enlarge upon his story as he went through life. In the original newspaper stories, he is reported as having been sent to the house, and as having found the body, so this part is obviously true. But blood is not mentioned in any of the original news accounts. Yet Jones, having been the first to see the dead woman, claimed proprietary rights to the story. It was he, at roughly the age of forty-five or forty-six, who told a reporter from the *Baltimore Sunday-American* of an autopsy lasting "three days and three nights," a "fact" too good to let drop. Perhaps the story of Trout's whittling throughout the autopsy was another of his fanciful additions. According to Harry Fields, caretaker of the Lewisburg courthouse, who knew Jones, Anderson would "add a little bit, and take away a little bit" each time he told someone new about the Shue murder. Anderson Jones "died sometime after the War"—crippled by arthritis for many years before his death, but still able to do odd jobs even while on crutches.

Radio and electricity came to Greenbrier in the twenties, though there had been some telephones for a decade or more. In 1927 Zona Heaster Shue's childhood home burned completely to the ground, taking with it all portraits, family Bibles, scrapbooks, or letters that might have afforded us important information. As has already been mentioned, somewhere along the line, someone removed the trial transcript, probably the only copy of it, from the Lewisburg courthouse. If it still exists, its whereabouts are unknown. A newspaper ad in September 1984, offering a reward of five hundred dollars for its return, did not smoke it out.

Girta Lucretia Shue Hendricks died in the early fifties, her daughter Frieda Hendricks King reports.

After a while, folks pretty much quit talking about the Shue murder, unless some stranger came to stir the story up again. The newspapers, constantly in search of fillers, from time to time revived the story of the Greenbrier Ghost, and trotted it out again for the delectation of new readers.

In April 1984, apple trees in bloom laced the hillsides and perfumed the cool air of Greenbrier County. Except for the obvious improvements of paved roads and running water, the Meadow Bluff area is still isolated, off the beaten track, primarily a section of small farms, a place where change is not necessarily synonymous with progress. At a local store where a stranger stops for a Coke, the storekeeper warns her that she needs a sweater on a day like this. And the people she visits are cordial but wary. Why would she want to go over all this again? they seem to be wanting to know. At one house she is offered a piece of cake. When she refuses politely, the man says, "You better eat something or you won't have nowhere to hang them clothes." Once when she asks directions, she is told, "There's two ways to git there. Whichever one you take, you'll wish you'd took the other." One day in Lewisburg, a man tells her, "This is a town where you can live and die, and never know which it is you're doing."

And yet, from time to time, somewhere in Greenbrier County, perhaps on a soft blue night on a wide porch where the moths flutter against the yellow light, one of the old-timers will review those events of 1897, and some stranger, maybe a cousin from over the mountains in Kentucky, or Virginia, will perk up and say, "What? What ghost? Tell me!"

And against the chorus of the tree frogs and amid the perfume of honeysuckle, the story will be told again, and a neighbor from down the road will say when it is over, "I always heard the sheets turned to blood when he tried to wash them . . ."

And someone else is bound to say, "My uncle Ben's mother's first husband was kin to some of those people. You know, it was summertime when they took her up. There were so many flies they had to break limbs off the trees to shoo them flies away . . ."

"Didn't they find some letters from another woman while he was still married to Zonie?"

"Why didn't anyone ever think it might have been that little colored boy did it?"

The first one will say, "Didn't Orph know that Anderson Jones fellow?" And maybe they'll get Orph on the phone, and maybe he'll come over and tell his version . . .

"One day over at Lewisburg I talked to Andy Jones. He was only nine years old when he found her. He said there was a trail of blood at the foot of the stairs, and that Shue pushed her down . . ."

In the words of "Lorena" that Jacob Shue just might have sung to while away the time awaiting Trout's arrival with his first marriage license, "But now 'tis past, the years roll on; / I'll not call back their shadowy forms, / But say to them, 'Lost years, sleep on, / Sleep on, nor heed life's pelting storms!'"

At length, they will all fall silent, listening to the creaking of the rocking chairs, watching the chips of wood curl down from Orph's whittling, each one alone pondering the events and watching the moon rise over the West Virginia mountains. Eventually, someone will sigh and stretch, and get going on the long goodnights. And finally, after the false starts and desultory remarks, they'll all go home and go to bed.

NOTES

p. 147: An analysis of the drawing by psychologists appears as Appendix VI.

p. 148: Wenona Shue McNeal is to be commended for her fierce family loyalty, but all in all, it doesn't seem likely that her view of her great-uncle is accurate.

p. 149: The anecdote about the horse thief being buried outside an Augusta County cemetery was told me by Ervin Shue, Staunton, Virginia, in March 1983. Of course that may or may not have been Trout.

p. 150: Jacob Shue's obituary is from the *Pocahontas Times*.

p. 150: Follow-up information on all the people who played parts in this story comes from interviews, newspaper articles, Greenbrier County records, Cole's *History of Greenbrier County*, and Daisy Kincaid Hume.

The story of Zona's death, burial, and return touches on many of Stith Thompson's categories of familiar themes in American and British folklore (*Motif-Index of Folk-Literature*, 1932). The return from the dead for revenge (E 233), a ghost disturbing a sleeping person (E 279.2), and a murdered person being unable to rest until the murder is divulged (E 413) are three of them. Ghost stories have long been familiar fare among the folks of Appalachia.

Part Seven

DID SHE SEE A GHOST ?

Your dead will come to life,
their corpses rise;
awake, exult, all ye
who lie in the dust,
for your dew is a radiant dew,
and the land of ghosts
will give birth.

Isaiah 26:19

There remains the question of the ghostly visits. How can we today account for Mrs. Heaster's story?

We have seen that there was already sufficient doubt within the community to prompt the inquest, once these doubts had been taken to the authorities. Preston quite certainly did not believe the ghost story, but it did bring to dramatic attention the widely held suspicions. Once the inquest was held, there was clear reason for a murder trial. Zona Heaster Shue's neck had been broken. Nothing discovered at the postmortem suggested any other cause for death, according to the newspaper accounts. There was no evidence of poisoning, of accident, of suicide, of illness, or of abortion, either accidental or induced. There was only the broken vertebra, the mashed windpipe, and the external bruises. The supposedly grief-stricken husband had not allowed a proper examination; and folks had noticed the instability of the corpse's head and Shue's peculiar behavior at the wake and in the weeks following.

Had Judge McWhorter been so minded, he could of course have ruled that the ghost testimony was inadmissible evidence that might, if heard, prejudice the jury. Or he could have allowed the testimony, but had the jury sequestered while the use of such testimony was discussed. He did neither, because clearly neither prosecution nor defense raised any objections to Mrs. Heaster's telling her story. The prosecution knew that everyone in town, including the jury, knew about the ghostly visits, and they had doubtless coached Mrs. Heaster in how to respond to the questioning. Preston and Gilmer believed—rightly, as it turned out— that her "evidence" would work in favor of their case against

Trout Shue. The defense wished to show the woman as insane, irrational, so Rucker brought up the ghost story.

Thus the testimony was allowed to be heard. There is no reason whatever to assume that either the prosecution or the defense placed any credence in the ghost story, or that the judge did—or, for that matter, that the jurors did. So, the highway department's marker and the local popular legend to the contrary notwithstanding, testimony by a ghost did not help to convict Trout Shue of murder. The slain girl's mother's claim to have seen the ghost did help to reopen the supposedly closed case of the girl's death, but only because there was an ample supply of nonectoplasmic evidence also available.

So how do we account for the alleged visits themselves? Did the distraught mother, resentful of her daughter's death and convinced of her son-in-law's guilt, dream them up? Did she then, prompted by counsel for the prosecution, extend her story to include details turned up by the inquest? Or did she see no ghost at all, but instead invent the story in an effort to force the authorities to reconsider the manner of her daughter's death?

The likely solution to this question seems ridiculously clear, yet so far as I know, has never been brought to light until now. It lies there in cold print in the *Greenbrier Independent* for January 28, 1897, and has been available for viewing all these years since. Yet no one has noticed it, or if noticed, grasped its implications.

The brief account of Zona's death appeared on page three of that same issue of the *Independent*. On page one there was printed another story. I quote it in full:

A Ghost Story.—J. Henneker Heaton tells in the London *Literary World* an interesting sequel to the most famous Australian ghost story, which came to his knowledge as one of the proprietors of the leading New South Wales weekly, "The Town and Country Journal." One of the most famous murder cases in Australia was discovered by the ghost of the murdered man sitting on the rail of a dam (Australian for horsepond) into which his body had been thrown. Numberless people saw it, and the crime was duly brought home.

Years after, a dying man making his confession said that he invented the ghost. He witnessed the crime, but was threatened with death if he divulged it as he wished to, and the only way he saw out of the impasse was to affect to see the ghost where the body would be found. As soon as he started the story, such is the power of nervousness that numerous other people began to see it, until its fame reached such dimensions that a search was made and the body found, and the murderers brought to justice.

The juxtaposition of these two apparently unrelated news stories, in the same issue of the *Greenbrier Independent*, goes far beyond the likelihood of coincidence. What does seem incredible is that, following Mrs. Heaster's subsequent report of her daughter's ghostly visitations and the reopening of the case, no one recalled having read the story of the Australian ghost. And no one brought it to the attention of the authorities—though perhaps people did read the story and make the connection between it and the story Mrs. Heaster was telling, and, because the circumstantial evidence against Shue was strong enough to convict him without resorting to ghosts, decided to remain silent. Pointing out that Mary Heaster was obviously lying would only have muddied the waters. The ends of justice have been served in stranger ways.

In any event, there are the two news stories: on page three, the notice of Zona Heaster Shue's death; on page one, the account of how the supposed intervention of a "ghost" had been used to bring a murderer to justice. That the slain girl's mother read both stories, and then decided to use the device described in the second to force the authorities to reopen the case, seems obvious.

Through the years it has been supposed that ghosts exist and that Mary Heaster saw one. It has been supposed that, in her grief, she hallucinated the vision of the girl as a projection of her accumulated bits of evidence that Zona's death was other than natural. It has been supposed that she merely had a vivid and convincing dream. But the evidence of the story clearly suggests that none of the above occurred.

What really happened is this: Mrs. Heaster suspected Shue, read or heard the ghost story, and consciously decided to use it to construct one of her own, in the hopes of collecting more "witnesses" to Zona's ghost, as had happened in the Australian story. Mary Jane Heaster, once her plan was formulated, went to Preston with a vague story of Zona's midnight appearance, believing that her real suspicions about her son-in-law were not enough.

We know her story was vague, because of the printed reason in the *Greenbrier Independent* for the autopsy, that "Trout Shue was suspected of having brought about her death by violence or in some way unknown to her friends." Once the autopsy was performed, Mrs. Heaster then elaborated on her original story, making sure it dovetailed with the autopsy findings. By the time of the trial, and the published ghost testimony, her story was "set in stone" for its hearers, who conveniently forgot its real evolution. Ironically, it was not a necessary ploy at all, nor was it a successful one, since no one else ever claimed to have seen Zona in ethereal form. Trout Shue was convicted on circumstantial evidence, not the testimony of a ghost.

The "mystery" of the Greenbrier Ghost now appears to have been solved.

NOTES

p. 158: I am extremely indebted to Fred Long, editor of the *Hinton News-Leader*, for pointing out to me the ghost story in the same issue of the *Greenbrier Independent* that printed the notice of Zona's death.

p. 160: The Greenbrier jury concluded that Shue killed his wife. Even the newspaper takes care to point out that no motive for his doing so was ever brought to light: ". . . with no other motive than to get himself another, more to his liking."

But a motive may have existed nonetheless. I believe that two possibilities or explanations are possible, and I conclude, after two years of exhaustive searching, that we can never know which of them was the case. (Of course, if Lucy Shue's grave could be located, dug up, and a crushed skull found, we would at least know she died of a head injury . . . but not if Shue killed her on purpose. And if we could raise poor Zona's bones once more and find a baby's skeleton within the coffin, also . . . we would then know that Zona gave Shue a motive, but still not certainly that he killed her . . . but an exhumation of a body is not legally possible.)

If I, who have followed Trout Shue for two years, may be allowed an opinion, extrapolated from all I have learned about this man, then one scenario seems to me the most likely one, though I feel it is appropriate only as a footnote to the book. I know that my guesses are only that: guesses.

It seems clear that, from the beginning, Shue tried to hide Zona's broken neck, thus indicating that he did kill her. He pleaded "not guilty" in a game of chance. There was, as the *Greenbrier Independent* observed, about a fifty-fifty chance of his getting off scot-free if his guilt could not be proven. Having pled not guilty, he of course could not then explain any mitigating circumstances or motives. So he took a chance, knowing that if he had pleaded guilty on a lesser charge, such as manslaughter (accidental murder), he would certainly spend some time in prison. For him it was all or nothing. Nonie Shue McNeal's explanation for this, "that he sacrificed himself to protect Zona, whom he loved dearly," does not make sense.

Shue killed Zona; this seems beyond doubt. But, maybe, given his personality, he didn't do it on purpose. Quite possibly he did love her dearly. And quite possibly he also loved his other two wives. And this is not just empty speculation. The remarkable testimony of Giles McKeever identifies Shue as a wife-beater. In the profile of wife-beaters, this fact emerges often: they are terribly sorry after, they truly love their wives, and are horrified at their own actions when reason returns to them.

We cannot know how it was that Zona aroused his fury, or whether her monthlong illness culminating in her death was fear of her husband's moments of irrationality and fury. But his grief at the time of her death seemed real to all observers, even extreme, and his strange behavior sounds very like terror coupled with grief. It is apparently not very difficult at all to break a neck with strong hands—and perhaps it really was one of those horrible accidents in which a man loses control of himself, and accidently kills the woman he loves.

For Zona was still on his mind in prison when he drew the picture of them and sent it to Charlie Tuckwiller back in the Richlands. His popularity with people of both sexes argues against his being simply an antisocial killer. From what few facts of his life we can know, my own extrapolation is what follows:

Trout Shue was, as a young man, artistic, intelligent, talented, mercurial, strongly attracted to women and by them, thus sexually motivated to a large extent. When only twenty-four he married a very young woman. They lived with her parents as he had few marketable skills. When she became pregnant, he felt threatened and jealous by the thing that was growing between them, and began to take out his sexual frustrations on his wife. Hence the vigilante group and the winter baptism. That he stole a horse may argue for his having been a person who believed he could get away with anything, and a person who intended to have what he wanted.

During his second marriage, he and Lucy lived with his parents. As has been shown, it is not possible to determine how she met her death. One version of the story is peaceable, and one violent. But even if the dropped rock story happened to be true, one questions why everyone assumed it was not an accident.

Marrying Zona, he was no different. Who knows what sparked his anger? Sexual problems, perhaps jealousy, are a possibility; her year-old illegitimate child may have been an issue between them. Mistreatment may already have occurred before she died, though her body at the autopsy so far as is known showed no indications of other abuse than the broken neck. Zona's mother seems to have known something was wrong. Had Zona sent her mother messages or letters?

Given that there is so little real evidence, one possibility is that Trout killed Zona in an out-of-control fury. When he realized what he had done, he panicked and tried to figure how to lay the blame elsewhere. In the panic of unreason, Anderson Jones came to mind, and Shue proceeded to try to frame the child. This was an irrational thing to do and indicates a lack of cold-blooded planning. Yet he was anxious enough about her to try four times that fateful morning to send Andy Jones to see about her.

I believe Mary Jane Robinson Heaster lied outright because she had not liked Shue from the start, because she had immediately assumed on hearing of Zona's death that "the Devil killed her," and because the week of Zona's funeral she found in the newspaper a story suggesting to her a way that she could "prove" that Shue had killed Zona. Probably most of us would agree she was justified in her lying—but all in all, there is enough evidence to conclude that she did. Furthermore, Mrs. Heaster planned a piece of physical evidence, the stained or dyed sheet, to impress anyone who remained unconvinced. Apparently, the Greenbrier County folks were not as gullible as the Australians.

In the end, I find the man Trout Shue not good, certainly, but not wholly evil either. He was reportedly well liked though a braggart; he was almost surely a man deeply troubled and very probably lacking in control, yet one who nonetheless has his family's regard and loyalty even unto the third generation. And I find the woman, Mary Heaster, not evil but not wholly good and pious either—a woman who was from the first determined to avenge the death of her only daughter, and found a way to do it. As for Zona, who remains a shadowy figure, although she did not deserve to die, yet she too was not the innocent virgin she is so often portrayed as being.

My research assistants also deserve to be heard. They too have spent a great deal of time helping me to reason through problems and find information. Interestingly, both Paul Shue and Bob Adams disagree with my conclusions. They prefer another explanation as the more likely one.

The official record says that Zona died of childbirth. This was the first reaction, what Knapp thought before anyone suspected that Zona's death was anything but natural. Knapp was the attending physician, so if he believed she had died of childbirth, that probably meant that he had been treating her in the weeks prior to her death for problems connected with pregnancy. Many versions of the story do say that the reason Shue dressed her himself was that her clothes were bloody. In later years Anderson Jones described a "trail of blood" leading into the house. There were, at the time of her death, two versions of the cause: the public one, printed in the papers, said she "died of an everlasting faint." The private, and official one, said she died of childbirth. At that point, of course, there was no knowledge of her broken neck.

Wenona Shue McNeal explains, "I really feel Zona was pregnant. I think that Uncle Trout was the father, and when he learned she was pregnant he did the right thing and married her. Her mother was indignant about him getting her daughter pregnant, and she and Dr. Knapp were trying to abort the fetus. She was mad because Trout had wronged her daughter."

To Bob Adams, a lawyer, it does not make sense that someone would casually record a woman's death as having been caused by childbirth. Had she been pregnant, Knapp would have known whether the child was too far along to have been legitimate. We know that Zona and Trout got married very soon after they met. Just perhaps, Zona was already pregnant when she met Trout. The one person we talked to who ever saw her alive, Lily Heaster Barlow, of Sweet Springs, W.V., saw Zona the Christmas after they were married, a month before she died. Though Lily was only eight or nine, she remembered Zona as fat.

Bob Adams's scenario gives Shue a motive for killing her—perhaps not an excuse, but a motive. But it is highly possible that neither side wanted to bring it out; the prosecution wouldn't have wanted to because it would weaken its case against Shue, and the defense would not have wanted to bring it out because it was embarrassing. And once the autopsy physicians found the broken neck, any sign of abortion or miscarriage became, as it were, irrelevant.

Paul Shue adds that, knowing what we know of Trout Shue's nature, and his past reputation as a wife-beater, he was probably capable of killing—but only in a rage. But noting that Zonie was reputedly young and pretty and popular, he believes that Trout would have had to have a very strong motive to kill her. Had Zona been pregnant by another man, he would have had a motive. That means he would have been tricked into saving her reputation as well as taking care of another man's child. By some, this might be regarded as the ultimate betrayal.

If it was true that Zonie miscarried a child more developed than was possible in the time they had been together, then each side had reason to suppress the information. Each side, therefore, in the trial, waited for the other side to bring it out. And finally, recall that Nonie Shue reported that her grandfather said, before the suspicion of murder, that there was a baby in the coffin with Zona. Just perhaps, that was what was in the wadding by her head.

Thus both Adams and Paul Shue believe that Zona was pregnant when she met and married Trout, and that he killed her when she miscarried and he realized that the aborted fetus could not possibly be his child.

You be the jury: you have heard more evidence than the Greenbrier jury heard. You must sort out for yourself what was truth and what were lies, what was likely and what was not.

The judge dismisses you. You rise, stretching your legs and back. You glance out at the sea of faces, and remind yourself that a life may be in your hands. You must act responsibly. Who is guilty, and of what? The question lingers in the air.

Appendixes

Appendix I

Chronology

Erasmus Stribbling "Trout" Shue born	1861 or 1862
Daisy Kincaid Hume born	April 3, 1885
Trout weds Ellen Estelline Cutlip	November 24, 1885
"The unlawful baptism"	Winter 1886–87
Girta Lucretia Shue born	February 22, 1887
Trout and Estie separate	March 1888
Trout steals a horse	Autumn 1888
Trout sent to prison for two years	April 11, 1889
Trout and Estie Shue divorced	November 5, 1889
Trout discharged from prison	December 20, 1890
Trout weds Lucy A. Tritt	June 23, 1894
Lucy Shue dies	February 11, 1895
Zona Heaster's child born	November 29, 1895
Trout moves to Greenbrier	Autumn 1896
Trout weds Elva Zona Heaster	October 20, 1896
Zona Shue dies	January 23, 1897
Zona's burial	January 25, 1897
Zona's body exhumed and Trout arrested	February 22, 1897
Grand jury hearing	April 22, 1897
Trial for murder	June 23–July 1, 1897
Lynching attempt	July 11, 1897
Trout goes to prison for life	July 14, 1897
Trout Shue dies	March 13, 1900

Appendix II

An Informal Bibliography and History of the Printed Articles

Stories of the trial of Trout Shue were carried, as has been seen, in the *Greenbrier Independent*, which served the area where the murder, and later the trial, occurred; and the *Pocahontas Times*, which served the area where the Shue family lived. Other nearby papers in the state, such as the *Monroe Watchman*, the *Greenbrier Dispatch*, the *McDowell Recorder*, and the *Beckley Herald*, picked up the stories, of course. Since then, from time to time, these papers and many others have revived the event, recognizing its appeal, and thus it has been kept alive for almost a century. Though this list is by no means a complete history of the story's publication, surely it will give readers a chance to go to other sources themselves.

On December 3, 1903, Judge McWhorter wrote to his friend, the editor of the *McDowell Recorder*, Joseph A. Swope, his account of the trial. This may have been the first "revival." (See Appendix V.)

On September 20 and 27, 1936, the *Baltimore Sunday-American* printed a two-part version of the story, by Eddie Ballard, complete with artist's renderings of Mary Jane in her bed, up on an elbow, and Zona floating lightly over the bed. This story was picked up in the next two or three years by at least a score of papers around the country, and became pretty much the standard version. In the thirty-nine years that had intervened since the trial, the story had taken on what was to become the standard form, incorporating many errors of fact which subsequent versions would repeat over and over. Many of these errors must, it appears, be attributed to the unimpeachable "respected" Anderson

Jones, the witness interviewed at the time, then said to be "graying." Shue is described as a "towering man of unknown strength," which we have seen to be untrue. That "the first two wives had both died mysteriously" was in fact not so. That the ghost gave her mother very specific information later confirmed by the autopsy is untrue. The autopsy did not take "three days and three nights." Original articles mention no "trail of blood" leading Anderson Jones to the body; this was a later embellishment. Shue died in the Moundsville penitentiary on March 13, 1900, yet all the standard versions from this one on say either that "he died in 1905" or that "he died eight years later." Of course, various details were added and exaggerations tacked on as years went by; Mrs. Heaster is frequently described as "aged," when she was in reality not yet fifty.

The *Greenbrier Independent* reprinted the story from the *Sunday-American* on June 12, 1942.

Another version was written during the mid-forties, which agrees in all the details of the other, but slightly changes the wording of Mrs. Heaster's testimony (I would venture to guess it was for clarification, not obfuscation). It seems to be heavily derivative of the first one, but adds from the original 1897 news story the three questions and answers of "re-cross-examination," which appeared originally at the time of the trial in the *Monroe Watchman*, and perhaps other papers in the area.

One of the papers that carried the second version was the *Greenbrier Dispatch*, and it may have been written for that paper. It was this printing of the story on June 2, 1944, amid news of the armed forces in Europe, that prompted one J. George Deitz, whose mother was Betty Deitz, first cousin to Zona Heaster Shue, to tape in June 1944 a reminiscence of two earlier episodes from Trout Shue's life, the story of his wedding to Estie and an event later in their marriage, which is corroborated by an article in the *Pocahontas Times* on March 12, 1897.

In 1950 the *Nicholas County News Leader* revived the ghost story, and in January 1951 the *West Virginia News* at Ronceverte picked up that version. The *Beckley Post-Herald* published a series of five articles by Eugene L. Scott on the subject of the Greenbrier Ghost in 1955, expanded from the 1942 version. His series added two personal testimonies, and mentions that the case was discussed in his column twelve years before.

The *West Virginia Hillbilly* prints a version of the story every few years, which appears in identical form in two editions of the

West Virginia Heritage Encyclopedia, edited by Jim Comstock in the one from 1974, on pp. 48–50, and in the one from 1976, on pp. 2031–41.

Shirley Donnelly, a popular West Virginia preacher and columnist, was fascinated by the story, and retold it several times in the sixties in his column in the *Beckley Post-Herald* "Yesterday and Today." He reprinted those columns in his book *Today and Yesterday*, in 1977. He says that in the sixties the trial transcript was still on file at the Greenbrier County courthouse, but he does not seem to have had access to any information not already known without that transcript. Miss Blanche Humphreys, a local historian and genealogist, claims that the transcript of *State* v. *Shue* had disappeared from the Greenbrier County courthouse by 1932 when she first went there to work.

The *Greenbrier Independent* trotted the story out yet again, on August 10, 1967. A year later, Edwin Ott, in his book *The Mountains Speak*, published a version of the story somewhat more accurate than most, and adding for the first time that Trout Shue owned a dog named "Perk." He told me in an interview in March 1983 that he obtained his information from Shue's collateral descendants, who have also done research on the events. On December 16, 1971, the *Monroe Watchman* printed a version of the story by Lester N. Lively.

In 1979 a group, headed by Mary Odell Phipps, of members of Soule Chapel United Methodist Church, in whose cemetery Zona rests, raised money for a tombstone for Zona Heaster Shue. Up until then, her grave had remained unmarked. This act rekindled interest in the story, and papers all over West Virginia once again published versions of it. The main speaker at the dedication was Shirley Donnelly. It was following this event that the West Virginia Department of Culture and History put up the highway marker about the Greenbrier Ghost.

Also in 1979, the *Charleston Gazette* on May 29 printed a version of the story by Robert Morris. On June 24, the *Meadow River Post* ran a story. A few months later, Jane Echols compiled a version of the story for the *West Virginia News* which was printed in two parts, on September 6 and 7. The same year, Fred Long of the *Hinton News-Leader* compiled a version of the story for his paper that is more carefully researched than any of the others. I am indebted to Fred for sharing his information with me. The *West Virginia United Methodist* magazine printed a version of the old story in its October–November 1979 issue.

In 1982 *Globe* Magazine stumbled onto the story, and printed a brief version on April 6, with the newly discovered drawing, which is discussed in Appendix VI.

Most recently, Jane Echols and Michael Clay Smith have published an article in *Case and Comment*, a law magazine, which was reprinted in the *West Virginia News Leader* of Richwood on July 20, 1983. Their article retells the story but raises the questions of how the hearsay testimony of the dead girl was first brought into evidence, and why there was no appeal questioning the sufficiency of the evidence. The answer seems obvious at last: the circumstantial evidence was quite strong enough to convict Shue of Zona's death. Only later accounts have Mrs. Heaster's testimony the deciding factor. And finally, the standard story of Zona Heaster Shue's murder appears in folktale collections from West Virginia by James Gay Jones (*Appalachian Ghost Stories*) and Ruth Anne Musick (*Coffin Hollow and Other Ghost Tales*).

To sum up, there is only one story, essentially. A few details differ, a few embellishments appear here and there, and occasionally one of the writers (Ott and Long, specifically) has questioned whether Mrs. Heaster really saw her daughter's ghost. But astonishingly, it seems that no one has ever begun with the assumption that there was no ghost, and attempted to discover how it was that the ghost story began.

In addition, I consulted the following books: Abrahamsen, David, *The Murdering Mind* (his profile of a killer fits closely the known traits of Shue); Brown, F. C., *Collection of North Carolina Folklore*, vol. 7 (I found the version of "Pretty Polly" in this close-to-home collection, as well as the lyrics to "Will You Love Me When I'm Old?"); Cole, J. R., *The History of Greenbrier County* (this source gave me information about Preston, Rucker, and Gilmer); Francke, Linda Bird, *The Ambivalence of Abortion* (this book offered some insights to husbands' reactions to abortion, and to the delicate subjects of paternity, paternal jealousy, and pregnancy); Levy, Richard, and Langley, Roger, *Wife-Beating, The Silent Crisis* (this source offers insights into at least one trait of Shue's that we can be fairly certain about); and Rawcliffe, D. H., *Illusions and Delusions of the Occult and Supernatural* (this book offers some insights into how the human mind works regarding supernatural events).

For genealogical information, I consulted the West Virginia Archives in Charleston, and the Greenbrier and Pocahontas County records.

I also found useful the marvelous profile of William Parkes
Rucker by Hal Walls in the *Journal of the Greenbrier Historical
Society*, vol. 3, no. 4 (1978).

Appendix III

Handwriting Analysis

There is one further piece of "evidence" that we can look at:
one handwriting sample on the card that Shue sent to his daughter
Girta in January 1889. Dorothy Sara is a handwriting expert, and
this analysis is based on her method. From its slant, the writer
was an extrovert. Some variations in the baseline indicate mercurial moods. The letters are connected, indicating a logical
mind. From the pressure, which varies even in this short note,
Ms. Sara would say the writer is jealous, self-indulgent, lacks re-
finement and sensitivity, but has lots of physical vitality. As it is
legible, he wishes to be understood. Since the writing is of normal
size, neither large nor small, the writer has pride but is not ego-
tistical, and has tastes that are good and unpretentious. The an-
gular letters suggest aggressiveness and a critical mind, prac-
ticality and shrewd judgment. The writer of such a hand may be
interested in "work which requires an analytical approach or the
use of hands in some skillful manner." The tight, closed letters
indicate caution and skepticism. His *i*-dots indicate that he is
careful with details, but the dot a bit to the right of the *i* suggests
he is reaching for things he doesn't have. The capital letters,
slighty elaborate, indicate a desire to be noticed. The back-
looping *y* indicates introversion or resentment or hesitation to co-
operate with others. Two of the letters are reversed, an *N* and a *Y*.

Appendix IV

Profile of a Murderer

Goethe once wrote that there was no existent crime the inclination towards which he could not trace within himself. In trying to understand Shue at this late date, is there anything that psychology or criminology can help us with?

In *The Murdering Mind* (New York: Harper & Row, 1963), David Abrahamsen writes:

Where a person resorts to violence, it is, in the last analysis, to achieve power. By obtaining power, he enhances his self-esteem, which fundamentally is rooted in sexual identity. In the murderer, this sense of true identity is inadequate or lacking. Those who have been unable to develop their genuine sexual role will try to compensate for it by asserting themselves in a field in which they have a special talent and in which they can hope to excel. In this way they attempt to regain vicariously what they have been unable to achieve sexually, a process that takes place mostly on the unconscious level. People who have developed a distorted sense of identity are unable to love genuinely, and therefore feel themselves unloved and unwanted. They react explosively to being sexually rejected, for it threatens their whole sense of self. The outcome may very well be murder.

Sexual inadequacy is a major reason for the intensity of the violence in murder. The degree of violent acting out employed in homicide is usually far greater than is needed to kill the victim, particularly because of revenge. (P. 26)

Among characteristics of the murdering mind, Abrahamsen lists "fantasies of grandiose accomplishments" (Shue frequently was described as a braggart); errors of spelling or speech related to early emotional disturbances (recall the reversed letters in the only handwriting sample we have); a tendency to transform identity (note his changing of his age and name more or less at will); suicidal tendencies (Shue threatened to kill himself in jail in May before the trial); and a history of previous antisocial acts associated with threatening or committing murder (not only had he been in prison for horse stealing, but he had also so enraged the neighborhood that vigilante action was taken over his treatment of his first wife.)

Appendix V

The McWhorter Letter

In 1903, Joseph Swope, then editor of the *McDowell Recorder*, wrote to Judge J. M. McWhorter for an account of the case, then six years in the past. Its original appearance is gone from any official source, but Shirley Donnelly reprinted it in the mid-fifties in the *Beckley Herald*. It seems a source more worthy of attention than most.

Lewisburg, W.Va.
December 1, 1903

Dear Joe:

Inclosed I send statement of facts proven in Shue murder case. Of course, this is not all that was proven, but the most interesting is what was brought out by defendant's counsel.

Yours very respectfully,
J. M. McWhorter

A very interesting murder case was tried in the Circuit Court of Greenbrier County at the June term, 1897. Some mysterious and unaccountable facts were developed upon the trial that can not be forgotten by those that heard the evidence through.

Shue, in November, 1896, married Miss Zona Heaster of Meadow Bluff District, in Greenbrier County, as his third wife, he being about 33 years of age, and settled at Livesay's Mill to work at the blacksmith trade. He and his wife occupied what room they needed in a two-story frame building which had been the residence of the late William Livesay.

On the 22nd of January, 1897, as he went to work, he called on a colored family who lived a few yards from his house and asked the mother to let her boy—some 12 years of age—go up to his house and do some chores there, and take some eggs to the store for Zona, his wife. About 11 o'clock he left his shop and went to the colored neighbor and asked if the boy had yet been up to his house, and the woman said he had not, but it was near dinner time. Shue said he was not going home to dinner that day and again requested the boy to be sent up.

In a short time the boy gave the alarm that Mrs. Shue was dead. She was found in the dining room, lying stretched out and her clothes pulled down, and apparently had been dead for some hours. The doctor was sent for and after making a cursory examination decided that she had died from heart failure, as she had been unwell and he had been attending her for a week or two.

It was decided that the remains should be taken for interment to her father's, about 14 miles distant. The remains were to be kept overnight at her father's and buried the following day.

After burial the friends, in talking over the circumstances connected with her death and burial and recalling the fact that no one was permitted to view the remains but in the presence of Shue, who always took his place at the head of the corpse, and when she was placed in the coffin, he had a sheet folded and placed alongside of her head and some garments placed on the other side, and her mother stating that her daughter had appeared and talked to her, her parents were not satisfied as to the cause of her death. So, after consultation, it was decided to exhume the body, which was just one month from the time of its burial.

And here comes the most remarkable part of the evidence introduced by defendant's counsel: Mrs. Heaster, mother of the deceased, who seemed a very pious lady, had told all she knew about her daughter's death and burial, and defendant's conduct on the night of the wake. Counsel for the defendant said to her: "Mrs. Heaster, did you not have a dream that aroused your suspicions and led you to have the body exhumed." [Sic]

She replied: "I had no dream for I was fully awake as I am at this moment."

"And did you not have a dream or vision that led you to have the body disinterred." [Sic]

"Well," she said, "I was not satisfied that my daughter came to her death from natural causes, and I prayed earnestly that it might be revealed to me how she came to her death, and after about an hour spent in prayer, I turned over and there stood my daughter and I put my hand out to feel for the coffin, but it was not there. She seemed to hesitate to speak to me, and departed. The next night, after I had prayed again that the manner of her death might be shown, she again appeared and talked more freely and gave me to understand that I should be acquainted with the whole matter, and disappeared.

"The third night she again appeared to me (her murdered daughter did) and told me all about the difficulty, how it occurred, and how her death was brought about.

" 'He (her husband) came that night from the shop and seemed angry. I told him supper was ready and he began to chide me because I had prepared no meat for supper and I replied that there was plenty; there was bread and butter, apple sarce [sic], preserves, and other things that made a very good supper, and he flew mad and got up and came toward me. When I raised up he seized each side of my head with his hands, and, by a sudden wrench, dislocated my neck.'

"She went on and described to me the location of the building and surroundings in the neighborhood, where they lived, so that it was fixed in my mind as a reality. I was telling someone about the situation of the buildings, etc., and he said to me, 'You have been there' and I replied, 'I have not' 'and he said, 'I have been there many times and yet I could not describe the place and surroundings so minutely as you have.'"

"Mrs. Heaster, was there not something about a sheet that you could not understand?" And she replied, "There was."

She said that when Mr. Shue was leaving from the burial for home she called his attention to the sheet that had been under the side of her head in the coffin, and he said, "Mother, you keep it." "I kept it for three or four weeks and while it looked clean and white I imagined it smelled badly, and I concluded to wash it. I washed it with my white clothes and when I pressed it down in the tub it turned red, and I concluded I had spoiled my other clothes, but when I dipped up water in my hand the water was not colored. I washed it and boiled it and hung it out and froze it three or four days, but it still had a reddish color." Counsel says, "Have you that sheet with you?" She replied that she had it at her boarding house. The sheet was brought in and exibited [sic] to the jury, and it was a decidedly reddish color.

When the body was taken and a post-mortem examination was made, it was found that her neck had been dislocated, which undoubtedly had caused her death. The trial occupied eight days and the jury found him (Shue) guilty of murder in the first degree, and [line dropped here, but it must have read "he was incarcerated behind the"] walls of the West Virginia Penitentiary, and he was accordingly sentenced for life. This murdered woman was his third wife, and he had boasted that he expected to have seven wives. In this, however, he was disappointed. He was passed to the Great Beyond to meet the three he treated so brutally here.

[Signed]
J. M. McWhorter

Appendix VI

The Drawing

I should point out that there is no proof that Shue actually drew this picture, but (1) Charlie Tuckwiller's daughter says he did, (2) his family all recall that he drew a lot, (3) the antiquity and fragility of the drawing are apparent when viewing the original, and (4) the subject of the drawing presses us to believe that Shue did it.

If I have, from the moment I heard of it, overvalued this drawing, it is because it is the only item (except for the card Shue sent his daughter Girta around her second birthday) I have seen by or about him that is not secondhand. In fact, there are almost no hints anywhere of the personality of Zonie, and only a few of Trout. So much must be extrapolated on the basis of known facts, and a handful of folk-memories handed down for nearly a hundred years, many of which contradict each other.

So, with certain understandable misgivings, I determined to try to see whether several trained psychologists might be able to "read" anything of the artist's character or of the relationship of the two figures in the drawing. It seems fair to try to understand Shue, to try to arrive at the nearest thing possible to truth, by any reasonable means available.

I sent copies of the drawing to five psychologists and one psychiatrist—three men and three women. Only the psychiatrist, a woman, declined to comment on the drawing, saying she "did not want to put her head in a noose." The men were Dr. James Worth, counselor and psychology professor at Washington and Lee University, who has worked in a prison and specifically used prisoners' drawings both diagnostically and therapeutically in his therapy with inmates; Dr. Lowry Michael Gilmore, who heads the Rockbridge County Mental Health Clinic, and has used drawings by children in therapy with them; and Dr. Dean Foster of the Virginia Military Institute, whose research on sleep and dreaming, and on smell, is widely known and respected. He also teaches general psychology at VMI. The two women who ended up taking part in the experiment are Dr. Maureen Rousset Worth, who teaches psychology and family classes at Southern Seminary, and has written two textbooks on midlife crises and the aging process, and Dr. Julie Adams Jennings, a family specialist and counselor at the Rockbridge County Mental Health Clinic.

None of them knew the story or anything about the case in advance. I wrote each a brief note, saying that the drawing was made between 1897 and 1900 by a man convicted on circumstantial evidence of killing his third wife. I then asked them to try to answer, on the basis of the drawing alone, three questions: (1) in your opinion, did he commit the murder? (2) what kind of man was he, judging solely from what he drew on this page? and

(3) what kind of relationship did he have with the woman in the drawing?

As I mentioned, one person sent the material back without comment. All the other five wisely urged caution about placing too much importance on one drawing. Dr. Gilmore's disclaimer is typical: "I am sure you realize the drawing only suggests answers to your questions about the person doing the drawing. I use projective drawings as tools to indicate areas that need exploration. They are not final tests of personality. Furthermore, I have no knowledge of what prompted the person to complete the drawing and will assume he initiated it spontaneously."

To the first question—did he murder his wife?—four replied yes; one said, "I don't see enough evidence to actually support . . . that he committed the crime," yet saw clearly the theme "of the expiation of guilt" in the drawing. The overall impression had by all the psychologists was of gloom, guilt, and punishment. One noted that the male figure's coffin is "sticking into him in two places, and he is in his coffin but exposed, while his wife is in hers yet out of sight." Perhaps, suggested one, that was because her case was "closed" by her death, and his "case" was as yet still open. Another said, in a sort of figurative statement about the drawing, that as her death was upon his head, so his death would be upon her head. Also mentioned by one was the oversized flower fragilely supported above his coffin, appearing ready to crash down upon him. The part of the flower pot next to his coffin is shaded, or dark. The vine leaves appear to be "raining down" on his coffin. Two respondents felt that there was enough bound-up power in the male figure to suggest that he probably killed her "with a gun or a knife" or "in a sudden fury." The death motif indicated to all five guilt and morbidity.

Second, what kind of man was he? This question drew the most lengthy comments. One found the man's body actually "threatening" in its thick heavyset darkness. One stated that he was hostile, with confused feelings about women as shown in the female figure's "secret smile." The bound-up distorted body, in contrast to the clearly drawn head of the man, indicates a distorted image of his own body (as opposed to the much clearer and more properly proportioned drawing of the woman's body) and he was therefore seen by all respondents as having "a diminished self-confidence," or a "poor self-image," or a "deformed sense of himself," which "demonstrated mental imbalance." The male figure, though handsome and broad-shouldered, looks stiff and bound-up. This suggested to all an "inability to express emotion—and therefore, probably affection." There is no smile on his face. The upper body is large, dark, "domineering," and "on the surface powerful. Yet how frail the supports upon which it is planted!" He makes no eye contact with the woman. Since he has no hands in the drawing, "perhaps he feels guilty about the use of them." The hands being out of sight suggested a man "who could not reach out and touch," or one "not in touch with his feelings." The "primitive" or "childish" or "inept" quality of the drawing of his body was noted by four of the five. His figure is "so precariously seated that it needed an additional support in the sofa legs." This suggested "poor 'understanding'" and that "those tiny legs could not support" the massive body. One spoke of a "reliance on primitive and crude defense mechanisms," and believed the man might have been alcoholic. Thus all five saw him as "anxious about his body image and his sexual ability," "a man who needed to feel powerful, and tried to appear so, but underneath was very frail." This implies a "man who could not have handled anger or intimacy very well."

He was seen as someone of "high intellectual abilities," "quite sensitive, with good powers of observation and a keen eye for details," which can be seen in the details of the drawing, especially the intricacies of the dress, and the accuracy of the hummingbird. "The abstract, or symbolic, nature of the drawing" argues that intellect is at work: "the tree of life and the philosophical concepts suggested by the placement of the coffins are, at the very least, interesting." The bodily distortions of both figures may point to a "schizoid" view of the world. One felt that the melancholy dark eyes and heavy eyebrows suggested a "serious nature." One person saw the artist as having "high religious values." One respondent said without explaining that from the drawing he appears to be "egocentric, social, and competitive." One person noted that he is literally poised to "kick the bucket" (in which the plant grows).

The third thing I asked about was his relationship to the woman. All mentioned the obvious separation that the picture portrays. "Marital relationship defined by the sketch is problematic and troubled." Of course she was dead and he was still in the land of the living, though this separation suggested to several respondents that the artist saw men and women as being "on opposite sides," or "from two different worlds" and therefore perhaps tended to view marriage not as a blending, but as a contest or battle of wills. As one person put it, "there seems to be no real connection between the two figures." At the time the drawing was made it was conventional in connubial portraits for the man to be seated and the woman to be standing, though usually the wife stands behind the husband with a hand on his shoulder, and surely not widely separated from him. But this picture is "essentially two portraits." This suggested that there may have been something "unobtainable" about this woman, that he perhaps "never 'had' her." Also, he is "lower" than she is, or, if he is grounded, then she appears "to float slightly above the ground." One commented at some length: "The relative sizes and positions of the two figures, the presence of the plants as barriers between them, and the contorted drawing of the woman lead me to think he felt threatened by this woman and great conflict over their relationship. She stands above and behind him. Her one hand looks like a knife; the other holds something that looks like a cup held away from the man—certainly not a nurturant gesture. The sexual theme of the hummingbird, the 'gaping mouth lined with teeth' depicted in the woman's dress, and the zipper-like appearance of the central plant reveal a concern with the threat of emasculation by the woman (one of his legs is missing). His feelings about her are so conflicted that her arms are completely distorted. If he did kill her it was probably with a gun or knife."

The female in the picture has energy, "airiness," and "much more life than the male," which is ironic in view of the fact that she was the one who was dead. Yet she too looks bound up in the upper body, suggesting that the artist saw her as ungiving, holding herself to herself. Her hair is not flowing free, but drawn into a tight little topknot. Her tiny little arms and hands and feet point to an "ungiving" nature, or as one put it, "she did too little for him." The funny little smile on her face may represent that she had "the last laugh" or it may indicate that "he saw her as laughing at him," or it may mean that "he saw her as someone whose thoughts were so secret" that he couldn't really "get to her." One of her hands points at him—perhaps in accusation. Her smile was seen by one as "puzzling"—but by another as "perhaps signifying that she is at peace while he is not."

Though both heads are detailed, her body is drawn with much more care than his. Two of the respondents, both male, noted the strongly feminine quality about the drawing: birds and flowers, with which the picture abounds, are "generally drawn by women but much less often by men," and are generally thought of in connection with women. But even more feminine, according to one, is the "painstaking detail of the female figure's dress, in contrast with the lack of detail of the male figure's clothing." This suggested to two of the five that the man was possessed by a latent homosexuality, "causing him great anxiety." (Here I add that his having had three wives may further hint that he was a man full of doubts about his manhood, and frantic about his masculinity. A man, especially in that era, hiding a secret of that sort, would have needed to be on guard and in control all the time, and to prove to himself and the world what a man he was.) One person saw in the details of the woman's dress and the plants a "compulsiveness," and "repression," and noticed that in his drawing he took "more care to emphasize the details of inanimate objects than he did in drawing the people." "Flowers stand for growth and beauty," and in the "symmetry of his drawing" for "unity." "Birds or insects," one observed, "fly around the flowers, around the casket, above the tree of life or tree of heaven. Somehow, above, the two dead bodies seem to be 'pushing up daisies.'" One respondent felt that all of this indicated "a strong faith, though not necessarily Christian."

This is everything that the respondents mentioned. I have left out nothing, only arranged the comments into an order of sorts. There are, as we can see, no serious disagreements about any single thing, with the possible exception of the female figure's smile. What is astonishing to me is the consensus in viewing this drawing—when the respondents knew nothing of the story, and had no communication among themselves on the drawing. Make of it what you will; perhaps it gives us a glimpse into that past which is never really dead.

Appendix VII

A Curious Interview

Note: Information in this appendix was obviously collected somewhere in the general vicinity of Brigadoon, Oz, and Sleepy Hollow, West Virginia, a remote area of many legends, lies, and ghostly visitations.

The sign creaks as I drive in. Clearview Manor stands out like a new bandage on the landscape: a shining, lying white. There's a chill in the West Virginia wind as the world turns again towards winter, as day by day the sun fades. That life should end in such a place strikes me as an indecency.

As usual, the name is supremely ironic. There is no clear view, and the building is depressing, square and unimaginative. Inside are pale green halls already dingy, and the sour smells of old age, incontinence, and rubbing alcohol.

At the desk I ask for Babbie F. Alcock, explaining to a lady in sequined glasses that it was she who called me. In a moment, there appears a squarish young girl with red cheeks, dressed in the same pale green as the walls. As she leads me down the hall, which is stifling, she says, "He's kind of unpredictable, so watch out. There he is. You just call me if you need anything." She waves breezily towards the corner of the lounge.

The old man sits right in a long square of sun filtering into the shabby room, hunched over in his wheelchair, not talking to the two old ladies in bathrobes in their wheelchairs nearby. He is peanut-sized, shriveled and ancient, a yellow lap robe hung between two knobs where his knees should be, making a hammock so deep there couldn't be anything underneath. Only his hands are large, spread out on the chair arms like huge white spiders. He stares straight ahead. But as I start across the room, already I can see that he has caught sight of me and is sizing me up, a crazy gleam in his eyes. I nod to the old lady who stares curiously at me, her mouth fallen open and toothless.

He had Nurse Alcock call me up and tell me to come over here, that he wanted to meet me. Had to do with the book I was writing. His name is Charles Shugue. They don't know his exact age, but they estimate well over ninety. And I don't know why I came, since I am through with the book; it's in production— except he's the first person who has called me for an interview. And of course I found the name, so close to the one I've been researching, intriguing.

I look around for a chair, find a molded orange one, drag it over, and sit down so as to be on a level with him. I say I am Katie Lyle, and he says, "I didn't think you was nobody else."

He has a deep voice for such an old man—and a handshake surprisingly strong, because he looks like a bag of bones covered with skin. "They tell me you writing about the Trout Shue case." I admit it. "What you find out?" he asks at once.

"Well," I say, not sure how to respond, "I guess I found right much. You know about it?" Quickly I do the arithmetic in my head: 1985 minus 90—1895. Make him two or even older at the time of the trial. If he's really that old, he could know something . . .

His washed-out blue eyes narrow, and his face in repose is like alligator hide. His skull is shiny beneath transparent hair.

"You going to put it in a book?"

I tell him I hope so. "I'd like to see that," he says, sarcastically, and I don't know why. It makes me uncomfortable.

"Well," I say, unable to sound anything but prissy, "I hope you will."

He stares at me, hard. "They say I'm on the way out. Old ticker's weak, liver's turned traitor on me, eyes like two holes in a old hollow log, nose veiny as a county roadmap. Seedy as a milkweed field. I know I'm no beautiful thing. They tell me I'm dyin'. I scratch too much, and my hands shake."

How must I respond? I change the subject. "Mr. Shugue," I say, "are you related to Trout Shue?"

"But I ain't forgot how to turn a phrase," he says, grinning and slicking his rheumy eyes my way. Then, almost to himself, "Ain't no reason not to tell now." He looks me up and down. "I don't feel no different'n I ever did. Well, maybe sicker is all."

"Tell what?" I prompt.

"Just hold your horses, girlie. I'm gittin' ready to tell you a story. He glances off out the window. "They was a time when I was thought of as the best around." I decide I sort of like being called *girlie* this close to fifty. "Once upon a time, you could git folks to listen to stories. No more. Now ever'body's too busy, got to git here, or git there." I nod, trying not to think about whether I will get home in time to fix supper . . . "They tell you he didn't die in prison?"

So, another one nuttier than a fruitcake. Maybe it has to do with being from Appalachia. I think back to all the lies, all the mistakes, all the exaggerations I've heard in the last four years since I took on this story. I try not to betray irritation, and shift in the uncomfortable chair. Immediately I see his eyes move up and down my legs, not missing a trick. The general rule I have come to expect in researching this book is, the wronger the story, the more insistent the teller. Am I going to bite?

"Actually," I say, being prim on purpose, trying to pull my denim skirt down farther over my knees, "the prison records say he died."

"Well, course they do," he says. "They ain't goin' to admit nobody escaped. They all turnt agin me, anyway. I was doin' time it was somebody else's to do. Said I stolt a horse. I never. It was a cow—and I didn't steal it nohow. But that's another story."

"Trout Shue escaped?" This is a new one. I settle myself, yellow pad and pen at the ready. Who cares if it's a lie? I can't resist a good story.

His eyes squint up, and he's already into it, clutching the wheelchair arms like he's going to spring out any minute. You couldn't prove it by me he's dying. In fact, it looks as if his body is saying, "If it weren't for this damn wheelchair—"

I have to write fast. "—this guard's sister. See, I already knowed to put cloths soaked in calamus extract on piles. You see a lot of piles in a prison. That's wild Irish—you know?— flags, some call 'em. Men thought I was crazy—'til it worked. Shrunk 'em right down. Then one day this guard's sister she come to me. See, she's heard I could doctor real good. She's got The Change. Her husband he don't understand. I'll never forgit how she jus' stood there hangin' on to the bars with both hands, cryin'. Just hangin' on. So I ask her what's ailin' her, and she tells me more'n I ever wanted to know. I don't know a thing to do. But I can't stand a woman to cry. Then I recalled how my

mama jes' loved the names of flowers, the longer the better—
and it just come to me sudden-like to tell her I figure she got a
blocked delphinium. And she quit cryin' then, once I named it,
and went to snufflin' and all, like they'll do. But she begun to
listen. I didn't want her to start up again, so I just made up how
inside of a woman's body sometimes the delphinium swells up
and can't get through this passage it got to get through. I told
her it was like a fat woman tryin' to git through a real narrow
door. She nodded, listening hard, and I had to keep goin' then
so she won't start to bawlin' again, so I just yanked nettle out of
clean air, told her to make a tea and drink some ever' hour.
They grows ever'where, God knows how many times in the dark
I have done stumbled into some goddamn patch of nettles . . ."

"Just a second," I interrupt. "I need to get some dates on
this. Are you saying you were in prison? When was that?"

"It eased her," he says, staring at me with those wicked old
eyes. "She was grateful to me 'til her dyin' day."

I am confused. Where are we? Who is this man? How did he
get my name? "Listen—" I begin. "I need to—"

"Girlie," he says, "all I ever had to do was listen. That's all a
woman needs. I could tell them medicine school doctors a thing
or two. That one told her friends. Before long, they was comin'
to see me in droves. Black nor white, both. One black lady,
name of Polly Henry, come all the way from down around Talcott
jes' to see me. She was near to dyin' but I fixed her. Some come
all the way from Ohio. Turned out the woods is full of women
with complaints. I couldn't beat 'em off with a stick. One I'd tell
she had a tuberous begonia, the next one I'd say she had a
dropped hollyhock. But I couldn't go on doctorin' without exam-
inin' them now, could I? So I gone to the warden, talked 'im into
lettin' me have this cell wasn't bein' used, for a office. I got
better 'n better once I could git my hands on 'em. I could burn
disease out of a woman's body with jest these hands." He holds
them up, flannel-covered bones, and grins over at me, frail and
rascally. "That's when I got the plan to ex-cape." Overhead a fan
moves the air just enough to keep the room from being too hot. I
decide to relax, get the story down. How many chances will I get
to interview some charlatan of a doctor?

"I knowed I'd git my chance sooner or later. It come in the
spring, lot of pnew-moanye going around. Folks called it 'the old
man's friend,' since it taken so many away, put 'em out of their
misery right quick-like. By then, I was given free run of the

entire prison, went around listenin' to them dyin' confessions. Couldn't nobody put a man to rest good as me. But my leanin's was still to the women.

"That night, the one I'm a-talkin' about, it was rainin' fit to kill. Water was already up in Tom's Creek, and gittin' up in the river, night they called for me to come. It was the warden's daughter, and they said she was real sick. Well, I hated to do it. I'd done seen her once or twice when she brung dinner to her old man, and she was purty and young, jus' the way I liked 'em. I could of helpt her out good! But I knowed my chance had come, and it might be my onliest one. Warden he lived maybe a mile away. I'd been sprang twice before, but in the daylight. But see, I'd tooken to teachin' Sunday school to the other fellers, with just a mind to this chance. Guards was feelin' ornery to have to go out in weather like that to begin with, and they wasn't half paying attention to me. I uz on a horse behind of ole Thurmond Newton. We wasn't hardly out of the place when I just slud right down off'n that old nag's rump. In all that rain, I jes' slipped into the woods. Darkness swollered me up in a gulp, and if they hollered for me, why I never heard 'em. Five minutes later I knowed I was safe. I headed for Ohio, swum that swollen river, damn near drownded. I holed up in a barn that first night, and I never will forget the way that hay smelled. I reckon nothing in my whole life ever smelt as good as that hay in that barn—"

I am staring at my yellow pad. Mr. Charles Shugue. If I'd learned anything in the last four years, it was that people back then changed their names all the time. The boy by Annie Williams? He was born just about a hundred years ago—that could be right. "Mr. Shugue—" I say, "was Trout Shue your father?"

"My father? Ain't you been listenin', girlie?"

I don't know whether to humor him or not. If I make him mad, he might quit talking to me. On the other hand, it appears that for his own reasons he is trying to tell me that he is a man—let's see—born in 1861 or '63—over 120 years old, and maybe 124! Well, it's entertainment. What can I lose by playing along?

So I settle down and say, "What actually happened to Lucy Tritt Shue?"

He opens his eyes, gives me a suspicious glance. "The law send you?"

"No," I say, smiling in spite of trying not to. "You sent for me, remember?"

He looks around, to see if we are being observed. The two old women have both fallen asleep. One snores gently. "That damn woman," he says under his breath. "Brown bean Lucy." He shakes his head. "I've eat poor in my time, but I ain't never ate that poor. She couldn't cook nothing but brown beans with molasses. Beans fer breakfast, beans fer dinner, and beans at night when I'd been plowing 'til I was like to drop with them dumb oxes her old man was so proud of. You think a jackass is stubborn? Farmin' is for fools, you ask me."

"Did you kill her?" I interrupt.

He only looks at me. "What'd they tell you about that?"

"Different things," I hedge.

"I bet they did," he says. "Well, it was a accident. I one time thought that woman was pretty. Musta been blind. Fact is, she was slack-jawed and fat, and had a breath could kill a mountain lion at fifty yards. Estie now, she was pretty. Course Estie was just a baby. She couldn't even cook brown beans, and that's the truth. I damn near starved to death, married to her. Puny little bitty thing. Never had no appetite."

He must have heard the stories so often he's identifying with Trout Shue. "Best bet—lost son," I write on my tablet.

Then I stare at my scrawling, already five long pages on the yellow legal pad. "Do you mind if I ask how old you are?"

"Age don't mean nothin'," he says. "I figure these lines jis' give my face character." And he grins.

He's quick: no doubt of that. "Mr. Shue," I say, "you always said you'd have seven wives."

"Did, too," he says without hesitation. "Wait. Maybe it was eight." He grins lewdly. "Them was the best years, doctoring and all. Black nor white, din't make no difference to me. I headed west. Went to Missouri. Missouri's a good state. I shoulda stayed in Missouri. But I went on. That is, I and Nellie did. Run off from her husband in Missouri. I never forget that place we camped that May in them Rocky Mountains, so full of apple blossoms looked like clouds from off the peaks when we was coming down, then lookin' up we could see how the wind had whipped the clouds into peaks—looked just like them apple blossoms. Me and Nellie stayed two days in that stand of the sweetest-smellin' blossoms you could think of, air was warm in the day, and cold at night . . . the bluest sky you ever seen. We was higher up than I ever been, before or since. We found some

of them morchella mushrooms, up there near Heaven, and at the
end of the first day in them mountains I killt a deer, and it was
the best meat I ever eat. We had some whiskey we done stole
from Nellie's husband, and that night at our campfire she drunk
my health, and I reckon I never was as happy agin in all my
life . . ." He sniffs, wipes his nose with the back of his hand.
Tears? "That is, 'til her old man caught up with us . . . Then it
was good-bye, Nellie.

"Yessir, a doctor's a good thing to be. A doctor's got standin'."

"You actually practiced medicine without any formal train-
ing?" I am writing as fast as I can.

"Shore I did. I done more'n practice. I done it. Nothin' to it.
When I seen how it was all just talk, I read two pamphlets once
back there on woman's anatomicals. Both of 'em a full eight
pages. Gyne—sump'n, it was called. I cain't recall. Didn't help
me much, jest give me some fancy words to use fer a while. I
didn't bother with no medicines, figured they was jes' a lot of
poisons. Herbs done them women jist as well. Peppermint fer
pregnancy, rhuberb if they uz bound up; I forgit—

"But I knowed what the hypocritic oath was, and I tooken that
serious: no matter what tima day, no matter what the weather is
or ain't, no matter what your circumstantial evidences is, who-
ever calls you, especially a woman, and especially if she's young
and purty—you is goin'. I got right good at child-deliverin' in
the early days, out in the lumber camps in Ohio. That was when
I was married to Belle. But that didn't work out. She started as
one of my patients. Trouble was, she wouldn't let me get on with
my doctorin' after we was married. See-uh, well, she was jealous of my other patients. That's when I went on to Missouri.

"And I didn't lose too many patients, neither, no more'n any
other doctor. I don' reckon a doctor ever lived didn't lose some
of his patients. You know anythang about baseball, Lady? Now
if'n a baseball player bats .400, they say he's doin' real good,
ain't that right? Well, say if I had ten patients which would normally be mostly women, I usually saved four outa ten, on the
average. So I say I batted about .400. Cain't nobody expect no
more'n that.

"I one time paid somebody a whole fifteen dollar for a P.H.
and D., and after that it was legal I was a doctor. Didn't nobody
ever ask to see it, though. Had faith in doctors in them days.
Buckets of water over the bridge since then. Ain't that way
today.

"I just reckon I always did lean to the females. You might say

I had special desires and special abilities in that area. Fact, I got so good that after five-six months I could tell right off a lady was pregnant."

I am writing fast, and admiring his gall. Suddenly he says, "I didn't kill Louise. She run away."

"Which one was she?" I ask. This whole thing amounts to the biggest lie I've heard yet.

"Louise? Hell, I cain't recall. Maybe six. She come before Carrie, I know that.

"They say I'm dying. But I ain't so sure. I been thinkin' too much lately and it's got me down is all." Again he peers around, then says, "They won't give you no whiskey in here. It's been I don't know how long since I had a drink. You got a car?"

"Well, yes—"

"You know what? They had the doc the other day, local quack, just to see about one-two little things been botherin' me. He told me I was 'depressed' and needed cheerin' up. I tole him a drink'd cheer me up jist fine. Y'know, I asked him if he ever heard of me—by my old name, I mean. Told me his father used to recall Trout Shue when he was a blacksmith around these parts, and said he told a mean story. Said word all over Greenbrier was that couldn't nobody tell a story gooder'n Trout Shue! Said we needed more folks like him around today. Said it was too bad he died up in the pen. Said if he was around, I could look him up and get him to tell me some stories, and he bet then I'd feel better. How about that, Lady? Lady, you married?"

I nod. "Hmmm," he says. "I shore wish your husband'd run you off."

At this point, I look up in disbelief. At that instant, out comes one of those spidery hands, and clamps down on my knee like a vise. "Hey, girlie, give me half a chance. I can do lots for you—"

I stare down at my leg in that bony vise, then try to wrench out of his grip. His faded eyes burn into mine. "I always liked blondes—" It feels unreal until I realize. He's crazy—

"Help!" I cry, wrenching around. Stupid, stupid, how do I get myself into these things? His hand slides down my leg, and the chair I've been sitting in shoots out, skidding, while I hit the floor with a smack, right at his feet. One of the old ladies wakes up and stares, puzzled. The other one jumps in her sleep, and lets out a little cry. As I pick myself up off the floor, I hear footsteps. In comes Miss—what was her name?—and I feel stupid and frightened. "He—he tried—"

The chubby nurse nods, smiles knowingly. "I know—"

"Girlie," he is saying, grinning with no teeth, struggling against her efforts to intervene, "you don't know what a good time—"

"Tammy!" calls the nurse. A black girl in an identical uniform comes running in. Now both of the old ladies are awake, alarmed. The two nurses at the back of his chair grab him, one by each arm. "He's strong, ain't he?" observes the one called Tammy. "Honey," Nurse Alcock says to him, "now you just calm down."

He tries to wiggle his way out of their grasp, as I recover my balance, and in his struggle his bathrobe top falls open to reveal his shrunken white chest, fallen tissue, skin as wrinkled as a bedsheet, no color except for a big brown mole on one sagging breast. He looks for just an instant like the crucified Christ. As I babble thanks, and gather up bookbag and legal pad to flee, he says, "Go on now, but if you ever have any female troubles, Lady, I'm the best there is. And don't you listen to no stories—they never could prove I done it!"